A LONELY
JOURNEY'S END

A LONELY JOURNEY'S END

An Oceanic Park Mystery

Geoff Cabin

ISBN: Softcover   978-1-6698-6932-0
                    eBook   978-1-6698-6931-3

Rev. date: 03/14/2023

To order additional copies of this book, contact:
Xlibris
844-714-8691
www.Xlibris.com
Orders@Xlibris.com
851675

Chapter 1. Tuesday, July 19, 2005

It was one of those mid-summer mornings in Oceanic Park that you can tell is going to develop into a scorching hot day. It hadn't cooled off much during the night and the temperature already was on the rise again. The sun was a fiery red ball starting to creep above the horizon and, by the middle of the day, would be beating down fiercely on the town, making the asphalt on the streets and the sand on the beach hot enough to burn the soles of people's feet.

As I did every morning, I made my way through the streets of the Old Town section of Oceanic Park toward Java Joe's Coffee Cafe. I walked past the familiar surroundings of old-fashioned storefronts, shingled fisherman's cottages, and Victorian-style hotels that dated back to the earliest days of the seaside resort, around the turn of the prior century. Interspersed among the older buildings, were pre-fab townhouses and semi-high-rise condos of the sort that were starting to encroach on the Old Town neighborhood and alter its character. At that hour of the morning, Old Town had yet to come to life. A few early-risers were out jogging or walking their dogs, but it still was too early for most vacationers to be out and about. Most of them probably still were recovering from the activities of the previous evening.

As I progressed through Old Town, it began to dawn on my still-foggy consciousness that the neighborhood been struck by a flyering campaign during the night. Flyers had been posted in a haphazard manner throughout the neighborhood by attaching them to whatever surface happened to be available - flyers had been stapled to telephone poles, placed under the windshield wipers of cars, and taped to mail boxes, newspaper boxes, and store windows.

I paused by a telephone pole, tore down a flyer, and glanced over it. The flyer looked like it had been created on a computer and then photocopied. Across the top of the flyer was a bold-faced headline that read "PRESERVE OCEANIC PARK'S HERITAGE - IMMIGRANTS OUT NOW!" Underneath the headline was a sub-headline that read "Protect Oceanic Park from Crime, Gang Violence, and Degenerate Third-World Culture." This was followed by a list of demands: "(1) End unchecked immigration; (2) Make English the official language of Oceanic Park; and (3) Ban foreign-language signs in Oceanic Park." Beneath the list of demands was a caricature of a sinister-looking Latin American immigrant wearing a sombrero and sporting a Zapata mustache with a gunsight superimposed over top of the image. Underneath of the caricature was another bold-faced headline stating that "YOU HAVE BEEN WARNED!" At the bottom of the flyer was the name "OCEANIC PARK VIGILANTES."

I crumpled the flyer into a ball and tossed it into a trash receptacle. This was the third time this summer that the neighborhood had been plastered with these anti-immigrant flyers. No one had ever heard of the group calling itself the Oceanic Park Vigilantes or had any idea who its members were. The police had announced that they were launching an investigation into the matter, but, so far, they had failed to turn up any information.

I brooded over the matter as I continued on my way toward Java Joe's. The cafe is housed in a shingled storefront with a large plate glass window that overlooks the sidewalk and a hand-painted wooden sign hanging over the door. As I approached the cafe, I saw Joe Laubach, the proprietor of Java Joe's, on the sidewalk in front of the cafe, using a putty knife to scrape scraps of flyers and strips of tape off the cafe's front window. His hair was disheveled, he was unshaven, and he was dressed casually in a loud Hawaiian shirt and khaki cargo shorts. He looked in my direction when he heard me approaching.

"Can you believe this?" he asked, waving his arms in exasperation at the storefront window. "These idiots have struck again!"

"So I see," I responded. "The flyers are all over Old Town."

"This is becoming really annoying," Java Joe continued. "They used heavy-duty packing tape to stick the flyers on the window and that stuff is really hard to get off. I don't understand how they're getting away with it. You'd think that someone would have seen or heard something."

"Whoever's posting the flyers must be very fast and well organized. Or else they've just been really lucky."

"Or some sympathetic members of the police force are looking the other way when it happens."

"Yeah, that could be."

"Have you heard anything more about who's behind the flyering campaign?"

"No. There's a lot of rumors and speculation going around, but no one actually knows anything."

"Well, I've got to finish cleaning the window before the breakfast rush starts," Java Joe sighed. He resumed scraping the remains of flyers and tape off the window and I proceeded to enter the cafe. The interior of the cafe has a casual and comfortable atmosphere that provides an outpost of bohemia amid the gentrification that is creeping through the Old Town neighborhood. A counter with stools runs the length of the room and separates the eating area from the kitchen. Large glass canisters of roasted coffee beans are displayed on a shelf behind the counter and the aroma of freshly-ground coffee permeates the air. The eating area is furnished with mismatched tables and chairs that look like they were picked up at flea markets and second-hand stores. A couch and a couple of easy chairs add a homey touch and a vintage jukebox in a back corner provides a wide variety of music. The walls are decorated with vintage travel posters for destinations known for producing coffee beans - Brazil, Columbia, Jamaica, Java, and Sumatra.

Karen Cardenay, the all-purpose cashier, counterperson, and short-order cook was at work behind the counter, making toast, frying bacon, and flipping pancakes. Karen is a former English teacher who had retired to Oceanic Park and taken a job at Java

Joe's to supplement her retirement income. Her short, dark brown hair was starting to turn grey at the temples and she hobbled bit when she walked due to pain in her knees. Wendy Stevens, the waitress, was taking orders and delivering food to the handful of early-rising customers who were scattered among the tables in the eating area. Wendy is an avid surfer who had moved to Oceanic Park after graduating from high school to be near the ocean. Her long, sun-streaked hair was pulled back into a pony tail and she was wearing a bright red baseball cap tilted back at an angle.

I called "good morning" to Karen and Wendy and walked to the jukebox in the corner. I went through my morning ritual of punching up Stan Getz and Charlie Byrd's classic recording of Antonio Carlos Jobim's "Desafinado" on the jukebox, before taking a seat at my usual table nearby.

"How's the training going?" I asked Wendy when she came to take my order. Wendy was training to compete in the Oceanic Park Surf Tournament, which was taking place the following week.

"Pretty good," she responded. "Terry's helping me to work on my arial reentry. I managed to nail a couple of them yesterday." Terry Mannering is a former professional surfer who had settled in Oceanic Park and opened a surf shop. He was coaching Wendy and a couple of other young surfers to help get them ready to compete in the tournament. "We haven't seen you out in the waves much this summer," Wendy added.

"I've been really busy," I said, "but I'll try to make it out as soon as I get a bit of time."

As we were talking, Java Joe entered the cafe carrying a bucket in one hand and a putty knife in the other and disappeared into the kitchen. After Wendy took my order, I settled down to read the *Oceanic Park Press*. The war in Iraq, now in its second year, continued to dominate the news. A fuel truck had exploded south of Baghdad, killing 98 people, and three car bombs driven by suicide bombers had exploded in the city...President Bush announced that he was nominating Judge John G. Roberts, Jr. to fill the vacancy on the Supreme Court created by the retirement of Justice Sandra

Day O'Connor. In local news, the Oceanic Park City Council was proposing to adopt a new emergency ordinance:

CITY COUNCIL PROPOSES EMERGENCY ORDINANCE TO LIMIT NUMBER OF ARTISTS AND PERFORMERS ON BOARDWALK. The Oceanic Park City Council is proposing to adopt an emergency ordinance that would limit the number of artists and performers on the boardwalk to 25. Under the ordinance, artists and performers would be chosen on a weekly basis by a lottery system and restricted to designated spaces on the boardwalk.

Oceanic Park has a long tradition of artists, musicians, jugglers, puppeteers, and other types of entertainers practicing their craft on the boardwalk. Recently, however, the number of artists and performers has increased, causing concerns about congestion, health and safety, and competition with businesses along the boardwalk.

"The number of artists and performers on the boardwalk has gotten totally out of control," said Kevin Sullivan, President of the Oceanic Park City Council. "They are impeding the orderly flow of pedestrian traffic and creating health and safety concerns by blocking the access of emergency personnel to the beach and properties along the boardwalk. We have to act to address the problem."

While brick-and-mortar businesses along the boardwalk have voiced support for the ordinance, it has come under criticism by artists and performers who ply their trade on the boardwalk.

"This is an outrage," said Roger Steadman, an Elvis impersonator who performs under the moniker of "Boardwalk Elvis." "The proposed ordinance is an infringement of our 1st Amendment right to free speech and we intend to fight it."

The text of the proposed ordinance has been posted on the City Council's website and a public hearing has been scheduled for Friday July 22 at 10:00 a.m. at City Hall.

After awhile, Java Joe emerged from the kitchen and took a seat in the chair across the table from me.

"I'm glad that job is done," he said, nodding his head toward the window, which was now free of flyers and tape. "And I hope that I don't have to do it again."

"Yeah, let's hope so," I seconded. "By the way, I've got something for you to put on the jukebox." I reached into my knapsack, pulled out a 45 rpm record in a black paper sleeve, and handed it to him.

"'Surfin' Hootenanny' by Al Casey with the K-C-Ettes," Java Joe read off the record's label. "I'm not familiar with this. Who's Al Casey?"

"He's a guitar player. He started out in Phoenix in the mid-fifties - he played guitar on 'The Fool' by Sanford Clark and did a bunch of stuff with Duane Eddy and Lee Hazlewood. Then he moved to L.A. and became a top session player and a member of the Wrecking Crew. He did session work for the Beach Boys, Glen Campbell, Phil Spector, and a whole bunch of other people. He also made some records under his own name on the side. This record, 'Surfin' Hootenanny,' actually was a minor hit back in '63, although it's pretty much forgotten now."

"Where on earth did you find it?"

"I got it at a record convention up in the city last weekend."

"Not another new record that you're obsessed with," Wendy interjected, when she brought my breakfast to the table.

"I'm afraid so," I responded

"I suppose we're going to have to listen to that record every morning from now on," Wendy said.

"Of course."

"Good grief," she muttered, before retreating to the kitchen.

The door to the cafe opened and Gary Rockwell stepped inside. Rockwell is a reporter for the *Oceanic Park Press* who covers the City Hall and courthouse beats. I often cross paths with him in the course of my work at the courthouse and we sometimes exchange information. When he spotted Java Joe and me, he came over and sat at the table next to us.

"Hey, what's happening?" he greeted us. Rockwell is forty-something with grey-streaked hair and was dressed in a business casual style with a pastel plaid shirt and Khaki pants. He was carrying a spiral-bound notepad in one hand and had a laptop case slung over a shoulder.

"You're in early this morning," Java Joe observed.

"Yeah, my editor rousted me out of bed in the middle of the night," Rockwell said. "Someone had called our news hotline to alert us to the latest flyer attack. I've been canvassing the neighborhood to see if anybody saw anything."

"Any luck?" I asked.

"Not much. As best I can tell, they struck around 3:30 in the morning. I spoke to a charter boat captain who lives in a cottage on Mediterranean Avenue. He was up early, getting ready to go down to his boat for an early-morning charter. He heard noises out in the street and went out onto his porch to see what was going on. He saw a guy putting flyers under the windshield wipers of cars that were parked on the street. When the guy with the flyers saw the captain on his porch, he hopped on a skateboard and tore away like lightening."

"Could the captain identify him?" Java Joe asked.

"No, he said it was too dark. All he could say was that it was a young guy, probably in his late teens or early twenties, wearing a backwards baseball cap."

"Given the number of flyers that were posted, there must have been more than one person involved," I said.

"Yeah, it looks that way," Rockwell agreed, "but no one else seems to have seen anything. The police department's information officer says that they're going to release a statement later this morning, but I wouldn't expect too much from that."

With that, Rockwell opened his notebook and started typing on his laptop, Java Joe returned to the kitchen, and I went back to perusing the paper.

By the time I left Java Joe's, Old Town was starting to come to life - there were more people out on the streets, stores were opening their doors and setting up displays of merchandise on the sidewalks, and the air was starting to buzz with the sound of voices, music, and traffic. A crew of city workers was making its way through the neighborhood, tearing down the anti-immigrant flyers, and tossing them into a trash truck. They were too late, however, to prevent vacationers from seeing the flyers. This incident would deal another blow to Oceanic Park's carefully-cultivated image as a family-friendly resort where people could escape the cares of the world.

Oceanic Park is located on a barrier island that is 12 miles long and half a mile wide. During the summer vacation season, Oceanic Park undergoes a transformation from a small, sleepy town of 7,000 residents to a bustling city with a temporary population of 300,000. A large, seasonal work force is needed to meet the demands of the increased population. A lot of seasonal positions are filled by high school and college students on summer vacation. They are joined by an influx of seasonal migrant laborers who come into the country on guest worker visas under the H-2B program. Two industries, in particular, rely heavily on migrant labor - hotels and seafood processing plants. Hotels employ migrant workers as maids, groundskeepers, and maintenance workers, while seafood processing plants employ migrant workers as crab meat pickers and oyster shuckers.

As nativism and anti-immigrant sentiment had increased in recent years, the use of migrant workers had begun to create a bit of friction in Oceanic Park. Up until recently, it mostly had been limited to cranks calling talk shows or writing letters to newspapers to complain about the presence of people who couldn't speak English or signs in Spanish.

Recently, however, things had escalated. A local radio station, WDSF Business Talk Radio, had hired an abrasive talk show host named Walter Braddock who hosted a morning drive-time show dubbed "Rude Awakening." Braddock had taken up the issue of immigration and was trying to be deliberately provocative, referring to migrant workers as "wetbacks" and saying that their presence was causing Oceanic Park to resemble a third-world country. When people demanded that he apologize, Braddock refused and reveled in the controversy that he created. His provocative style appeared to be popular with listeners and his morning drive-time show was doing well in the ratings.

Now, the anti-immigrant flyer campaign was escalating things still further. There was something particularly nasty and ugly about it. And there were a lot of unanswered questions. Who were the Oceanic Park Vigilantes? Was the flyer campaign a stupid prank by some thrill-seeking kids? Was it a publicity stunt organized by Walter Braddock to stir up more interest in his talk show? Or was there something more serious and sinister behind it?

My law office is located in Old Town, overtop of a tourist shop called the Pirate's Den, which sells t-shirts, beach apparel, suntan lotion, sand chairs, beach umbrellas, and all sorts of tacky souvenirs. I noticed that there still were some fragments of anti-immigration flyers stuck to the display window of the Pirate's Den. I climbed the wooden stairs on the side of the building to the landing and entered my office's reception area. My assistant and law clerk, Phoebe Blackwell, was seated behind the reception desk, clattering away at her computer. Phoebe was in her mid-twenties with short dark hair and wire rim glasses. She has a degree in computer science from Bay County College. Since she had been working for me, she had been modernizing and updating my practice by bringing it into the computer age - converting paper files to electronic format, setting up an electronic calendar to track the status of cases, and upgrading the phone system.

"Did you see those flyers all over Old Town?" Phoebe asked.

"Yeah," I responded. "Java Joe's got hit by them. They had a bunch of flyers taped on the front window."

"So did the place downstairs."

"Yeah, I noticed that, they didn't quite get them all off."

"Do you know if anyone saw anything last night?"

"As far as I know, no one saw anything much." I recounted what Gary Rockwell had told me about the charter boat captain who had seen a skateboarder placing flyers under the windshield wipers of cars.

"Anything happening here?" I asked.

"Roger Steadman called," Phoebe responded. "He wants to talk to you about the emergency ordinance that the city council is proposing to limit the number of artists and performers on the boardwalk. I scheduled him for ten o'clock."

"O.k. thanks," I responded.

I was casually acquainted with Steadman, aka "Boardwalk Elvis." He had been doing his Elvis impersonation act on the boardwalk for several years. He sang along to karaoke-style backing tracks through a portable, generator-powered PA system. His act was quite popular and tended to attract big crowds. I supposed that he did pretty well with all of the tips that people left in his beach bucket.

I went into my office and sat down at my cluttered desk. The office had pine-paneled walls, which gave it a retro-fifties look. The walls were decorated with posters for old surfing movies like *The Endless Summer*, *Five Summer Stories*, and *The Innermost Limits of Pure Fun*. Through windows in front of my desk, I could look out over the street and, through windows to my right, I could see, between the intervening buildings, a small strip of the boardwalk, beach, and ocean, a couple of blocks away.

"Roger Steadman is here," Phoebe announced from the reception area around ten o'clock.

"O.k.," I said. I started to get up to go out to the reception area and greet him, but, before I could get out from behind my desk, Steadman burst into my office waving some papers in his hand. Even out of costume, Steadman bore something of a resemblance to Elvis. He wore his hair in a pompadour with long sideburns and a duck tail in back, had the collar of his shirt turned up, and wore blue jeans with cuffs on them overtop of two-tone shoes.

"Hey, Jackson, have you seen this emergency ordinance that the City Council is proposing to adopt?" Steadman demanded. Steadman had a habit of addressing everyone as "Jackson," regardless of their actual name.

"I saw the article in the paper this morning," I said, "but I haven't actually read the proposed ordinance."

"Well, it's worse than anyone could have imagined," Steadman declared. He tossed the papers onto my desk with disgust and then took a seat in a chair opposite me. "They're going to limit the number of artists and performers on the boardwalk to 25. And they're going award the 25 places by holding a weekly lottery. You have to reapply every week. With all the competition for the 25 places, I'll be lucky if I'm able to work one week per month. If I don't work every day, I won't be able to afford my rental. And I've got a lot of money invested in costumes and a PA system."

"I take it that the Merchants Association is behind this," I said.

"Of course. They're afraid of competition. They're always talking about the free market and how competition is a good thing, but then they try to gain an advantage by restricting access to the market and eliminating competition. A bunch of us are banding together to form a group called the Coalition to Preserve the Boardwalk. We'd like you to represent us and challenge the ordinance on the ground that it violates our 1st Amendment right to free speech. I know that, a couple of years ago, you got the ordinance that prohibited panhandling struck down as an unconstitutional restriction on free speech. We'd like you to do the same with this ordinance."

I picked up the copy of the proposed ordinance and quickly skimmed through it.

"So, what do you think, Jackson?" Steadman asked. "Can we challenge it as a violation of the 1st Amendment?"

"Yes, we should be able to. Courts have held that the 1st Amendment applies to public forums. The boardwalk should qualify as a public forum because it's publicly owned and there's an established tradition of artists and musicians performing there. That means that the city council can't prohibit people from performing on the boardwalk, but they can impose reasonable time, place, and manner restrictions. The issue is going to be whether the ordinance constitutes a reasonable time, place, and manner restriction."

"There's nothing reasonable about it!" Steadman declared. "It's totally unfair! And it's really inconvenient to implement a new system like this in the middle of the summer. If it takes effect, it's going to screw up all of the plans that I made months ago."

"Time, place, and manner restrictions are required to be narrowly tailored to infringe on 1st Amendment rights as little as possible," I explained. "They also are subject to strict scrutiny by the courts. I think that we can make a strong argument that the proposed ordinance is overly broad for the purpose that it's intended to serve."

"So, how should we proceed?"

"The hearing's on Friday, right?"

"Right."

"O.k., we don't have much time to prepare. I'll need to do some research on the 1st Amendment issue. I'll submit a written memorandum of law in support of our position to the City Council and I'll testify as to the legal issues at the hearing. Some artists and performers also should testify at the hearing. They should be prepared to explain how the ordinance will affect them - they need to stress that, for most weeks of the season, they will be totally banned from exercising their right to free speech on the boardwalk. We need to demonstrate that, rather than acting as a reasonable restriction on speech, the ordinance actually will act as a *de facto* ban on speech."

"Right. I'd like to testify and I know that there's a few other people who would like to testify as well. I'll tell them to work on putting their testimony together."

"That sounds good. Why don't we get together tomorrow afternoon and review our plans for the hearing?"

"O.k. What do you think our chances are?"

"I doubt that we have much of a chance in front of the City Council. They generally take their marching orders from the Merchants Association. But we stand a pretty good chance when we get into court, in front of a judge."

"Won't that take a lot of time?"

"No, it shouldn't. If the City Council adopts the ordinance and the mayor signs it, we can file a petition for an emergency injunction to prevent them from enforcing the ordinance until a court can hold a hearing on it. We should be able to get a ruling on the petition for an emergency injunction from a judge in a matter of days."

"If the ordinance goes into effect, it's going to cost me a lot of money and really screw up my summer."

"We'll try to make sure that it doesn't."

I rose and shook Steadman's hand as he prepared to leave.

"Oh, by the way, are you coming to the block party for the reopening of the Chimera Gallery tonight?" Steadman asked, pausing as he headed toward the office door. "I'm going to be performing."

"Oh, yeah, I'll be there."

Steadman's mention of the reopening of the Chimera Gallery took me back to the events of the previous summer. The Chimera Gallery had been run by a friend and client of mine, Count Rupert St. Cyr, and located in the historic Asher mansion on a bay-front lot in Old Town. In the early morning hours of August 3rd, the gallery was destroyed by a fire. After the fire had been extinguished, firefighters found Count Rupert's body among the ruins of the building. When fire department investigators concluded that the fire was caused by arson, I had gotten involved in investigating the cause of the fire and Count Rupert's death. The investigation had not ended particularly well.

After Count Rupert's death, the gallery property was inherited by his former wife, Elizabeth Birkin, a professor of art history at

Faber University. When Count Rupert had purchased the Asher mansion back in the mid-'90s, it had been a derelict property that no one else had wanted. In the decade or so since then, Old Town had begun to undergo a process of gentrification and redevelopment and the bay-front lot where the mansion had been located now was a desirable piece of real estate. A local real estate developer named Eric Burns tried to coerce Elizabeth Birkin into selling him the property, but she rebuffed his offers and, instead, decided to rebuild and reopen the Chimera Gallery.

A lot of people had expressed skepticism about whether the rebuilding project was feasible, but Elizabeth had been determined to make it happen. She managed to locate the original plans for the Asher mansion in the archives of the Bay County Historical Society. Working from the plans and photographs of the building, she had the mansion rebuilt as close as possible to the original. During the winter, spring, and early summer, I had watched as the gallery had been rebuilt, progressing from a skeletal framework to a completed building that now appeared almost indistinguishable from the original and was scheduled to reopen that evening.

At the time of the fire, the gallery had been hosting an exhibition of paintings by Captain Dan Chapman. Captain Dan was one of the originators of Tiki art. He was a former member of the Navy and the merchant marine who had ended up in Hawaii back in the mid-fifties, where he lived the life of a beachcomber and took up painting. There, he developed his style of Tiki art, which portrayed a romanticized portrait of island life. During the Tiki craze back in the late '50s and early '60s, Captain Dan's paintings had been popular with tourists, but dismissed as "kitsch" by art critics. When the Tiki fad faded, however, Captain Dan's popularity had faded along with it. A couple of years ago, with Tiki art coming back into style, Count Rupert had decided it was time for Captain Dan to make a comeback and tracked him down at his current home in Key West. Count Rupert had given Captain Dan his first exhibition in more than 40 years, and it had proved to be a hit before it was cut short by the fire.

With the publicity generated by last summer's events, Captain Dan had become something of a celebrity again. His old paintings were selling for big prices now. People were digging through their attics and basements looking for his old paintings, while collectors were scouring church bazaars and flea markets for them. People were kicking themselves for having discarded his paintings as worthless junk

Since Captain Dan's exhibition had been cut short by the fire, Elizabeth Birkin had decided to pick up where matters had left off and invited Captain Dan reopen the gallery with an exhibition of his recent work. Given his renewed celebrity status, Captain Dan could have chosen to hold his exhibition at a more trendy and prestigious gallery in New York or Los Angeles, but instead accepted Elizabeth's invitation to return to the Chimera Gallery. He wanted to express his gratitude to Count Rupert for giving him a break and lend support to the gallery. It was a nice gesture on his part.

In conjunction with the reopening, the town was holding a block party in the 1200 block of Jamaica Avenue, where the gallery was located. There would be musical acts performing and booths selling food and arts and crafts.

I knocked off work around 6:30 p.m. and walked home to the restored fisherman's cottage in Old Town where I lived, changed my clothes, and then headed to the Chimera Gallery.

When I left the house, I could hear the faint sound of music coming from the block party in the distance. As I headed north along the bay front, I strained my ears and was able to make out the sound of "Baja" by the Astronauts. I took my usual shortcut under the drawbridge that connects Oceanic Park to the mainland.

"Hey!" A familiar voice called out to me and saw I Buffalo Smith, along with a few other people, sitting on the rock breakwater that bordered the small, crescent-shaped beach underneath the bridge. Buffalo Smith was one of a number of homeless people who used the area under the bridge as a hangout and shelter.

I walked over to where he was sitting. Buffalo Smith's face was weatherbeaten and wrinkle-lined, he had long hair and a beard, and was wearing a shabby old raincoat. I had first met him a couple summers before, when I had filed a suit on behalf of the town's homeless population to strike down an ordinance that prohibited panhandling as an unconstitutional restriction on free speech. Then, the previous summer, he had been an important witness in the investigation into the death of Count Rupert.

"What's happening?" I said by way of greeting.

"Oh, we're just hanging out, listening to the music," he responded.

"Aren't you going to join the party?" I asked.

"I don't know," he shrugged. "The cops came around and warned us against panhandling during the block party."

"The ordinance that prohibited panhandling was struck down by the court."

"Yeah, I know, but that hasn't stopped the cops from hassling us about it. They like to hassle us and push us around. It makes them feel big."

"I'll have to have a word about that with Sergeant Bartlett." I took out my wallet and handed him some money. "Here, take your friends and go and join the party."

As I emerged on the other side of the bridge, the music was louder and more distinct and the block where the Chimera Gallery was located came into view. The near end of the street had been blocked off by sawhorses and orange traffic cones and, at the far end of the street, a bandstand had been set up with a banner across the top that read "Oceanic Park Block Party." Each side of the street was lined with booths selling food, artwork, and handicrafts. An eating area with folding tables and chairs had been set up to one side of the bandstand. Lee Ellison, a disc jockey with local radio station WVOP, was manning the sound system on the bandstand. As "Baja" faded out, he put on "Mr. Moto" by the Belairs.

A fairly big crowd already had gathered; people were seated in the eating area, milling around in front of the bandstand, and drifting up and down the rows of booths. A t.v. camera crew and a couple of news photographers were on hand to document the event. I joined the crowd, got a hot dog and cup of coffee from one of the booths, and sat at a table on the eating area.

"Good evening, everyone, and welcome to the Oceanic Park block party" Lee Ellison announced when "Mr. Moto" ended. "I'm Lee Ellison from WVOP, the Voice of Oceanic Park. Tonight, we are celebrating the reopening of the Chimera Gallery as well as the continued renaissance of the Old Town neighborhood. Right now, we have a special treat for you. A favorite on the boardwalk here in Oceanic Park - please welcome Boardwalk Elvis."

Roger Steadman strode onto the stage with a confident swagger that came from years of performing for crowds on the boardwalk. He was wearing a rhinestone-studded jumpsuit of the sort that Elvis wore during his Las Vegas period, with an acoustic guitar slung over his shoulder. Steadman's entrance was greeted by a smattering of polite applause from the people gathered in front of the bandstand. Without pausing, Steadman launched into "Viva Las Vegas," singing and strumming along to a karaoke-style backing track. He managed a pretty good imitation of Elvis' voice and had Elvis' stage mannerisms down cold. What he lacked in skill, he made up for with conviction and enthusiasm. When he concluded "Viva Las Vegas," the audience erupted into enthusiastic applause.

"Thank you ladies and gentlemen," Steadman said in his best Elvis drawl. "Right now, I'd like to take you back to where it all began, at Sun Studios at 706 Union Avenue in Memphis, Tennessee on July 5, 1954, with this song." He then launched into "That's Alright," the A-side of Elvis' first single, a cover of a rhythm and blues song that originally had been recorded by Arthur "Big Boy" Crudup in 1946. Steadman's performance captured the raw energy and excitement of Elvis early rockabilly style and was well received by the audience.

"In late 1955, Elvis' contract was bought by RCA Records," Steadman said. "I'd like to do the first song that Elvis recorded for RCA, which went on to become his first big hit, going to number one in the spring of 1956." Steadman then launched into "Heartbreak Hotel."

As the set progressed, the crowd in front of the stage grew larger as more people, attracted by the music, stopped to listen. Steadman's set featured songs from throughout Elvis' career, ranging from early rhythm and blues and rock 'n' roll numbers to schmaltzy ballads from his Vegas years.

Steadman concluded his performance with "Suspicious Minds," a song from Elvis' late-sixties comeback period. Toward the end of the song, Steadman dropped into a crouch and performed some karate-inspired moves the way Elvis had done. When the song ended, Steadman stepped forward, took a dramatic bow, and then exited the stage.

The crowd started to clap and chant "Elvis," almost as if Steadman were the real thing. When the clapping and chanting persisted, Steadman came back onstage and sang the ballad "Can't Help Falling in Love" from *Blue Hawaii* for an encore. He took another bow before exiting the stage.

"Let's hear it for Boardwalk Elvis," Lee Ellison said, stepping up to the microphone again, as Steadman left the stage. "You can catch him performing most evenings on the boardwalk. Coming up in a little while, we'll have reggae music with another local favorite, the Island Breeze Rhythm Band. In the meantime, I'll be spinning some discs. Here's 'I Live for the Sun' by the Sunrays."

I decided to head over to the gallery and check out the exhibition.

On entering the gallery, I was greeted by Antonia Lambert from behind the reception desk. Antonia is a young artist who had worked as an assistant for Count Rupert prior to his death and had been kept on by Elizabeth Birkin when she took over the gallery. Antonia had spiky henna'd hair and a gold stud in her nose. As usual, she was dressed almost entirely in black - she was wearing a black t-shirt with the name and logo of the Irish punk band, Stiff Little Fingers, on the front of it, black jeans, and black, high-top Chuck

Taylor All Star sneakers. For the past year, she had been working to assist Elizabeth with the reopening of the gallery.

I congratulated Antonia on the opening, noting that all of the hard work that she and Elizabeth had done had paid off.

"It almost didn't happen," Antonia said. "When I came in this morning, the front window was covered with those stupid flyers. I had to spend half of the morning cleaning them off. I wasn't sure that we would be ready to open, but we made it."

The first floor of the gallery houses the reception area, a gift shop, and the administrative offices. I made my way up the stairs to the exhibition room, which is located on the second floor. In the days of Lee Asher, the exhibition room had been a ballroom - it had a hardwood floor for dancing and French doors that opened onto a balcony with a panoramic view of the bay. Captain Dan's paintings were displayed on the walls and on display boards arranged around the room. Strings of colored tiki lights were suspended from the ceiling and some plastic palm trees and pink flamingoes were scattered about the room to give it the tiki-bar atmosphere. The room was crowded with people and buzzing with conversation.

I wandered around the room, looking at the paintings. The new paintings were in the classic Captain Dan style - hula girls strumming ukuleles under palm trees; an ocean liner cruising past a verdant tropical island; a carved Tiki figure next to a jungle waterfall; a shipwreck in a deserted cove; an outrigger in full sail against a clear azure sky.

"Hey, how're you doing?" I was greeted by a middle-aged guy wearing a baseball cap, a polo shirt, and khaki pants, looking like he had just come off a golf course. He appeared vaguely familiar, but I couldn't place him. "Good to see you," he declared, grabbing my hand and shaking it as if I was a long-lost friend. He was giving off alcohol fumes like a distillery.

"Uh...good to see you, too," I managed to stammer, while frantically searching my memory trying to figure out who this guy was.

"Are you in town for the meeting?" he asked.

"The meeting?"

"The annual meeting of the Economic Freedom Foundation."

"Oh, no, I live here."

"You *live* here?" He sounded shocked.

"Yeah, I have a small law practice here."

"Oh, man, what're you doing here? You should be where the action is."

"And where's that?"

"Corporate security," he announced. "Since 9/11, multi-national corporations have become concerned about the threat of kidnappings and terrorist attacks. There's a lot of money to be made providing risk assessment and security services to corporations all over the world."

"Uh-huh," I said. I had finally managed to remember who this guy was - his name was Stuart Nichols and we had been in law school together back in the '80s. After law school, he had gone into lobbying. I occasionally had crossed paths with him back when I worked for the state legislature. The overly chummy, gregarious manner was part of his lobbying schtick and he never turned it off. The last time I had seen him, he had been lobbying on behalf of a group of payday lenders who were trying to kill legislation that would have prevented them from charging exorbitant interest rates and fees to their customers. Apparently he had moved on to bigger and better things.

"Let me tell you something," Nichols continued, jabbing me in the chest with an index finger. "Those poor saps who flew the planes into the World Trade Center thought that they were striking a blow against the heart of capitalism. Instead, they created the first great business opportunity of the 21st century. We couldn't believe our luck. It provided the justification that we needed to gear up the military-industrial machine and get the money flowing again. Do you know how many people have made fortunes from 9/11?"

"Uh...no...I don't know." I glanced around the room, trying to find some way of extricating myself from this conversation.

"A hell of a lot. There's still the opportunity for a lot more people to make fortunes, and I intend to be one of them. The next big thing is going to be providing contractors and support services to the military. War's going corporate. It's going to be privatized just like everything else. The war on terror means that the country will be in a permanent state of war and the money will never stop flowing. The Pentagon and the CIA will have more money than they know what to do with. You need to think about how to position yourself to get a piece of that money. That will be one of the main topics of discussion at the meeting of the Economic Freedom Foundation - economic opportunities created by the war on terror."

"Well...that sounds interesting."

"Damn right. It should be a great meeting. Some of the greatest business leaders and economic minds of our time will be there."

"Uh-huh."

"Well, I'll be in town for a week or so. Maybe I'll see you around." With that, he whacked me on the shoulder and wandered off into the crowd.

I breathed a sigh of relief and resumed my perusal of the paintings, sincerely hoping that I wouldn't run into him again.

As I drifted about the gallery, I overheard a couple of women discussing who they thought was responsible for posting the anti-immigrant flyers.

"It's those redneck farmers from over on the mainland," the first woman said. "The ones who drive around with Confederate flags on their pickup trucks. Those guys are still fighting the Civl War."

"No, I think it's those skinheaded skateboarders who hang out around the skatebowl," the second woman responded. "They're all a bunch of neo-Nazis. They really give me the creeps."

This was typical of the sort of speculation that was floating around. While there were plenty of theories about who was responsible for posting the flyers, no one had yet to produce any evidence to back them up.

When I had finished looking at the paintings, I started to make my way through the crowd toward a far corner of the exhibition room where Elizabeth Birkin and Captain Dan were holding court, shaking hands, and exchanging greetings with people. Elizabeth

Birkin looked elegant with her long red hair pinned up and wearing a lime green sun dress and sandals. Captain Dan was in his usual beachcomber getup of loud Hawaiian shirt, cut offs, harachi sandals, topped off by an ancient, grimy captain's hat.

I congratulated Elizabeth on the reopening and noted that she had proved wrong all of the skeptics who said that the gallery couldn't be rebuilt.

"Thank you," she said. "I just wish that Rupert could be here to see it."

"I'm sure that he's here in spirit."

I moved on to greet Captain Dan and congratulate him on the exhibition. I had gotten to know Captain Dan a bit during the previous summer when he had come to Oceanic Park to attend the opening of his earlier exhibition.

"It's good to be back again," Captain Dan declared, shaking my hand with his vice-like grip.

"How long are you going to be staying?" I asked.

"Oh, I'm going to be here for about three weeks."

"Any plans for fishing?" Captain Dan was an enthusiastic sport fisherman. The previous summer, I had helped him find a charter boat captain, Buddy Emerson, to take him deep sea fishing.

"Oh, yeah, I've chartered Buddy Emerson's boat again," Captain Dan replied. "We're going out first thing tomorrow. I'm really hoping to bag a white marlin this year."

"Well, good luck."

"By the way, I ran into your friend, Sophie, down in Key West. She's playing in a bar called Trader Dan's Beach Shack and living on her boat. She told me to say 'hello' to you and tell you that she'd see you when she plays the Crow's Nest in a couple of weeks."

I was totally blindsided and disconcerted by this news about Sophie and felt as if the earth had shifted out from under my feet. I struggled to find my voice.

"Did she say anything else?" I finally managed to stammer.

"No, that's all," Captain Dan replied.

I thanked Captain Dan for relaying the message and drifted across the gallery and out onto the balcony. I leaned my elbows on the railing, and looked out over the bay, watching the headlights of cars as they streamed across the drawbridge into town. My mind was reeling while trying to come to terms with contradictory thoughts and feelings swirling about in my mind.

I had met Sophia Ambrosetti the previous summer when she was playing piano and singing in a local club called the Crow's Nest, while living on her sailboat. We immediately had hit it off. It turned out that, in addition to being a musician, she was an investigator and researcher. I asked her to help with the investigation into Count Rupert's death and it was largely due to her efforts that we had solved the case. It turned out, however, that she was pursuing an agenda of her own and things had not ended particularly well.

I subsequently learned that Sophie was a notorious computer hacker known as "Pirate Girl" and had worked for Amaranthine Consulting, an investigative research firm that engaged in industrial espionage and political black operations.

Given the circumstances under which we had parted, I had assumed that I would never see or hear from Sophie again. Back during the fall, however, I had received a post card from her in Key West with a somewhat cryptic message on it. I couldn't quite make up my mind whether to respond or not, and I had ended up not responding.

I knew that she was scheduled to return and play at the Crow's Nest this summer, but I couldn't quite believe that she would have the audacity to show up. Now it appeared that she actually was going to show up. I supposed that I shouldn't have anything further to do with her; in spite of everything that had happened, however, she still exerted a strong emotional pull on me and I wasn't sure that I could resist the temptation of seeing her again.

My attention was diverted from my thoughts when, out of the corner of my eye, I noticed movement at the top of the water tower a couple of blocks south of the gallery. As I watched, a gigantic banner was unfurled from the top of the tower. The banner billowed out, hesitated for a moment, and then unfurled down the side of the water tower. Across the top of the banner was the spray-painted headline "Immigrants Out Now!" Underneath the headline was a crudely rendered drawing of a stick figure hanging from a gallows by a noose. At the bottom, the banner was signed, "Oceanic Park Vigilantes."

"Oh, my God!" a woman standing nearby exclaimed. "Look at that!" There were audible gasps from other people on the balcony as they crowded against the railing to get a better view.

Barely visible in the fading light, I could see the figure of a man climbing down the rung ladder affixed to the base of the water tower. The man was wearing a dark hooded sweatshirt with the hood pulled up over top of a baseball cap and the brim of the baseball cap tilted low over his face. The hooded figure jumped the last ten feet or so to the ground, dropped to his knees, and did a shoulder roll. He quickly got to his feet, climbed the chain-link fence that surrounded the water tower, and sprinted down the street toward the bulkhead, where the street dead-ended into the bay. I could see that another person was waiting on the other side of the bulkhead, bobbing in the water on a jet ski. The hooded figure climbed over the bulkhead and lowered himself onto the back of the jet ski. The operator of the jet ski tore away from the bulkhead, sending a geyser of water shooting up behind them. When they got out into the channel in the middle of the bay, the operator of the jet ski turned in an arc toward the north and they soon disappeared from sight.

Attracted by the astonished exclamations of people who had seen the banner unfurled, the crowd from the exhibition room began making its way out onto the balcony to see what was happening. Going against the tide of people, I quickly made my way off the balcony, through the exhibition room, and down the stairs to the street. Outside, I ran a couple of blocks to the water tower. I paused and looked through the chain link fence at the ground around the base of the water tower, but the ground was covered with loose gravel that wouldn't have retained any footprints. I walked down the sidewalk to the bulkhead where the jet ski had been, but there were no traces left behind to indicate that anyone had been there. It had been a well-planned and neatly-executed operation.

I headed back down the block toward the water tower. By that time, a crowd of people from the block party and gallery reopening had started to gather on the street and sidewalk alongside the water tower. People were talking excitedly and taking photos of the banner with their cell phones. The news photographers and t.v. camera crew that had been covering the block party also arrived on the scene and began photographing the banner.

Shortly, the sound of a siren cut through the air and a flashing blue light illuminated the night sky, as a police cruiser arrived on the scene. A young African-American officer in uniform, emerged from the car. I recognized the officer as Sergeant Bartlett; I had become acquainted with him the previous summer, when he had been involved in the investigation of the fire at the Chimera Gallery. Another officer followed Sergeant Bartlett out of the car.

"Please clear the area," Bartlett directed the crowd. "Everyone move to the other side of the street." The officer with Sgt. Bartlett herded the crowd to the sidewalk on the other side of the street.

When Sgt. Bartlett saw me, he greeted me and we shook hands. "Did you see what happened?" he asked.

I told him about the banner being unfurled and the figure climbing down the water tower and fleeing on the jet ski.

"Could you identify the person who climbed down from the water tower?"

"No, it was too dark and he was too far away."

As we were talking, a fire engine arrived from the nearby volunteer fire station and parked behind the police car. After conferring with Sergeant Bartlett, a couple of firefighters climbed the water tower to remove the banner. After the banner came down, the crowd started to disperse and drift back to the block party and the gallery and I did the same.

Back at the gallery, I found Elizabeth Birkin seated at her desk in her office on the first floor. She appeared distraught over the disruption of the reopening.

"I can't believe this," she said, on the verge of tears. "We worked so hard to make the reopening happen only to have it ruined by something like this. It really seems like someone has it in for us. Why did they pick the reopening to do this?"

"I doubt that the people who hung the banner were targeting you or the gallery," I said. "They probably were just taking advantage of an opportunity. They knew that there would be a big crowd here for the reopening and the block party, and that the event would be covered by the news media. It was a chance to make sure that the banner was seen by a lot of people and got a lot of coverage in the media."

"I guess you're right, but still...I wanted so much for the reopening to go smoothly, particularly after everything that happened last year. This can't help but leave a sour taste in my mouth."

"It shouldn't, the reopening still was a success. It drew a big crowd, people enjoyed themselves, and they liked Captain Dan's paintings. In any event, this is just the opening night. The exhibition still has three weeks to run. It will be a success."

"Yes, but coverage of the opening often determines how an exhibition is received. The anti-immigrant banner will end up getting all of the attention and dominating the news coverage. That's what this will be remembered for."

I tried to reassure her that things would work out o.k., but I'm afraid that I wasn't very successful.

After leaving the gallery, I headed out on my customary evening walk. I avoided the boardwalk, which was crowded with tourists at this time of night, and took my usual route through Old Town along the bay front. I walked past the marinas, which were largely quiet now that most of the boats had returned for the night; past the yellow-brick Coast Guard station; and past Bond's Amusement Park, filled with the flashing lights of the various thrill rides and the blare of carnival music. I paused for awhile when I reached the inlet at the southern end of the island and watched a few fishing boats that were returning late and headed for marinas in the bay, and a couple of big cruise boats that were leaving the bay for an evening cruise up the coast.

On my way back along the bay front, I took a detour and walked out onto the municipal fishing pier. Several people were fishing the evening tide under the light cast by street lights placed at intervals along the pier. I spotted Amanda and William Price, an elderly African-American couple who lived down the street from me. The Prices were avid fishing enthusiasts and regular habituates of the fishing pier. They were seated in folding chairs, their rods propped on the railing in front of them, a cooler and bucket on the ground next to them.

"How's it going?" I asked after we had greeted each other.

"Not bad," William replied. "We've gotten a few bites."

"What was all of that commotion over at the water tower?" Amanda asked. "We heard sirens and saw flashing lights."

You could see the water tower from the fishing pier, but the banner had been hung on the north side of the water tower, which faces away from the pier. I told them about the banner being unfurled on the water tower with a figure hanging from a gallows on it and the man climbing down the water tower and fleeing on a jet ski.

"A gallows?!" Amanda exclaimed. "That's really nasty stuff. What's going on around here? I don't understand what this place is coming to."

"Oh, it's nothing new," William said. "That sort of stuff has been going on around here for a long time."

"But not like this," Amanda said. "It's gotten worse lately."

"It's come out in the open more, but it's always been there," William stated. "Bay County has a long history of lynchings and racial violence, but people aren't familiar with it, it tends to get swept under the carpet." He turned toward me. "Do you know when the last lynching took place in Bay County?"

"No," I admitted.

"August 1937," William stated. "Orphan Leroy. I was nine years old when it happened and I still remember hearing about it very clearly. It sent terror through the Black community in Bay County. The case received a lot of publicity at the time, but it's largely forgotten now."

"What happened?"

"It took place in Bellwether Hill over on the mainland. That summer was really hot and humid and there was a lot of tension between the Black and White communities in Bellwether Hill. There had been a number of incidents where Blacks had been accused of committing crimes against Whites, including the murder of a chicken farmer and his family. A Black man named Bill Grainger was arrested for the murder of the chicken farmer and supposedly confessed. The International Labor Defense League subsequently got involved and provided Grainger with a lawyer. After that, Grainger recanted his confession and claimed that it had been coerced out of him, and the lawyer had the trial postponed and moved to another venue.

"That infuriated members of the White community. As far as they were concerned, the International Defense League was a bunch of anarchists and Communists.

"Then in early August, the International Labor Defense League held a rally in the Black section of Bellwether Hill and told members of the Black community that they were being exploited by their White employers. The day after the rally, the owner of a sawmill named Owen Matthews was shot and killed.

"The sheriff suspected Orphan Leroy of killing Owen Matthews. Orphan Leroy worked at the sawmill, had attended the rally, and, afterwards, had been overheard saying that he had a score to settle with Matthews. Apart from saying that he had a score to settle with Matthews, there was no evidence to indicate that Orphan Leroy actually had shot Matthews, but that was enough for the sheriff. The sheriff and some deputies went to Orphan Leroy's home to arrest him. It's not clear exactly what happened, but a shootout took place and Orphan Leroy was shot in the shoulder and arrested. He was taken to the Bellwether Hill Community Hospital.

"When word spread that Orphan Leroy had been arrested and was in the hospital, a mob formed and went to the hospital to seize Orphan Leroy. The sheriff and a couple of deputies were guarding the front door of the hospital and turned the mob away. A few members of the mob, however, went around to the side door of the hospital, which had been left unguarded - whether intentionally or not is unclear - and entered the hospital. They seized Orphan Leroy and dragged him out of the hospital.

"The mob dragged Orphan Leroy to the town green. Along the way, a few members of the mob stopped at the fire station to pick up a rope. They tossed the rope over a branch of a tree, placed a noose around Orphan Leroy's neck, and then hoisted him up and down until he was dead while the crowd cheered them on. According to reports, there were about 2,500 people in the crowd.

"When the crowd started to drift away, some people cut down Orphan Leroy's body and dragged it to an empty lot in view of Bellwether Hill's Black community. Then they poured gasoline on the body and set it on fire. They wanted to make sure that members of the Black community got the message."

"That's really chilling," I said, although that was hardly an adequate description. "It's shocking that they could do it so openly and brazenly."

"The members of the mob knew that they could act with impunity," William said. "There was widespread support the for the lynching in the White community - most of the White residents turned out to see it. In the unlikely event that the participants were charged with murder and went to trial, they would be in front of an all-White jury that never would have convicted them."

We fell silent for awhile, brooding over what we had heard. The story of Orphan Leroy seemed to add an even more sinister dimension to the image of the figure hanging from the gallows on the banner on the water tower. Was it possible that something like that could happen today? How far was the group calling itself the Oceanic Park Vigilantes was willing to go? Were they just trying to stir up trouble or were they planning to follow through on their threats?

Chapter 2. Wednesday, July 20, 2005

"We're gonna have a surfin' hootenanny!" The sound of the K-C-Ettes came blasting out of the jukebox at Java Joe's, followed by Al Casey's thundering surf guitar, doing imitations of the guitar styles of Dick Dale, the Ventures, and Duane Eddy.

"Surfin' hootenanny?!" exclaimed William Bywater, looking up from the musical score that he was studying at a nearby table. "What on earth is this?!" In addition to being a music teacher and a violinist with the Bay County Symphony, Bywater was a composer and a self-proclaimed musical genius. He cultivated the look of an 19th-century bohemian maestro with a Van Dyke goatee and was constantly complaining that the unenlightened musical establishment failed to recognize the brilliance of his compositions.

"It's Al Casey with the K-C-Ettes," I informed him.

"Not another record that you've gotten Joe to put on the jukebox," he groaned. "Where do you dig up this stuff?"

"I came across it at a record show last weekend."

"I suppose that you're going to tell me that this is some sort of rock 'n' roll classic."

"That's precisely what I was going to tell you."

"Good grief," he groaned. "The level of musical literacy in our society is appalling."

He returned to studying his musical score and I returned to perusing the *Oceanic Park Press*. Elizabeth Birkin had turned out to be right - news coverage of the reopening of the Chimera Gallery was overshadowed by coverage of the anti-immigrant flyer campaign and the banner hanging, which were covered in a front-page article by Gary Rockwell. I read the article, but didn't learn anything that I didn't already know. It appeared that the police still had no idea as to the identity of the Oceanic Park Vigilantes.

Glancing up from the paper, I noticed that Adam Pulman had entered the cafe and was standing at the counter placing a carryout order. Pulman is an attorney who works for the City Council. After placing his order, he glanced around the cafe and, when he saw me, came over to my table.

"Hey, how're you doing?" he asked. Pulman appeared to be in his forties, wore wire-rimmed glasses, and had close-cropped hair and a goatee flecked with grey.

I returned his greeting and we shook hands. The two of us crossed paths fairly regularly regarding City Council business and usually were on the opposite sides of issues. The previous summer we had come into conflict over the City Council's refusal to issue a permit to the local chapter of the United Human Rights Coalition to hold an anti-war demonstration. Pulman wasn't a bad guy, though, and we maintained a cordial relationship in spite of our differences.

"I understand that you're going to be representing that riff-raff on the boardwalk at the hearing on the emergency ordinance on Friday," Pulman said in a good-natured manner.

"Yeah, that's right. How did you know?"

"I ran into that Boardwalk Elvis character at the block party last night. He was haranguing me about violating his 1st Amendment right to free speech. He kept calling me 'Jackson,' for some reason. He said that you're going to represent them and that you're going to kick my butt."

"Well, he's right about that," I laughed.

"Look, do you have to challenge everything that the City Council does? Why can't you be reasonable for a change? We're not trying to take away anyone's right to free speech, we're just trying to restore a little bit of order and sanity to the boardwalk."

"You *are* taking away people's right to free speech. The ordinance isn't just regulating speech - the way that it works, it will totally prohibit most artists and performers from exercising their right to free speech on the boardwalk most weeks of the season. You know that the ordinance is not going to stand up to a constitutional challenge in court; you should advise your clients to withdraw it."

"There's no way that that's going to happen. Particularly not with the Economic Freedom Foundation in town for its annual meeting this week. If Oceanic Park wants to attract more big-name convention business like that, it needs to demonstrate that it's serious about cleaning up the boardwalk."

"So, that's what this is about. I wondered about the timing of it."

"Look, I know that people have a sentimental attachment to the carnival atmosphere on the boardwalk, but it's time for Oceanic Park to leave that behind and move into the 21st century."

"From what I've seen of the 21st century so far, we'd be better off not moving into it."

"Oh, that's very witty."

Karen Cardenay called across the room to tell Pullman that his carry-out order was ready.

"Well, I've gotta run," he said, 'but I'll be seeing you around."

That was the second time in two days that someone had mentioned the annual meeting of the Economic Freedom Foundation to me. Then, as I continued to go through the paper, I ran across an article about it.

ANNUAL MEETING OF ECONOMIC FREEDOM FOUNDATION BEGINS TOMORROW. The annual meeting of the Economic Freedom Foundation, which is being held at the new Oceanic Park Plaza Hotel and Conference Center in northern Oceanic Park, begins tomorrow and runs through Sunday. Founded in 1947, the Economic Freedom Foundation is a think tank that advocates in favor of free trade and less government regulation. Topics on the agenda for this year's meeting include business opportunities created by the war on terror, deregulation of business, and reform of corporate tax policy. Among the scheduled speakers are Clifton Safir, CEO of the Rubicon Consortium; Victor Huang, professor of Constitutional law at Monterey University Law School and a former Justice Department official; and Robert Oakley, a Republican congressman from Montana.

The meeting is the first major event to be held at the new Oceanic Park Plaza Hotel and Conference Center, which was built by local developer Eric Burns and had its grand opening over Memorial Day weekend.

"We are pleased to be hosting the annual meeting of the Economic Freedom Foundation," said Mayor Joseph O'Connor, who had worked to bring the event to Oceanic Park. "A high-profile event like this will help to establish Oceanic Park as a leading destination for meetings and conventions."

Not everyone, however, is welcoming the meeting to Oceanic Park. Helen Marwood, president of the local chapter of the United Human Rights Coalition said that her group was planning demonstrations against the meeting and organizing a boycott of the Oceanic Park Plaza. "The Economic Freedom Foundation is an elitist and undemocratic organization that wields tremendous power without any accountability," she stated. Marwood further stated that her group objected to the presence of Victor Huang as a speaker at the meeting. "When Victor Huang worked for the Justice Department, he was one of the architects of the Bush Administration's torture policy," she stated. "He should be on trial for war crimes, rather than speaking in Oceanic Park."

In a rare interview, Everett Nowell, the Executive Director of the Economic Freedom

Foundation, defended the decision to invite Victor Huang to speak at the meeting.

"Professor Huang has been on the front line of the war on terror," Nowell stated. "It has given him unique insight into the workings of terrorist organizations. That is a subject that is of interest to a lot of our members, who have to do business in a world where terrorism is a constant threat." Nowell called allegations that Huang is a war criminal "preposterous."

Nowell also scoffed at the suggestion that the Foundation is a shadowy organization that secretly governs the country. "We simply provide a forum for the discussion of issues related to business and economics," Nowell stated. "We don't tell anyone what to think or what to do."

After leaving Java Joe's, I checked in briefly at the office and then headed over to the Bay County Historical Society to do some research on the history of artists and performers on the boardwalk. I wanted to demonstrate that the boardwalk has an established tradition of serving as a public forum for artists and performers and, therefore, is protected by the 1st Amendment.

The Bay County Historical Society is housed in the town's old railroad station, which dates back to the early days of Oceanic Park, when the resort was accessible only by train or ferry. Use of the railroad declined after a drawbridge was built in 1948 and Oceanic Park became accessible by car. In 1953, the railroad bridge was badly damaged in a storm. Since the bridge wasn't used much anymore, the town decided to demolish what was left of it rather than rebuild it, ending the era of train service to Oceanic Park. The railroad station had sat empty for a few years before it was taken over the by Historical Society.

The old station is a two-story frame structure built on an elevated concrete slab that used to serve as a boarding platform for the train. The platform now is used to display some of the Historical Society's larger artifacts. On display were a heavily-corroded 12-pounder cannon mounted on a wheeled, wooden platform and a gigantic two-and-a-half-ton anchor, both of which had been salvaged from shipwrecks. Also on display, in a glass-sided case, was a huge shark, posed by the taxidermist with its mouth open, showing off its enormous bite span and nasty-looking teeth.

As I entered the lobby of the Historical Society, a buzzer sounded and Margot Peterson looked up from behind the old ticket counter, which now served as a reception desk.

"Good morning," Margot said in her raspy croak of a voice, removing her reading glasses and allowing them to hang from the cord around her neck. She was in her late sixties with steel grey hair cut into a bob, wearing a jacket against the chill of the air conditioning. For generations, Margot's family had run the Atlantic Hotel, one of the first hotels to be built along the boardwalk. The hotel had been established by her grandparents and then run by each succeeding generation of the family. At this point, Margot was largely retired and the next generation had taken over running the hotel. Margot volunteered at the historical society, where she was a font of knowledge on local history, some passed down from her family and some acquired through her own experience as a lifelong resident of Oceanic Park.

"What can we help you with?" Margot asked.

"I'm doing research on the history of the boardwalk," I told her.

"Well, we've got lots of information about the boardwalk," she said. "Anything in particular?"

"I'm interested in information about artists and performers on the boardwalk."

"So, you're going to challenge that ordinance."

"Yes, some of the artists and performers on the boardwalk have asked me to represent them. I need to show that there's an established tradition of artists and performers working on the boardwalk."

"Well, you shouldn't have any trouble doing that. There have been artist and performers on the boardwalk practically since it was built. I can remember my grandmother talking about a blind banjo player who used to play on the boardwalk with a tin cup attached to the end of his banjo for tips. Let me check our subject matter files and see what we have." She went down the hall to the file room and returned shortly with a couple of thick files stuffed with newspaper clippings, magazine articles, promotional brochures, and other items.

"Start taking a look at these while I check the catalog and see what else we have," Margot said, handing the files to me.

I took the files and entered the library. At one end of the library was a reading area that was furnished with a few wooden tables and reading lamps and, at the other end of the library, were rows of shelves filled with books. A large nautical map was mounted on a wall in the reading area and, underneath the map, was a glass-topped display case that housed an old ship's log, a compass, a sextant, and some other objects.

The reading area was deserted at that hour of the morning. I sat down at one of the tables, turned on the lamp, and started going through the files and taking notes.

"Here's a few more things that you may find helpful," Margot said and placed a small stack of books on the table next to me.

"Thank you," I said.

"I'm pleased to see that someone is going to challenge that ordinance."

"It's good of you to say so."

"You seem a bit surprised."

"Well, I wasn't sure how you'd feel about it, given your family business. I thought that the businesses along the boardwalk were supporting the ordinance."

"Hah! I prefer the boardwalk the way that it is. We've gotten along with the artists and performers on the boardwalk as long as I can remember. Why has it become a problem all of a sudden?"

"The Merchants Association wants to transform Oceanic Park from a carnival town to an exclusive, upscale resort."

"Those people with the Merchants Association really rub me the wrong way. That new executive director they hired - he's always in the newspaper and on the radio, talking about his 'vision' for Oceanic Park, as if he owned the place. And that lobbyist of theirs - she tried to get us to support the ordinance. She said it's important that the business community speak with one voice on this issue, meaning their voice, of course. They don't speak for me, let me tell you. The two of them are a couple of snake oil salesmen."

"It's the era of the celebrity business executive. They want to make a name for themselves. Oceanic Park is just the first step on the way to bigger and better things."

"Well, the sooner they get on their way to other things and leave us alone, the better."

"Perhaps you'd be willing to testify against the ordinance at the hearing on Friday."

"Oh, I plan to, believe me."

Margot returned to her post behind the counter and I continued going through the material that she had brought me. An article in the August 9, 1906 issue of the *Oceanic Park Press* reported that a strolling banjo player named Blind Georgie Wilkinson, led by a seeing-eye dog, entertained people on the boardwalk during the summer. The following summer, the paper reported that he was joined by a guitar player named Stanley Remington. Over the years artists, jugglers, magicians, puppeteers, and numerous others have entertained people on the boardwalk. I took notes and made photocopies of some of the articles.

As I was leaving, I paused at the counter to thank Margot for her help.

"By the way, did you get hit with those anti-immigrant flyers yesterday?" I asked.

"Yeah, we did," Margot responded. "It was a pain having to clean those things off the windows."

"Have you ever heard of this group, the Oceanic Park Vigilantes, before?"

"I've been doing some research in our archives, and I've managed to find a few references to a group called the Bay County Vigilantes in the period after the Civil War. It appears that they were involved in terrorizing Black families in the farming communities over on the mainland. They are reported to have posted flyers on the doors of the homes of former slaves warning them to leave the county or be killed. I haven't been able to find out much more about them. There are no references to them at all after the Reconstruction period."

"It's interesting that this new group has adopted a similar name. Perhaps someone in the new group is familiar with local history."

"That could be."

My next stop was the law library in the Bay County Circuit Court building, which is located in the northern part of Old Town, near City Hall. The Circuit Court building is a traditional-looking brick courthouse with a portico supported by Roman columns in front. The law library is located in the rear of the courthouse on the first floor in a high-ceilinged room with tall, narrow windows fitted with shutters on the inside.

I greeted Helen Marwood, who was seated at the reference librarian's desk in the front of the room. Helen previously had worked as a librarian at Bay County College, but recently had taken on a new job at the law library. She also served as president of the local chapter of the United Human Rights Coalition, an advocacy organization that holds seminars on human rights issues and organizes letter-writing campaigns on behalf of political prisoners. The previous summer, I had helped the organization obtain a permit to hold an anti-war demonstration in Pelican Park, after the City Council had denied their application for a permit.

"What brings you here?" Helen asked. She was in her thirties, with light-brown hair held in a clasp, wearing retro-looking tortoise-shell-framed glasses, and dressed in business casual style.

"I need to get up to speed on the most recent case law on the 1st Amendment," I responded. "I'm going to challenge the City Council's proposed ordinance regulating artists and performers on the boardwalk."

"Oh, yeah, I read about that ordinance in the paper."

"Speaking of the paper, I saw that you were quoted in that article about the annual meeting of the Economic Freedom Foundation."

"Yes, we're holding a demonstration against the meeting and trying to organize a boycott against the Oceanic Park Plaza for hosting the meeting."

"I take it that you didn't have a problem getting a permit for the demonstration."

"No, I don't think that they would have dared to deny us a permit after what happened last summer."

"How about the boycott?"

"It's really hard to find support for that. Most local people seem convinced that this meeting is going to be a good thing for the town. They think that it will help attract more meetings and conventions to the town. We've been trying to get businesses to put a sign in their windows supporting the boycott, but hardly anyone will do it. We're going to be running an ad for the boycott in tomorrow's edition of the *Oceanic Park Press* to coincide with the start of the meeting. Hopefully, that will drum up some support."

"This meeting certainly seems to be attracting a lot of attention."

"Yes. The Economic Freedom Foundation has been around for awhile, but lately it's become a very influential organization and is starting to get attention from the media. Are you familiar with them?"

"Vaguely. As I understand it, they're some sort of right-wing think tank that was formed back during the early days of the Cold War."

"That's right. The organization was founded by Marshall Rankin, who was the head of Amalgamated Steel Company. He was a Nazi sympathizer and continued to do business with Germany in secret during World War II by routing steel shipments through third countries. After World War II, with the rise of the Soviet Union, Rankin became a virulent anti-communist. He founded the Economic Freedom Foundation in 1947 to promote his economic and political ideas. He touted free-market capitalism, even though his company engaged in monopolistic practices. The Foundation published a quarterly journal called *Freedom Forum* that was distributed to high school economics and history teachers and college professors. It contained articles purportedly written by Rankin that promoted his economic views. The articles actually were ghost written by a free-market economist named Dean Longworth, who taught at the University of Urbana. Longworth is the one who really is responsible for developing the economic theories that the Foundation promoted. His ideas were primarily economic, but he cloaked everything in patriotic language - practically every sentence that he wrote had the word 'freedom,' 'liberty,' or 'independence' in it somewhere. Longworth used a lot of academic jargon in his articles, but his economic policies boiled down to one simple objective - making sure that the poor stay poor and the rich get richer."

"That seems like an idea that's becoming increasingly popular these days."

"That's true. Initially, the Foundation was considered part of the far-right lunatic fringe and most people dismissed them as a bunch of crackpots. During the past 25 years, however, as the Republican Party has moved farther and farther to the right, the Republican Party increasingly has embraced the Foundation's ideas. Nowadays, the Foundation's theories are standard Republican orthodoxy."

"I seem to remember that the Foundation was known for having some sort of seminar program."

"Yes, that was one of the smartest things that they did. They had a series of week-long seminars in the summer that they used to groom adherents to their economic theories. The Foundation would use sympathetic high school teachers and college professors to talent spot for them. The teachers would identify students who were likely candidates. The Foundation would offer fellowships to students and teachers. They held the seminars at their headquarters on the Hudson River in upstate New York. They would use the seminars to indoctrinate people with their economic theories."

"So they gained a lot of followers?"

Geoff Cabin

40

"Yes. To give them due credit, the people who ran the Foundation were long-range planners, and now they're getting to the point where their planning is paying off. Over the years, veterans of their seminar program have risen to positions of power and influence in government and industry. And they serve as a hiring network, hiring young alumni of the seminar program. Politicians come and go, but these people are embedded in the bureaucracy that runs the country. They wield a lot of influence. They were instrumental in pushing for the U.S. to invade Iraq."

"How did they end up holding their meeting in Oceanic Park?"

"Eric Burns offered them really good rates to hold their meeting at the Oceanic Park Plaza. He's using the event as a loss leader. He'll probably lose money on it, but he thinks it will establish the Oceanic Park Plaza a go-to location for conventions and meetings and he'll end up making money in the long run."

"No doubt he's right. Unfortunately, it's people like him who seem to be determining the future of the town."

I spent the next couple of hours checking the subject matter index, going through recent cases interpreting the 1st Amendment, and taking notes. As I was getting ready to leave, I paused by Helen Marwood's desk.

"Has your organization ever heard of this group, the Oceanic Park Vigilantes?" I asked her.

"No. We monitor nativist and anti-immigrant groups, but we've never heard of this one. We've been checking with other human rights organizations and monitoring alt right and nativist websites, but we haven't been able to find any mention of them."

"What do you make of them?"

"I'm really not sure. They may be a new group or they may have made an effort to remain below the radar. It's also possible that the whole thing is some sort of hoax."

Back at the office, I started going through my research and writing a legal memorandum to submit to the City Council. In the middle of the afternoon, Roger Steadman arrived at the office for our meeting, accompanied by a couple other performers from the boardwalk - Patti Aldin, a woman who dressed in a gypsy costume and told fortunes, and Eric Henderson, a juggler and magician.

"Hey Jackson, I've had a really great idea!" Steadman exclaimed, as soon as the three of them were seated in my office. He was leaning forward in his chair, nearly bursting with excitement. "I thought that what we need to do is to get a celebrity to support our cause. I wracked my brains trying to think who we could approach. Then I remembered that I had met Belinda Restivo when she was here last summer for the opening of Captain Dan's exhibition." I nearly groaned out loud at the mention of Belinda Restivo's name. Belinda Restivo was one of the stars of a reality show called *Bimbo Beach House*. Count Rupert had invited her to the opening of Captain Dan's exhibition the previous summer as a way of attracting media attention.

"So, I thought that we could get in touch with her and invite her to come down to Oceanic Park for a few days and testify at the hearing," Steadman continued.

"Uh...I'm not sure that that's a very good idea," I said.

"Of course it is, it's a great idea," Steadman countered. "Anyway, I managed to get hold of her last night and she's agreed to come down and testify. It will give her an opportunity to publicize her show. And she was particularly pleased to hear that Captain Dan is back in town." Last summer, Belinda Restivo had hit it off with Captain Dan.

"Wait a second," I said, "I think that we ought to reconsider this. I'm not sure that having a celebrity is the right approach for a hearing that deals with legal issues."

"What do you mean? It'll cause a sensation. We'll get a lot of press coverage and it will help focus attention on the plight of artists and performers on the boardwalk."

"Look, we're going to be appearing in front of a bunch of pompous and self-important politicians. They are not going to react well if they think that we are trying to turn the hearing into some sort of reality t.v. show event."

"They'll love it. They're precisely the sort of people who will be impressed by a celebrity. Politics is nothing but show business. Anyway, it's all set. Belinda Restivo will be arriving tomorrow evening. And I've already notified the local media."

"What?! You should have spoken to me about this first."

"Oh, c'mon, Jackson, don't be so stuffy. This will work out great."

"But Belinda Restivo doesn't know anything about Oceanic Park or the situation on the boardwalk," I objected. "What is she going to say when she testifies?"

"It doesn't matter what she says. All that matters is that she puts in an appearance."

"Yes, but she's going to have to give some testimony to the City Council."

"Look, if you're worried about what she's going to say, you can write something for her to read when she testifies."

"But..."

"Don't give me anymore 'buts,' we've made a decision."

I appealed to Patti Aldin and Eric Henderson for support, but they were in agreement with Steadman.

"Look at all of the publicity Belinda Restivo generated last summer when she attended the opening of Captain Dan's exhibition at the Chimera Gallery," Patti Aldin said. "She created a sensation. Her appearance will shine a spotlight on the activities of the city council and make them look really bad if they follow through with this ordinance. It will put a lot of pressure on them to change their position."

"Oh, alright," I conceded, slumping back in my chair.

We spent the next hour or so discussing our plans for the hearing. I explained the format and procedure that would be followed at the hearing and summarized the legal arguments that I would make. I also told them that I had spoken to Margot Peterson, whose family owns the Atlantic Hotel, and that she planned to testify against the ordinance. "That will show that not everyone in the business community supports the ordinance," I concluded.

Roger Steadman, Patti Aldin, and Eric Henderson all stated that they planned to testify, along with a few other artist and performers from the boardwalk. We decided that we would conclude our case with testimony from our star witness, Belinda Restivo.

After Roger Steadman and the others left, I sighed and buried my head in my hands. I was losing control of the proceedings and didn't like the direction in which they were headed. I had a feeling that the hearing was going to be a disaster. Still, I supposed it didn't matter that much. We didn't have any chance of winning in front of the City Council anyway; our real chance of succeeding would come later, in court in front of a judge.

In the evening, I took my customary walk along the bay front to the inlet and back again. On my way back, I walked out onto the fishing pier and found the Prices in their usual spot.

"How's it going tonight?" I asked after we had greeted each other.

"It's a slow night," William replied. "Nothing's biting. Nothing at all."

I looked into the large plastic bucket on the ground next to William and saw that it was empty.

"Well, your luck's bound to change," I said.

"I wouldn't count on it," William replied. "Is there any news about the group that hung that banner on the water tower, the Oceanic Park Vigilantes?"

"No, nothing," I responded. "As far as I know, the police investigation hasn't made any progress."

"I wonder if they want to make any progress. I wouldn't be surprised if members of the police force are involved."

"Oh, don't be so cynical," Amanda admonished him. "I'm sure that the police are doing everything that they can."

"Huh," William responded.

We fell silent, waiting for a strike to occur, but the rods propped against the railing remained motionless.

"Hey! Take a look at that!" Amanda exclaimed suddenly, standing up and leaning against the railing.

A large, gleaming-white yacht had entered the bay from the inlet. The yacht was huge in comparison to the sport-fishing yachts that one usually saw in Oceanic Park and had an array of antennas, radar equipment, and satellite dishes on the roof of the cabin. Both the interior and exterior of the yacht were brightly illuminated and throbbing, bass-heavy dance music was blaring from a sound system on the yacht and drifting across the water.

"Wow, that's amazing!" Amanda declared. "I've never seen a boat like that around here before."

"It's going to scare away all the fish," William complained.

"Oh, you weren't catching anything anyway," Amanda said.

"Now I'm definitely not going to catch anything," William responded.

"I wonder who owns that boat," Amanda said.

I squinted my eyes and managed to make out the name painted on the bow of the yacht - The Gold Standard. It seemed like a suitably ostentatious name for such a monument to conspicuous consumption.

We got a closer look at the boat as it went past the end of the fishing pier. A man in a blue-and-white striped shirt and white duck pants was piloting the boat from the wheel on the flying bridge with a woman in a tiny black dress standing next to him. The man had one hand on the steering wheel and the other resting on the woman's hip. The woman was holding a flute of champagne in one hand, alternating between taking sips from it herself and holding it up to the pilot's lips for him to take sips. The afterdeck of the boat was crowded with people who were dancing to the music with wild abandon. A few other people were lounging around the foredeck.

As the boat continued past the fishing pier, some of the revelers onboard waved and some of the people fishing on the pier waved back.

"They shouldn't wave back, it only encourages them," William grumbled. "People like that are going to ruin the place."

"Oh, lighten up," Amanda told him.

"No, I mean it. More and more rich people like that are coming here and trying to turn the place into some sort of upscale resort. They're going to drive up property values and make it unaffordable for everyone else."

As the Gold Standard approached the drawbridge, it sounded its foghorn as a signal to the bridgekeeper. On the drawbridge, bells began to toll and the red lights on the zebra-striped traffic barriers began to flash. The traffic barriers were lowered and traffic on the bridge came to a stop. Then the two sections of the drawbridge began to rise. When the two sections of the drawbridge were fully elevated, the Gold Standard started forward.

While the Gold Standard had been idling and waiting for the drawbridge to be raised, it had drifted out of the center of the channel and toward the shore. When it started forward again, it was out of position. Since it was such a large boat, it had very tight clearance going through the drawbridge. As the boat approached the bridge, it was apparent that the boat was too close to the side of the bridge.

"What's that guy doing?" William asked.

"If he keeps going like that, he's going to hit the bridge," Amanda said.

At the steering wheel on the flying bridge, the man piloting the boat seemed oblivious. He and the woman next to him were becoming increasingly entangled and she now was using her free hand to undo the buttons of his shirt. None of the revelers on the boat seemed to notice the danger either. As the boat neared the bridge, Keith Threlkeld, the bridgekeeper, appeared to realize what was happening. He leaned out of a window of the bridgekeeper's booth and began frantically yelling and waving his arms, but his voice was drowned out by the loud music.

The man piloting the boat finally seemed to notice Threlkeld's frantic waving and to realize what was happening. He shoved the woman to the side, grabbed the steering wheel with both hands, and tried to correct course, but it was too late. The Gold Standard hit the wooden barrier on the side of the bridge with a loud crack. The force of the impact jolted people onboard the yacht. On the crowded afterdeck, dancers collided and were knocked to the deck on top of each other like bowling pins. On the foredeck, people who had been lounging about were sent sprawling across the deck grasping for handholds. A woman who had been leaning against the railing of the foredeck was flipped over the railing by the force of the impact and hit the water with a splash. We heard the sound of screams and yells above the pulsating music.

"Someone's fallen overboard!" a voice yelled.

A man appeared at the railing of the foredeck. There was something familiar about him and then I realized that it was Stuart Nichols, my old law school classmate who I had run into the previous night at the reopening of the Chimera Gallery.

"Don't worry," Nichols called to the woman who had surfaced and was treading water alongside the boat. "I'll rescue you."

"Don't you dare!" Another woman appeared at Nichol's side by the railing on the fore-deck and grabbed his arm. "You're too drunk to swim."

"Don't worry," Nichols called to the woman in the water, jerking his arm free from the other woman. "I'll help you."

"I don't need any help," the woman in the water responded and began swimming toward the wooden ladder that was attached to the rear of the yacht. Nichols ignored her refusal of help and dove off the boat's deck. He hit the water flat on his stomach in a massive belly flop that sent a plume of water shooting into the air.

"Aargh!" Nichols let out a loud yell when he hit the water. Apparently incapacitated by the alcohol and the impact, he began flailing about, splashing and waving his arms.

"Help!" Nichols yelled. "Somebody help me!"

"You don't deserve any help!" the woman on the deck yelled down at him. "Let him drown!"

The woman who had been swimming toward the ladder, reversed course, got Nichols into a lifesaving hold, and pulled him along with her to the ladder. Nichols struggled up the ladder. As he reached the top of the ladder, people helped him onboard and he collapsed in a heap on the deck. The woman followed him up the ladder and boarded the boat with no difficulty.

Now that the two people were safely back on board, the man piloting the boat put it in reverse and started positioning it to make a second attempt at going through the drawbridge. He was interrupted, however, by the sound of a siren and the flash of a blue light cutting through the night. A police launch was approaching the yacht from the direction of the inlet.

"Stop the vessel immediately!" a woman officer in the bow of the police launch commanded through a bullhorn. "Do not proceed any further!"

As the police launch approached the rear of the yacht, a man ran to the foredeck of the yacht and began frantically going through the pockets of his tuxedo jacket. He extracted a couple of packets from an inside jacket pocket and tossed them into the water. Several other people followed suit, running to the railing of the foredeck, rapidly going through pockets and purses, and tossing things overboard.

"Stop immediately!" the officer on the police launch commanded through the bullhorn. "Do not throw any objects overboard."

The police launch pulled up behind the yacht and the officer in the bow of the launch laid down the bullhorn and began to climb the ladder to the afterdeck of the yacht. The yacht's pilot climbed down from the flying bridge and hurried across the afterdeck to the ladder. He positioned himself at the top of the ladder to block the officer from climbing aboard. Someone shut off the music as people on the boat waited to see what was going to happen.

When the officer reached the top of the ladder, she was blocked from boarding the yacht by the pilot.

"Please move aside and allow me to board," the officer instructed. Her voice carried clearly across the water to the fishing pier.

"Do you know who I am?" the pilot demanded.

"It doesn't matter who you are," the officer responded. "You were operating a vessel in a reckless manner."

"I'm Clifton Safir, the CEO of the Rubicon Consortium," the pilot declared. "My guests and I are here to attend the annual meeting of the Economic Freedom Foundation."

"Please move aside," the officer said, seemingly unimpressed.

"Is this how you treat guests who are in town to attend an important meeting?" Safir demanded.

"Please move aside," the officer repeated for the third time. When Safir failed to move, she grabbed him by the shoulders, moved him to the side, and climbed aboard the yacht. Another officer followed her up the ladder and onto the yacht, while a third officer remained in the police launch.

"The mayor and City Council will hear about this!" Safir declared. "You'll be back directing traffic tomorrow morning!"

After taking stock of the situation, the woman officer climbed onto the flying bridge and took control of the yacht. She put the yacht into reverse, repositioned it, and took it through the drawbridge. The police launch followed close behind.

"Can you believe that?!" William declared. "What a bunch of clowns! I hope that they throw the book at the guy who was piloting the boat."

Chapter 3. Thursday, July 21, 2005

By the next morning, word of Belinda Restivo's planned appearance at the City Council hearing had spread. It was the main topic of conversation at Java Joe's and there was an article about it by Gary Rockwell on the front page of the *Oceanic Park Press*:

> REALITY TV STAR TO APPEAR AT CITY COUNCIL HEARING. Belinda Restivo, star of the reality tv show *Bimbo Beach House*, announced that she will appear at tomorrow's City Council hearing to testify against the proposed ordinance to limit the number of artists and performers on the boardwalk. Restivo first visited Oceanic Park last summer to attend the opening of an exhibition by Captain Dan Chapman at the Chimera Gallery.
>
> "I fell in love with Oceanic Park last summer," Restivo said in statement posted on her website. "The boardwalk is one of its best features. The artists and performers on the boardwalk help to give the boardwalk its unique character. I want to show support for my fellow artists and performers."
>
> "We are pleased to have the support of a great artist like Belinda Restivo," said Roger Steadman, an Elvis impersonator who appears on the boardwalk under the name "Boardwalk Elvis." "Support from the wider arts community is important at a time when

the 1ˢᵗ Amendment rights of artists and performers on the boardwalk are under attack by the City Council."

"I see that you've invited Belinda Restivo to testify at the hearing," Wendy sneered when she brought my breakfast.

"I'm not the one who invited her," I protested.

"Uh-huh. I suppose that she'll explain the finer points of the 1ˢᵗ Amendment to the City Council."

"I suppose so."

I returned to perusing the paper. Family members of 28 children killed by a suicide bomber in Iraq the previous week had gathered at the scene of the explosion to honor the memory of the deceased children....In an appearance at the port of Baltimore, President Bush praised the USA Patriot Act and urged Congress to extend provisions of the Act that were due to expire, claiming that the Act had not compromised civil liberties...At the same event, Bush promoted the nomination of Judge John G. Roberts, Jr. to replace retiring Supreme Court Justice Sandra Day O'Connor, trying to pre-empt criticism of Roberts for consistently favoring business interests and being opposed to women's reproductive rights. There also was an article about the yacht that collided with the drawbridge:

YACHT COLLIDES WITH DRAWBRIDGE.
Last night, a yacht attempting to pass through the Oceanic Park drawbridge collided with the wooden barrier designed to protect the bridge from boats passing through the channel. The yacht, the Gold Standard, is owned by Clifton Safir, CEO of the Rubicon Consortium. Safir, who was piloting the yacht at the time of the collision, is in Oceanic Park to speak at the annual meeting of the Economic Freedom Foundation, which is being held at the Oceanic Park Plaza Hotel and Conference Center.

No injuries were reported, but a woman was knocked overboard by the impact of the collision. "I had to dive in and rescue her," said Stuart Nichols, a passenger on the yacht. "If it hadn't been for me, she would have drowned."

Following the collision, police seized control of the boat and arrested Safir, who has been charged with operating a vessel while intoxicated. Safir admitted that he "may have had a few drinks" but blamed the collision on an outdated drawbridge and incompetence of the bridge keeper.

"Those old drawbridges are too small to handle modern-day yachts," Safir stated. "If Oceanic Park wants to become a go-to destination for conventions, it needs to build a new bridge that can accommodate larger yachts. And the bridge keeper was asleep on the job and failed to give adequate warning. This is an outrageous way to treat an important guest who is in town for a convention." Safir demanded that the bridge keeper be fired and that the city pay for the damages to his yacht.

City engineers examined the bridge and reported that there is no structural damage.

After awhile, I glanced up and saw Adam Pulman, the attorney for the City Council, headed across the room, glaring at me and waving a copy of the newspaper.

"What's the idea of pulling a cheap publicity stunt like this?" he demanded.

"What are you talking about?" I responded.

"You know perfectly well what I'm talking about. Having that reality-t.v.-show bimbo testify at the hearing."

"Why should you object to that?"

"This is going to turn the hearing into a media circus."

"I would have thought that City Council would be pleased at getting some media attention."

"This is the wrong sort of attention. We'll get a lot of people from the national media who don't understand the local issues. You know what they're like. Everything will end up getting distorted and mischaracterized. The ordinance will end up being portrayed as powerful business interests picking on struggling artists and performers."

"Isn't that what's happening?"

"That's not what's happening at all. You're being impossible, as usual."

"Reverend Haycroft called," Phoebe informed me when I got to the office. "He said that they're holding a community meeting in the church hall at 8:00 o'clock this evening to discuss the anti-immigrant flyer campaign. Representatives of the town government will be there."

"O.k.," I responded. Reverend Haycroft was the pastor of the Oceanic Park United Methodist Church and played an active role in community affairs.

Phoebe and I spent the remainder of the day preparing for the hearing. I completed work on my legal memorandum and Phoebe ran off and collated copies. She then took them to City Hall and submitted them to the clerk's office, for distribution to members of the City Council prior to the hearing. Meanwhile, I reviewed my notes and worked on my oral presentation for the hearing. In the late afternoon, I held a final meeting with Roger Steadman, Patti Aldin, and Eric Henderson to review our plan for the hearing. Roger Steadman informed me that Belinda Restivo was due to arrive in Oceanic Park that evening and I gave him the testimony that I had drafted for her to present to the committee. By the end of the day, I felt like we were in pretty good shape.

After knocking off work, I headed back to my cottage, changed clothes, and grabbed a quick bite to eat. Then I headed over to the Oceanic Park United Methodist Church for the community meeting on the anti-immigrant flyer campaign.

The Oceanic Park United Methodist Church campus occupies half a block in the northern part of Old Town, not far from City Hall. The church was established in the early days of the resort, when the town consisted of a few hotels and vacation cottages at the southern end of the island. The congregation initially held services in the parlor of the Breakers Hotel. After a few years, they had raised enough money to be able to build a small meeting house on some nearby property. As the resort grew, however, the congregation grew along with it and soon became too big for the meeting house. During the 1920s, the church purchased a piece of land in what was then the northern part of town and built a proper church - a shingled structure that, in accordance with local custom, had a bell tower over the entryway. They also built a small cottage alongside the church to serve as a rectory. Both the church building and rectory still are in use today, having been renovated and modernized a few times over the years. In the 1950s, the church expanded by purchasing a boarding house that was located next door to the church and converting it into a church hall.

Like a lot of churches, the Oceanic Park United Methodist Church was experiencing a decline in membership and struggling to make ends meet. About two-and-a-half years ago, Eric Haycroft had been appointed to lead the church. Haycroft held a degree in something called "congregational re-vitalization" and was attempting to turn the church around. His strategy included getting the church more involved in the life of the community and doing more outreach to residents of the town. The meeting on the anti-immigrant flyer and banner campaign appeared to be an example of their efforts to engage with the community in a useful way.

I was greeted at the door of the church hall by Melissa Haycroft, Reverend Haycroft's wife, who helped to run the church. She had shoulder-length black hair streaked with grey and a quick, friendly smile that exuded a welcoming attitude toward everyone she met. She ran the church's thrift shop, which sold donated goods and used the proceeds to fund the church's programs, and oversaw the church's weekly soup kitchen, which provided a hot meal to the homeless and others in need. Tonight, she was stationed by the door of the church hall to greet arrivals and direct them down the hall to the auditorium.

I was a bit early and there was only a handful of people in the auditorium, some seated in the rows of folding aluminum chairs facing the stage and others milling about the room. I spotted a few familiar faces among the early arrivals - Gary Rockwell from the *Oceanic Park Press* was standing off to the side of the stage along with a news photographer and a couple of other people; Margot Peterson from the Bay County Historical Society was speaking to a man I didn't recognize; and Helen Marwood was seated on a chair, working on a laptop while waiting for the meeting to get underway.

I said hello to Helen, who looked up from her computer and greeted me.

"I'm glad you're here," she said. "I need to talk to you. Do you remember, yesterday, I told you that we were running an ad for the boycott of the Oceanic Park Plaza in today's paper?"

"Yes," I said, and it belatedly dawned on me that I hadn't seen the ad in that morning's paper.

"Well, yesterday afternoon, I got a call from the advertising manager at the paper. She told me that they had decided not to run the ad because it violates the paper's policy on advertisements."

"What did they object to?"

"She wouldn't say. She just said that the decision of whether to run an ad is within the discretion of management."

"She wouldn't give you any further explanation?"

"No. She referred me to a statement in the advertising material on the paper's website that says that the publisher reserves the right to reject or cancel any advertisement at any time."

"Yeah, that's pretty standard language."

"Can they do that? Is it a violation of the 1st Amendment?"

"No, it's not a violation. The 1st Amendment applies only to the government. What the the 1st Amendment actually says is that Congress can't pass a law that abridges the freedom of speech or freedom of the press. It doesn't say that a privately-owned entity, like a newspaper, can't adopt policies that place limits on speech."

"This is infuriating. Somebody must have found out about the ad and put pressure on the paper not to run it."

"Yeah, it sounds like it. Newspapers are desperate for advertising revenue these days. Somebody must have really put a lot pressure on the paper to get them to give up the revenue from the ad. I can talk to people at the paper and see if I can get any more information."

"Thanks, but don't bother. It's too late to do any good at this point. We'll just have to carry on with the boycott as best we can."

I left Helen to resume work on her laptop. By now, the auditorium was starting to fill up bit and I drifted about and exchanged greetings with people I knew. Among the attendees were Java Joe, Karen Cardenay, and Amanda and William Price.

A few minutes after eight o'clock, Reverend Haycroft walked onto the stage, accompanied by Joseph O'Connor, the Mayor of Oceanic Park, Tom Hadley, the Chief of the Oceanic Park Police Department, and Sergeant Bartlett. Reverend Haycroft stepped up to a podium located front and center of the stage, while Mayor O'Connor, Chief Hadley, and Sergeant Bartlett sat in chairs arrayed behind the podium. Haycroft was a slight, forty-something man with a receding hairline and frameless glasses that gave him a professorial air.

"May I have your attention everyone," Reverend Haycroft announced. "Please take your seats, we are about to begin."

There was a bit of commotion while the people who had been milling about found seats and settled down. I took a seat in the back row, next to the Prices.

"I wonder if we'll learn anything new tonight," Amanda mused.

"I doubt it," William responded. "If there were any news, we already would have heard it. I think that the purpose of this meeting is to try to reassure people that the authorities are on top of the situation."

"Good evening and thank you for coming," Reverend Haycroft said, when everyone had been seated. "As you know, our community has experienced some unpleasant incidents recently. Many of you have expressed concern about what is going on in the community and have asked what is being done to address it. As a result, we have organized this meeting to bring together representatives of the city government and members of the community. I'd like to thank Mayor O'Connor, Chief Hadley, and Sergeant Bartlett for attending. They will explain the steps that city government is taking to address the issue and then answer your questions. I'd like to start by introducing Mayor O'Connor."

Mayor O'Connor got up and walked to the podium. He was balding, middle-aged and overweight, wearing a sports jacket and a shirt with an open collar. O'Connor had an easy-going, jovial personality that allowed him to interact easily with voters. People tended to like him, even if they didn't agree with his politics.

"Good evening everyone," he began. "I'd also like to thank you for coming and thank Reverend Haycroft and the Oceanic Park United Methodist Church for organizing and hosting this meeting. I know that you all are concerned about the incidents that have occurred lately. I want to be clear that these kind of incidents have no place in Oceanic Park - Oceanic Park is a place where all are welcome. Those of us in city government are doing everything that we can to address the problem. I want to assure you that, in spite of these incidents, Oceanic Park remains a safe and family-friendly resort.

"I have been meeting regularly with Chief Hadley and the leaders of the Police Department to oversee the investigation of these incidents and formulate strategy for preventing future incidents. I am committed to ensuring that the police department has adequate resources to deal with the situation. Chief Hadley and Sergeant Bartlett will explain the plans of the police department in more detail.

"I also have directed the City Solicitor to review the laws that apply to these sort of incidents to determine whether adequate laws exist to address them. If additional laws are needed, I will work with the city council or state legislature, as appropriate, to try to get necessary laws enacted.

"I'd like to turn things over to Chief Hadley, who will explain the steps that the Police Department is taking."

Chief Hadley walked to the podium. He also was middle-aged and heavy-set, with ramrod-straight posture that suggested a military background. He wore his hair in a military-style buzz cut and was dressed in a sharply-pressed blue uniform. Hadley had been elevated to Police Chief the previous summer as a result of the upheaval caused by the investigation of Count Rupert's death.

"Thank you for the opportunity to address this issue," Hadley began in a clipped, rapid-fire cadence. "I know that there has been some frustration over the failure of the police department to apprehend the perpetrators of these incidents. I understand that there even has been some suggestion that the police have turned a blind eye to these incidents. Let me assure you that that is not the case - the police department takes these incidents very seriously. The investigation of these incidents and apprehension of the perpetrators are among the department's top priorities. To that end, I've created a special working group within the department, which is headed by Sergeant Bartlett. Sergeant Bartlett has worked as both a foot patrolman and supervising officer in Old Town and is very familiar with the neighborhood. Many of you already know him. I'd like to ask him to explain in detail what the working group will be doing."

Sergeant Bartlett exchanged places with Chief Hadley at the podium. Bartlett was in his late thirties, with a wiry, athletic build and, like Chief Hadley, dressed in a sharply-pressed blue uniform.

"Thank you," Sergeant Bartlett began. "As Chief Hadley noted, investigation of these incidents is one of the department's top priorities and we are making every effort to identify the perpetrators responsible for these incidents. As part of our effort to obtain information about the Oceanic Park Vigilantes, we are monitoring nativist and anti-immigrant websites, but the Oceanic Park Vigilantes do not appear to have any online presence. We also have spoken to both local and national organizations that monitor nativist and anti-immigrant groups and none of them have ever heard of the Oceanic Park Vigilantes.

"We currently are working with experts to develop a profile of the sort of person who would be involved in a group like this. And we are reviewing records of past incidents to try to identify any local people who have a history of involvement in these sort of activities.

"In order to prevent any future incidents, we are stepping up foot patrols in the Old Town neighborhood during the late night and early morning hours. We also are asking residents of the Old Town neighborhood for their assistance. Please keep a watch out for any suspicious activity and, if you see anything, please report it immediately. The department has set up a special hotline number for that purpose. The number is 410-782-3171. If you see anything, please do not try to intervene or take matters into your own hands. Call us. Reports will be relayed to foot patrols in the area, who will respond quickly. Thank you."

Sergeant Bartlett returned to his seat and Reverend Haycroft stepped up to the podium again.

"I'd like to again thank the representatives of city government for taking time to appear this evening," Reverend Haycroft said. "Now, does anyone have any questions for them?"

After a brief period of silence during which people glanced about to see who would be the first to break the ice, a smartly-dressed, middle-aged woman with short dark hair and glasses hanging from a cord around her neck stood up.

"My name is Idelle Arman and I run the Heirloom Antiques in Old Town," she said. "My store was hit in two of the three flyer attacks. Am I correct that all of these incidents have taken place in Old Town? And, if that is the case, do you have any idea why Old Town has been targeted and not other areas of the town?"

Sergeant Bartlett stood up to answer the question.

"You're correct, all of the incidents have taken place in Old Town," Bartlett said. "We're not sure whether the neighborhood is being intentionally targeted for some reason or whether it was chosen simply as a matter of convenience for the perpetrators."

The next person to stand up and speak was a thirty-something man with curly, sun-streaked hair and the dark tan of someone who spends a lot of time on the water.

"My name is Sean Taylor and I'm the owner of Deep Seas Dive and Salvage Shop," he said. "My shop also was hit by the flyer attacks. If the perpetrators are apprehended, what crimes can they be charged with?"

Chief Hadley stood up to field this question.

"When we apprehend the perpetrators, it will be up to the State's Attorney's office to decide what crimes to charge them with. My understanding, however, is that they can be charged with vandalism and posting flyers without a permit."

This prompted Helen Marwood to stand up.

"My name is Helen Marwood and I'm the president of the local chapter of the United Human Rights Coalition," she said. "Given that these incidents appear to be racially motivated, why can't the perpetrators be charged with hate crimes?"

"That's possible, but my understanding is that hate crimes are difficult to prove because you have to show intent," Chief Hadley responded.

"Why should anyone be charged with a hate crime simply for exercising their 1st Amendment right to free speech?" a loud, overbearing voice demanded. Everyone turned in the direction of the voice, which belonged to a man seated a couple of rows in front of us. The owner of the voice stood up - he was a middle-aged man wearing a loud, plaid sports jacket, which clashed with his salmon pink pants. His outfit seemed calculated to attract attention and offend anyone with good taste.

"My name is Walter Braddock," the man announced, "and I'm the host of Rude Awakening on WDSF Business Talk Radio." A decidedly unfriendly murmur went up from the crowd with a few muffled "boos" mixed in with it. Braddock looked around the room and smirked, savoring the reaction that he had provoked. "I don't understand why everyone is so upset about this flyer campaign. People post advertising flyers around town all the time and nothing is ever done about it. These flyers are being singled out for attack because of their content. This is nothing but censorship, trying to impose politically-correct standards on us and restrict people's 1st

Amendment right to freedom of speech. The people posting the flyers should be supported rather than condemned."

"Do you have any information about who is posting the flyers?" Chief Hadley asked.

"I don't know who is posting the flyers, but, if I did, I certainly wouldn't tell the police," Braddock responded. "I don't want to see people persecuted for exercising their 1st Amendment rights. While city government is focusing all of its attention on the flyer campaign, it's failed to address the real issue - out-of-control immigration. Every day here in Oceanic Park, you have to deal with people who don't speak English, who don't respect our culture and our way of life, and who refuse to assimilate into our society. I'd like to know what actions city government plans to take to stem the flow of out-of-control immigration and preserve the culture of Oceanic Park."

"I'll respond to that," Mayor O'Connor said, getting to his feet. "I understand the concerns expressed by you and your listeners. While out-of-control immigration may be a problem in some parts of the country, however, it is not a problem in Oceanic Park. Migrant workers in Oceanic Park are here legally under the H-2B guest worker program. These workers are very important to the economy of Oceanic Park. The fact is, without our migrant workers, Oceanic Park couldn't function in the summer."

The mayor was attempting to do a political balancing act, trying to avoid incurring the wrath of Braddock and his listeners, while, at the same time, avoid alienating members of the business community that relied on migrant workers.

"Migrant workers are taking jobs away from Americans and driving down wages," Braddock asserted. "They are bringing crime and gang violence here and replacing European-American culture with degenerate third-world culture."

"Migrant workers are not taking jobs away from Americans," O'Connor responded. "Before a business can employ migrant workers under the H-2B program, the business has to show that there are not enough American workers able, willing, and qualified to fill the positions in question. And we have not had any problem with crime and gang violence by immigrants in Oceanic Park."

"How do you know that all of the migrant workers in Oceanic Park are here legally?" Braddock countered. "What kind of enforcement procedures do you have in place to ensure that migrant workers have obtained an H-2B visa?"

Chief Hadley rose to respond to this question.

"Enforcement of immigration law is primarily the responsibility of federal immigration agencies," Hadley stated. "If you have any evidence that migrant workers are here illegally, we will look into it. But we can't investigate without probable cause for doing so."

"Listen, these people are coming here with an agenda," Braddock snarled. He was becoming increasingly angry and frustrated that his arguments were being so deftly parried by O'Connor and Hadley. "They want to replace us and our way of life. We need to preserve our American-European culture."

"What do you know about American-European culture?" Helen Marwood demanded, standing up again. "You're not using your radio show to promote American-European culture, you're using it to promote ignorance and vulgarity. You're the one who is destroying the community."

"Hah, I know all about you and your pathetic little organization," Braddock sneered. "It's typical of left-wing organizations on college campuses that want to stifle free speech and enforce political correctness. Organizations like yours are the ones that are spreading hatred and intolerance. You have no respect for the 1st Amendment."

"Hate speech is not protected by the 1st Amendment."

"You don't know anything about the 1st Amendment, you stupid bitch."

"Everyone, please calm down," Reverend Haycroft implored from the podium. "There is no place for the sort of language here. I understand that people have strong feelings about these issues, but, please, let's discuss them in a cordial manner."

"The time for being cordial is over," Braddock retorted. "It's time for people to take action. I'm not going to stand here and be insulted by this stupid bitch."

Sean Taylor, who was seated in the row in front of Walter Braddock, stood up, turned around and confronted Braddock.

"We've had enough of your invective," Taylor said. "You owe her an apology."

"I'm not going to apologize for standing up for America."

"I said that you owe her an apology."

"Are you going to make me apologize?"

"If I have to."

"You want an apology? Alright, here's your apology." Braddock reached into an inside breast pocket of his jacket, whipped out a small canister of pepper spray, and sprayed Taylor in the face with it. Taylor threw up his hands to try to shield his face and staggered backwards, knocking over a couple of chairs and falling onto the floor.

"That will teach you!" Braddock crowed and threateningly waved around the canister of pepper spray. "Does anybody else want the same treatment?"

Java Joe, who was seated in the row behind Braddock, stood up, grabbed Braddock's arm, and tried to wrest the canister of pepper spray out of his hand, but Braddock resisted.

"Get off of me, you jackbooted thug!" Braddock yelled, "I won't stand for this!"

Another man who was seated nearby joined in; he and Java Joe struggled with Braddock, knocking over more chairs and sending people scurrying out of the way.

"Help!" Braddock yelled. "I'm being assaulted!"

Java Joe and the other man managed to pin Braddock to the floor, amidst a bunch of overturned chairs, while he writhed against them. Sergeant Bartlett jumped off the stage, dashed across the floor, and knelt down next to Braddock. Bartlett grabbed Braddock by the arm with one hand and, with the other, pried the canister of pepper spray out of Braddock's grip.

"I'm placing you under arrest for assault," Bartlett informed Braddock.

"Don't be stupid," Braddock responded. "I was acting in self defense. You should arrest these people for assaulting me."

"Let him up," Bartlett instructed Java Joe and the other man who had Braddock pinned to the floor. The two of them let go of Braddock, stood up, and backed away from him.

"Please stand up and come with me," Bartlett instructed Braddock.

"I have no intention of going with you," Braddock said as he lifted himself off the floor.

"Would you prefer I use handcuffs?"

"Do you know who I am?" Braddock demanded.

"Yes, I know who you are."

"You are making a huge mistake. I have the highest-rated radio show in Oceanic Park. Tomorrow morning everyone in town will hear about this. Your career will be over."

"Please come with me," Sergeant Bartlett said calmly in a measured tone of voice, refusing to allow Braddock to provoke him.

By this point, Chief Hadley had joined Sergeant Bartlett.

"Are you going to allow this?" Braddock appealed to Hadley.

"You are not above the law, Mr. Braddock," Hadley responded.

"I'll call for transport," Sergeant Bartlett said. He instructed Braddock to have a seat in the back of the auditorium until the transport arrived and pulled out a cell phone to make a call.

Meanwhile, Melissa Haycroft and Helen Marwood had helped Sean Taylor off the floor and into a chair, where he was sitting, rubbing his eyes with his hands, tears running down his cheeks.

"Don't rub your eyes, that's the worst thing that you can do," Melissa Haycroft said. "Come back into the kitchen and we'll bath your eyes with water." She and Helen Marwood led Taylor out of the auditorium.

The members of the audience were milling about in stunned confusion. Gary Rockwell was seated on a chair, typing furiously on a laptop, no doubt trying to record events while they still were fresh in his mind. Chief Hadley was conferring with Mayor O'Connor, who was looking grim and worried. O'Connor had been placed in a position where he had little choice but to back up his police officers, but, no doubt, he was concerned about the political fallout from arresting Braddock.

"Could I have your attention please," Sergeant Bartlett announced after he had completed his phone call. "Before you leave, we need to get everyone's name and contact information in case we need to get a witness statement from you."

Sergeant Bartlett positioned himself by the door with a pen and notepad and had everyone write down their name and contact information as they left.

After leaving the church campus, I walked back through Old Town with William and Amanda Price.

"Can you believe that?" Amanda asked. "Braddock must be insane. Assaulting someone right in front of a couple of police officers."

"He wants to stir up controversy and generate news coverage," I said. "His followers will love it. And more people will tune in to his show out of curiosity. His ratings will go through the roof."

"I wonder whether Braddock is behind the flyer campaign," William said. "Whether the whole thing is a publicity stunt to attract attention and improve the ratings of his radio show."

"I wouldn't put it past him," I said. "He's certainly benefitting from all of the controversy that's been generated."

Chapter 4. Friday, July 22, 2005

When I arrived at Java Joe's the next morning, a few of the regulars already were there, scattered about eating area - William Bywater, immersed in a musical score; Heather Kaylin, a clerk at the Bay County Circuit Court, working on a laptop; and Lee Ellison, the WVOP disc jockey, poring over a notebook and assembling the play list for his afternoon show.

After exchanging greetings with everyone, I punched up a few songs on the jukebox and settled down at my usual table to eat breakfast and read the paper.

"Hey, I haven't heard that one in a long time!" Lee Ellison declared when "Surfin' Hootenanny" came blaring out of the jukebox.

"You should consider yourself lucky," William Bywater responded. "I've had to listen to it three mornings in a row."

"Why should you complain about that?" Lee asked. "It's a great song."

"A great song?" Bywater countered. "A chorus chanting the same thing over and over again, some simple guitar lines, and a crude, primitive beat?"

"In other words, all of the elements for a great song," I interjected.

Bywater groaned in response.

"This gives me an idea," Lee said. "I think I'll add it to the playlist for my show this afternoon."

"You're just as bad as he is," Bywater told Lee. I returned to perusing the paper. In Iraq, two high-ranking Algerian diplomats had been kidnapped from outside a restaurant in Baghdad...A second wave of bomb attacks had struck London's transportation system, bringing much of the city to a standstill…There were increasing calls for presidential advisor Karl Rove to be fired for disclosing the identity of an undercover CIA officer. In local news, there was an article by Gary Rockwell about the community meeting at the Oceanic Park United Methodist Church the night before:

RADIO TALK SHOW HOST ARRESTED AT COMMUNITY MEETING. Walter Braddock, host of the morning drive-time show "Rude Awakening" on WDSF Business Talk Radio, was arrested last night following an altercation at a community meeting held at the Oceanic Park United Methodist Church.

The meeting was organized by Reverend Alex Haycroft of the church to give residents of the community the chance to talk to city leaders about the recent campaign of anti-immigrant flyers by a group calling itself the Oceanic Park Vigilantes. The discussion became confrontational when Braddock came to the defense of the Oceanic Park Vigilantes and claimed that immigrants were destroying Oceanic Park's cultural heritage and bringing crime and gang violence to the town.

Braddock got into a heated exchange with Helen Marwood, president of the local chapter of the United Human Rights Coalition, and Sean Taylor, owner of the Deep Sea Dive & Salvage Shop. The exchange ended with Braddock spraying pepper spray in Taylor's face.

"I acted in self defense," said Braddock, who was released on his own recognizance. "When you're attacked by a rabid dog, you have to defend yourself."

Braddock said that he has no connection to the Oceanic Park Vigilantes and does not know the identities of members of the group, but he praised the group for trying to preserve the culture of Oceanic Park. Braddock said that he would plead not guilty and fight the assault charges. WDSF Business Talk Radio issued a statement saying that it stands behind Braddock, whose show is WDSF's top-rated show.

"I see that you're reading about the events of last night," Java Joe said, pulling out a chair and taking a seat across the table from me. "Did you hear any of Braddock's show this morning?"

"No."

"I was just listening to it while I was working in the kitchen. He was boasting about how he stood up to the forces of political correctness and made fools out of them. The callers to his show all were congratulating him and voicing their support for him. This is going to make him more popular than ever."

"Do you know anything about this guy?" I asked. "Where he came from? What he did before he got this talk show?"

"No, I don't know."

"He used to be a local news reporter for WCRX up in the city," Lee Ellison interjected.

"Yeah, I used to hear him on the radio occasionally," Karen chimed in from behind the counter. "He actually was a pretty good reporter back then."

"How did he end up down here?" I asked.

"He was being considered as the host of a public-affairs talk show on WCRX, but the job went to someone else," Lee explained. "He quit and came down here because it's a small market where he could get his foot in the door and have his own show. At first Braddock's show didn't do very well in the ratings. It looked like WDSF wasn't going to renew his contract. Then Braddock started making all of these inflammatory statements about immigrants, his show started to get some media attention, and his ratings took off."

"So all of these attacks on immigrants are just a cynical ploy to get better ratings?" I asked.

"It looks that way. He saw what type of talk shows were popular and jumped on the bandwagon. He's killing us in the morning drive-time ratings. The station management at WVOP is really concerned about it. They're considering making some programming changes."

"It won't affect you, will it?" I asked.

"I hope not," Lee replied.

After leaving Java Joe's, I checked in at the office and then headed to the Oceanic Park City Hall for the hearing on the emergency ordinance. City Hall is located on the northern edge of Old Town and housed in a white brick building that is topped by an aqua blue dome and set back behind a brick courtyard. The building began life in the '40s as the Oceanic Park School - a combined elementary, junior high, and senior high school. In 1961, with the student population growing, the school was moved to a new location and the building was converted into City Hall. A few alterations were made to the old school building, including capping it with a somewhat pretentious dome, patterned after that of the U.S. Capitol, to give the building the proper appearance of the seat of government. Large metal letters that spelled out "City Hall" were affixed overtop of the main entrance in case the dome left any doubt as to the function of the building.

Usually, no more than a handful of people turned up to watch City Council proceedings, but today a large crowd was milling around in the courtyard. Some people actually were carrying signs that said things like "Save the Boardwalk" and "Stop the Gentrification." A camera crew from the local t.v. station was filming the crowd and press photographers were snapping pictures.

I spotted Roger Steadman among the crowd, waving a hand to get my attention, and walked over and to join him.

"Hey, Jackson, what did I tell you about inviting Belinda Restivo?" Steadman asked. "Just take a look at this crowd. Isn't it great?"

"Not bad," I conceded. "Has she arrived yet?"

"She should be arriving any moment. She's being driven over from her hotel in a limousine."

"Where's she staying?"

"At the Majestic."

"The Majestic? That's only two blocks away. Why does she need to be driven in a limousine?"

"She wants to make a grand entrance for the cameras."

"Oh, good grief."

Exclamations went up from the crowd as a black limousine with highly polished chrome pulled to a stop at the curb in front of City Hall. A uniformed chauffeur got out of the driver's side, walked around the vehicle, and opened the rear door on the passenger's side. Belinda Restivo emerged from the limousine to enthusiastic cheers from the crowd. She appeared to be dressed for some sort of red-carpet premier rather than a legislative hearing in a clinging black dress and spiked heels.

She posed for photographers, draping herself provocatively over the limousine. Then she walked over and greeted Roger Steadman. He introduced her to me. I had met her briefly the previous summer, but she gave no sign of remembering me.

The chauffeur reappeared at Belinda Restivo's side, leading a tiny, rat-like dog on a rhinestone-studded leash. He handed her the leash and she began walking toward the door of City Hall.

"Uh...you'd better leave your dog with your chauffeur," I told her.

"Don't be ridiculous," she snapped in response.

"They're not going to let you take a dog into the hearing room."

"Winston goes wherever I go."

She proceeded toward the entrance of City Hall and I followed her and Roger Steadman through one of the imposing double doors and into the building. As we were making our way across the lobby, Karen Lutrell, the lobbyist for the Oceanic Park Merchants Association, emerged from the hallway that leads to the offices of the council members.

"What was she doing back there?" Steadman wondered.

"She's probably been meeting with the council members and coaching them on what to say during the hearing," I responded.

At the entrance to the hallway that leads to the hearing room, we had to go through a metal detector and have our bags searched by a security guard.

"I'm sorry, ma'am, but you can't bring a dog into the hearing room," the guard told Belinda Restivo.

"His name is Winston," she replied indignantly, seemingly offended that the guard didn't know her dog's name.

"Whatever his name is, you can't bring him into the hearing room."

"What am I supposed to do? I can't leave him behind."

"I'm afraid that you'll have to."

"You don't understand. Winston was badly traumatized when we visited Oceanic Park last summer. He has separation anxiety. He can't be left by himself."

"Maybe you can find someone to look after him."

"That would never do. He has to be with me and I have to be with him. I need him for emotional support."

"Everyone else seems to be managing alright without their dog." The guard smirked at his witticism and Belinda Restivo flew into a rage.

"How dare you!" she screamed. "You're being cruel and unfair! Why can't you understand that I need Winston for emotional support?!

The guard took a step backwards and blinked his eyes as if someone had just thrown cold water in his face. I decided to try to intervene.

"Look," I said, "the prohibition on dogs in the hearing room doesn't apply to service dogs."

"That's not a seeing-eye dog," the guard responded.

"It's not just seeing-eye dogs, the exception also applies to emotional-support dogs."

"Well…" the guard hesitated. He glanced apprehensively at the long line that was forming behind us due to the delay in admitting us to the hearing room. "Alright, but keep the dog quiet and under control. If it causes a disturbance, I'll have to ask you to remove it."

"Winston would never cause a disturbance," Belinda Restivo informed the guard, and we proceeded into the hearing room.

The hearing room is a large room with dark wooden paneling on the walls, narrow slit windows, and a high ceiling. The desks of the members of the City Council are arranged in a semi-circle in the front of the hearing room. A heavy wooden witness table faces the semi-circle of desks and, behind the witness table, rows of chairs are set up for spectators. Behind a railing on the far side of the room, is a press gallery.

I sat next to Belinda Restivo and Roger Steadman in the front row of the spectator gallery, and made sure that Belinda Restivo had a copy of the testimony that I had prepared for her to read. Before long, the spectator gallery was packed with people and there was an overflow crowd out in the hallway, crowding around the doorway so that they could hear. The press gallery was packed as well, and I spotted Gary Rockwell among the reporters and photographers.

A few minutes after 10:00 a.m., the members of the City Council entered the room and took their seats behind the desks. Kevin Sullivan, the President of the City Council, took a seat at the desk in the middle of the semi-circle. Sullivan was a heavy-set, middle-aged man with short curly hair, wearing a seersucker suit. When not performing his duties as President of the City Council, Sullivan was the manager of a convenience store. Lynn Kelleher, the Vice-President of the City Council and its only woman member, took a seat at the desk to Sullivan's right. Kelleher's hair was cut in a short bob and she was wearing a dark, sharply-tailored business suit. Outside of the City Council, she worked as a marketing consultant. Adam Pulman, the attorney for the City Council, took a seat at the desk on Sullivan's left. The remaining five members of the City Council - all middle-aged White men - filled in the rest of the desks around the semi-circle.

"Good morning everyone," Sullivan announced, and banged his gavel to get people's attention. "I'm Kevin Sullivan, President of the Oceanic Park City Council. On behalf of myself, Lynn Kelleher, the Vice-President of the City Council and the other members of the

City Council, I'd like to welcome you to today's hearing. The purpose of the hearing is to receive public testimony regarding proposed emergency ordinance number 9-301, which would regulate artists and performers on the boardwalk.

"I'd like to start by providing a bit of background information on the concerns that gave rise to the proposed ordinance. As many of you know, we always have had artists and performers on the boardwalk; they are part of what gives the boardwalk its colorful character. Recently, however, the number of artists and performers has increased significantly and is creating problems. The town government has experienced a large increase in the number of complaints regarding artists and performers from citizens and from merchants on the boardwalk. The artists and performers are attracting large crowds, causing congestion, and impeding the orderly flow of pedestrian traffic on the boardwalk. The congestion on the boardwalk is creating health and safety issues. The boardwalk is the primary means of ingress and egress to the beach and to the properties located along the boardwalk. The town's police, firefighters, beach patrol, and emergency personnel need unimpeded access to the boardwalk for emergency situations, such as fires in properties located along the boardwalk and rescue operations on the beach.

"We also have had problems with artists, performers, and the crowds that they attract leaving behind trash. In addition, there have been altercations between artists and performers fighting over prime locations on the boardwalk. In a couple of instances, the police had to be called to prevent the matter from getting out of hand.

"As a result of these concerns, we have proposed an ordinance that will regulate artists and performers on the boardwalk. A draft of the ordinance has been posted on our website and circulated to interested parties. Now, I will turn things over to our counsel, Adam Pulman, who will explain the provisions of the ordinance."

"Thank you President Sullivan, Vice-President Kelleher, and members of the City Council," Pulman began. "Historically, the boardwalk has served as a public forum, and, under the 1st Amendment, people have the right to be heard in a public forum.

Courts have held, however, that governments can impose reasonable time, place, and manner restrictions on speech in a public forum. That is what the town government is doing with this ordinance. In drafting the ordinance, we have tried to strike a reasonable balance between the artist's and performer's right to free expression and the town's interest in maintaining the orderly flow of pedestrian traffic on the boardwalk and ensuring access to the boardwalk for law enforcement and emergency personnel.

"Under the ordinance, the Director of the Department of Public Works will designate 25 ten-foot-by-ten-foot spaces on the boardwalk to be used by artists and performers. Permission to use the spaces will be granted through a lottery system. Each Monday, a lottery will be held in the office of the Town Clerk to award spaces for the following week. Artists and performers who wish to participate in the lottery should arrive at the Clerk's office between 9:30 a.m. and 10:00 a.m. They will be required to fill out an application on which they must state the nature and scope of the activity for which they propose to use the space. At 10:00 a.m. a lottery will be held to award spaces for the following week.

"Artists and performers must remain within their designated space while creating or displaying artwork or performing. The ordinance prohibits the display of any artwork or performance that is obscene or offensive and performances may not exceed a decibel level of 75 decibels between the hours of 10:00 a.m. and 10:00 p.m. or 60 decibels between the hours of 10:00 p.m. and 10:00 a.m. A person who has not been awarded a space is prohibited from creating or displaying artwork or performing on the boardwalk. Any person who violates the ordinance is subject to a civil penalty of not less than $100 or more than $1,000."

"Thank you, counselor," Sullivan said when Pulman had concluded his explanation of the ordinance. "We will now hear from interested parties. We will start with with supporters of the ordinance and then hear from opponents of the ordinance. Please restrict your testimony to five minutes, so that everyone has a chance to testify."

Karen Luttrell, the lobbyist for the Merchants Association, was the first to take a seat at the witness table. Luttrell was a slender thirty-something woman with long blond hair, dressed in a tailored business suit. She displayed an ease and confidence that came from several years experience appearing in front of the council and getting them to do what she wanted.

"Good morning President Sullivan, Vice-President Kelleher, and members of the City Council," Luttrell began. "I'm Karen Luttrell, Senior Executive Director of Government Relations for the Oceanic Park Merchants Association." Notwithstanding her grandiose title, which made it sound like she was in charge of a large lobbying operation, Luttrell actually constituted the Association's entire lobbying staff.

"The Merchants Association has more than 1,200 members," Luttrell continued. "Our members include hotels, retail establishments, and restaurants and are the main drivers of the economy of Oceanic Park. They attract loyal customers who return to Oceanic Park year after year." She tactfully omitted mentioning the amounts of money that the Association had contributed to the campaign funds of members of the City Council, but they probably didn't need to be reminded.

"The Merchants Association strongly supports the proposed ordinance," Luttrell went on. "Boardwalk performers unfairly compete with brick-and-mortar businesses along the boardwalk. Unlike boardwalk artists and performers, brick and mortar businesses pay property taxes and license fees that support the running of the town. The proposed ordinance will help to level the playing field.

"While boardwalk performers once may have added some color to the boardwalk, they now have gotten out of control and become a nuisance and a health and safety hazard. The boardwalk has taken on the atmosphere of a third-rate flea market and is in danger of being turned from an asset into a liability." A discontented murmur went up from the crowd at this.

"Please remain silent in the hearing room," Kevin Sullivan interjected. "If people cannot remain silent, they will be asked to leave."

"In conclusion, the Merchants Association believes that the proposed ordinance strikes the correct balance between preserving 1st Amendment rights and addressing health and safety concerns," Lutrell resumed. "It will benefit the economy of Oceanic Park and help to bring it into the new century. I reiterate the Merchants Association's strong support for the ordinance."

The next person to take a seat at the witness table was Eric Burns. Burns was in his late fifties or early sixties and was wearing a loose-fitting blue blazer designed to hide his paunch and a tie with the logo of a local baseball team on it. I had had a few run-ins with Burns the previous summer while I was investigating the fire at the Chimera Gallery and the death of Count Rupert. Burns had coveted the bay-front property where the gallery was located and, prior to the fire, had been hounding Count Rupert to sell the gallery property to him so that he could knock down the gallery and replace it with a high-rise condominium. When the gallery burned down, Burns had been one of my prime suspects. After Elizabeth Birkin inherited the gallery, Burns began to hound her to sell it to him as well. She refused, however, and went ahead with plans to rebuild and reopen the gallery. Burns must have been galled at the successful reopening of the gallery the other night.

"Good morning," Burns began. "My name is Eric Burns and I am the head of Eric Burns and Associates, the largest property development company in Oceanic Park. I also strongly support the ordinance." Burns had benefited greatly over the years from the cozy relationship between the City Council and developers.

"As you are aware, my company recently opened the new Oceanic Park Plaza Hotel and Convention Center," Burns continued. "This is a state-of-the-art convention and meeting center designed to attract corporate clients. The Oceanic Park Plaza is the type of facility that represents the future of Oceanic Park. It will make Oceanic Park a go-to destination for corporate conventions, not only during the summer, but all year 'round.

"We already have made great strides toward attracting convention business to Oceanic Park. This week we are hosting the annual meeting of the Economic Freedom Foundation. Getting the Economic Freedom Foundation to hold their annual meeting in Oceanic Park was a major coup for the town. If we expect to attract additional corporate convention business, however, we must improve the image projected by the boardwalk, so that convention goers have a good experience and aren't assaulted by a bunch of third-rate, would-be performers every time they venture out onto the boardwalk."

"I object to that!" Roger Steadman shouted and leaped to his feet. "That is an outrageous insult!"

"Quiet, please!" Kevin Sullivan called and banged his gavel.

"I will not be called a third-rate, would-be performer!" Steadman continued. "I demand an apology!"

"Please sit down," Sullivan responded, banging his gavel again. "Do not interrupt people when they are testifying. You will get your chance to testify. If you engage in another outburst like that, I will have you removed from the hearing room."

Steadman glared at Sullivan for a few moments before reluctantly sitting down again.

Burns glanced around the room, gloating in triumph at the reaction he had provoked.

"Please continue with your testimony," Sullivan instructed Burns in a solicitous voice.

"Thank you, Mr. President. We must accept the fact that Oceanic Park's days as a small carnival town are over," Burns resumed. "We need to meet the challenges of the future. As we move into the new century we need to modernize and upgrade the image of Oceanic Park. The proposed ordinance will be an important step in that direction by cleaning up the boardwalk."

Steadman started to rise out of his chair again, but I put a hand on his shoulder to restrain him this time.

"Wait until it's your turn to testify," I whispered to him.

Steadman resisted for a few moments, but finally settled back into his chair.

The next person to take a seat at the witness table was an elegantly-dress, middle-aged woman.

"My name is Eleanor Moranta," she said, "and I am the proprietor of Expressions Beach Boutique, which sells designer fashions and swimwear. I also wish to express my support the ordinance.

"My shop is located on the boardwalk near 13th Street. Every afternoon, a rather uncouth-looking young man sets up a microphone and amplifier on the boardwalk across from my shop. He then proceeds to sing and play guitar at an ear-shattering volume. The worst thing about it, though, is that he only knows five songs! He stands out there all afternoon and evening and plays the same five songs over and over again! People walking up and down the boardwalk don't notice because they aren't there long enough for him to get through his entire repertoire, but me and my staff are stuck there and have to listen to the same songs over and over again. It's torture - he's driving me and my staff crazy! And he's also destroying the atmosphere in my shop. We strive to provide our customers with an elegant and sophisticated atmosphere and instead they have to listen to this awful racket.

"Once again, I support the ordinance and believe that it is necessary to address this type of problem and restore some semblance of order to the boardwalk."

Next up was a middle-aged man with grey-flecked hair and a three-day stubble.

"My name is Anthony DiPietro," the man said, "and I run Tony's Pizza on the boardwalk. I also want to register my support for the ordinance.

"Last year, I installed a webcam on the front of my building overlooking the boardwalk. People who went to our website could view the webcam and see what is happening on the boardwalk in front of the restaurant 24 hours a day. Earlier this summer, a pole dancer would come every day, position herself on the boardwalk right in front of my webcam, and do her act. My God! You wouldn't believe the things she was doing on that pole! And all of this was getting picked up by my webcam and streamed over the internet! People who visited our website and saw it thought that I was responsible for it! I pleaded with the dancer to take her act somewhere else, but she refused. I ended up having to put a cover over my webcam because I didn't want to be associated with her. She's stopped now, but I'm afraid if I take the cover off my webcam she'll come back."

"Take it off!" someone in the audience shouted.

"Yeah, take it off!" another person shouted. "We want her back!"

"Silence!" Kevin Sullivan shouted and banged his gavel on his desk. "I want silence in the hearing room! I will not tolerate any more outbursts like that." Sullivan glared at the spectators as if daring anyone to make a sound.

"Please continue with your testimony," Sullivan said to Anthony DiPietro.

"I just want to conclude by saying that we desperately need this ordinance to regulate the nature of performances on the boardwalk to protect the family atmosphere of Oceanic Park," DePietro said.

Anthony DiPietro was followed by several more members of the Merchants Association who relayed similar stories about problems with performers on the boardwalk and expressed their support for the ordinance.

"Thank you for your testimony," Kevin Sullivan said when the last supporter of the ordinance had finished testifying. "We now will hear from the opponents of the ordinance."

A cheer went up from the crowd and people started clapping their hands, stomping their feet, and chanting "We want Belinda!" Kevin Sullivan pounded his gavel on this desk and demanded silence.

"Perhaps some of you have never attended a hearing like this before," Sullivan said. "This is not a sporting event. We do not allow cheers or chanting. If you have anything to say, you can testify. Otherwise, please remain silent. If anyone makes noise, I will order the sheriff's deputy to remove the person from the hearing room." There were a few muffled chortles and snickers, but the crowd quieted down. Sullivan glanced around warily, sensing that the crowd was not taking him seriously.

I sat down at the witness table, introduced myself, and explained that I was representing an informal coalition of boardwalk artists and performers.

"We oppose the proposed ordinance as an unconstitutional restriction on the 1st Amendment rights of artists and performers on the boardwalk," I stated. "I have submitted a written legal memorandum that explains our position in detail and cites the applicable legal authority, so I will just give you a summary of the important points.

"There is a long-accepted tradition of people performing on the boardwalk dating back to the turn of the prior century when the boardwalk was first built. An article in the August 9, 1906 issue of the *Oceanic Park Press* reported that a strolling banjo player named Blind Georgie Wilkinson performed for people on the boardwalk that summer. The following summer, he was joined by a guitar player named Stanley Remington. Over the years artists, jugglers, magicians, puppeteers, and numerous others have entertained people on the boardwalk. It is one of the things that gives the boardwalk its unique charm.

"Due to this tradition of public performances, the boardwalk is established as a public forum, which means that it is protected by the 1st Amendment. As counsel noted during his presentation, a government may impose reasonable time, place, and manner restrictions on speech in a public forum. Courts, however, have held that the restrictions must be tailored to apply as narrowly as possible, to avoid infringing on individual's 1st Amendment rights. Rather than narrowly-tailored provisions, the proposed ordinance imposes broad and sweeping restrictions. The proposed ordinance would drastically reduce the number of persons who may perform on the boardwalk. It also would impose an extremely burdensome and cumbersome lottery system that would require performers to reapply every week and leave them uncertain as to whether they can perform from one week to the next. Furthermore, the City Council proposes to implement the new ordinance in the middle of the summer season, disrupting the plans of performers and causing them to lose income.

"The City Council claims that it is not banning people from performing on the boardwalk, only regulating them. But those who lose the lottery will, in fact, be banned from performing on the boardwalk for the following week. Given the number of artists and performers who will be competing for a limited number of spaces, the majority of them will be banned for most weeks of the season. An individual's right to free speech should not be dependent on winning a lottery."

As I spoke, I looked around at the members of the City Council. They had been fairly attentive when supporters of the ordinance had testified, but, now, only Kevin Sullivan, Lynn Kelleher, and Adam Pulman appeared to be paying attention. The rest of the members of the City Council weren't even bothering to make a pretense of paying attention. One of them was reading the newspaper, and another was talking on a cell phone. A third had simply gotten up and walked out of the hearing room. It seemed that they wanted to send a clear message that they weren't interested in what opponents of the ordinance had to say.

"The ostensible reason for the ordinance is to address problems caused by congestion on the boardwalk," I continued. "It's true that the boardwalk has become congested in recent years. That is not due, however to the presence of artists and performers on the boardwalk. Rather, it is due to the City Council's planning and zoning policies, which have allowed rampant overdevelopment, cramming numerous high-density occupancy units into a small space along the boardwalk. The City Council is trying to shift blame for a problem that it has created through its planning and zoning policies onto performers on the boardwalk and using this as a pretext to get rid of the performers."

"In conclusion, if the City Council adopts this ordinance as currently proposed, we will challenge it in court. I am confident that any court will strike down the ordinance as unconstitutional."

"Thank you for your testimony," Kevin Sullivan said through clenched teeth. He was glaring angrily at me with a sour expression on his face that made it look like he had been sucking on a lemon.

I returned to my seat in the spectator area and Margot Peterson took a seat at the witness table.

"My name is Margot Peterson and my family owns the Atlantic Hotel, located on the boardwalk in Old Town," she said. "I am strongly opposed to the proposed ordinance. The Atlantic Hotel is one of the oldest hotels in continuous operation in Oceanic Park. It was established by my grandparents in 1903 and run by my family ever since then. For more than a hundred years, businesses along the boardwalk have coexisted with artists and performers. The have had a symbiotic relationship from which both benefit. The boardwalk is one of Oceanic Park's strongest assets and it would be a shame to lose it.

"I want to make it clear that the Merchants Association does not speak for all of the businesses in Oceanic Park. Many businesses would like to preserve the unique culture of Oceanic Park. If this ordinance is adopted, we will lose part of what makes Oceanic Park special. I urge you not to adopt it."

Next up at the witness table was Roger Steadman.

"Good morning," Steadman began. "My name is Roger Steadman and I perform on the boardwalk under the name 'Boardwalk Elvis.' Seven years ago, Elvis appeared to me in a dream and directed me to carry on his work. Since then, I have been performing on the boardwalk, carrying on the musical legacy of Elvis and introducing his music to a younger generation of listeners. During that time, I have built up a following and become one of the most popular attractions on the boardwalk. I have been featured in articles in the local as well as the national media. The *New York Examiner* named me as one of the top 100 Elvis impersonators in the country. I have brought nation-wide attention to Oceanic Park. And yet, at this hearing, I have been attacked as a 'third-rate, would-be performer.' I will not be insulted like that. An attack on me, is an attack on the musical legacy of Elvis."

"No one is attacking Elvis," Sullivan interjected.

"Don't give me that, Jackson," Steadman responded. "Back in the fifties, people like you tried to stop Elvis, but they couldn't stop him then, and you won't stop me now."

Sullivan, who wasn't familiar with Steadman's habit of addressing everyone as "Jackson," glanced around in confusion, trying to figure out whom Steadman was addressing.

"We're here to receive testimony about the proposed ordinance," Sullivan said. "I won't have the hearing turned into a referendum on Elvis. Please restrict your testimony to the topic of the hearing." Sullivan appeared to be getting increasingly agitated that the hearing wasn't going the way that he would have liked it to go.

"Alright, Jackson," Steadman continued. "During testimony today, we heard proponents of the ordinance compare the boardwalk to a 'third-rate flea market.' People have testified that, if we want to attract corporate conventions to Oceanic Park, the town needs to cultivate a more upscale image. When that so-called property developer testified, he boasted about bringing the annual meeting of the Economic Freedom Foundation to Oceanic Park. Well, the night before last, one of the people in town to attend that meeting got drunk and crashed his boat into the drawbridge. Are these really the sort of people we want to attract to Oceanic Park?"

Shouts and hoots of encouragement went up from the crowd and Sullivan furiously banged his gavel with an alarmed expression on his face.

"Please refrain from making personal attacks on people," Sullivan commanded.

"Come off it, Jackson," Steadman admonished. "You didn't gavel that so-called property developer into silence when he attacked performers on the boardwalk."

"Why do you keep calling me Jackson!?" Sullivan yelled. "My name is Sullivan! I'm the President of the City Council! I demand to be treated with respect!"

"Then you should treat witnesses at this hearing with respect," Steadman responded. "Look around Jackson, the members of your

City Council aren't even listening to what we say. You've already made up your minds. I have nothing more to say."

With that, Steadman returned to his seat. Several other artists and performers from the boardwalk followed Steadman to the witness table and testified against the ordinance. Many had complaints that the weekly lottery system was too clumsy and disruptive and the ordinance would destroy their ability to make any money.

Finally, Belinda Restivo took a seat at the witness table. She left the testimony that I had written for her on the seat of her chair in the spectators' gallery.

"My name is Belinda Restivo and I am the star of the hit t.v series *Bimbo Beach House*," she began. "Our new season premiers on Thursday, September 8 at 9:00 p.m. on the Vox Populi Network. This is our best season yet. On this season, we delve more deeply into the real lives of fashion models - the conflicts, the friendships, the rivalries. This season is filled with drama and suspense and..."

"Could you please keep your testimony focused on the topic of the hearing?" Sullivan prompted her.

"Excuse me?"

"Could you please keep your testimony focused on the topic of the hearing?"

"What's that?"

"The ordinance regulating artists and performers on the boardwalk."

"Oh, yes. I'm here to support...er..... I mean, I'm here to..." She glanced at Roger Steadman for guidance and he mouthed the word "oppose" at her. "I'm here to oppose the ordinance. I think it's very bad. I visited Oceanic Park for the first time last summer and fell in love with it. One of the things that I loved most about it was the boardwalk. There's also a boardwalk in Seaside Heights, New Jersey, where *Bimbo Beach House* is filmed. We've filmed a bunch of scenes on the boardwalk. There's one scene where we ride bikes on the boardwalk. I hadn't ridden a bike since I was twelve years old and..."

"Get that thing out of here!" Sullivan suddenly exploded, glaring furiously at the back of the gallery.

I turned and looked behind me. Some people in the back of the gallery were tossing around a giant inflatable beach ball as if they were on the beach.

"That's it!" Sullivan declared. "I'm going to adjourn this hearing. I'd like to thank everyone for their testimony…"

"I'm not finished yet!" Belinda Restivo yelled.

"We will take all of the testimony into consideration before making a final decision on the ordinance…"

"I haven't used my five minutes yet!"

"I expect that we will take a vote on the ordinance in the next day or so." With that, Sullivan banged his gavel on the desk, pushed back his chair, and stood up.

"Don't ignore me, you beastly little man!" Belinda Restivo yelled.

Sullivan turned and started walking toward the door in the back of the hearing room. Winston, who had been sitting quietly throughout the hearing, stood up on all four legs. Suddenly, he streaked across the floor as if shot out of a cannon and sank his teeth into the bottom of Sullivan's right pants leg. Sullivan looked down with a horrified expression on his face, as if he couldn't believe what was happening. He started shaking his leg, trying to free his pants from Winston's teeth, but to no avail. Sullivan shook his leg more violently, but Winston's teeth tenaciously retained a solid hold on his pants. Looking increasingly desperate, Sullivan started shaking his leg so violently that he lost his balance and fell over backwards. Now, he was lying on his back on the floor, frantically waving his leg in the air with Winston, still clinging to the pants leg, getting whipped back and forth through the air like a flag in the wind.

"What are you doing to Winston?!" Belinda Restivo screamed. She got up from the witness table and ran across the room to where Sullivan was lying on the floor. She grabbed Winston who then released his bite on Sullivan's pants leg.

"How dare you treat Winston like that!" Belinda Restivo yelled at Sullivan. She strode indignantly back across the room, clutching Winston to her chest.

Sullivan got up off the floor, turned, and glared at Belinda Restivo. His face was purple with rage. He looked as if he was about to say something, but then he seemed to realize that everyone in the room was staring at him and he thought better of it. He turned and fled the hearing room. The other members of the City Council followed him out of the room.

Belinda Restivo was mobbed by fans and members of the press. Reporters shoved microphones in her face and bombarded her with questions. Press photographers set off a barrage of flash bulbs. Fans snapped photos with their cell phones, inquired about Winston's condition, and pleaded for autographs.

I conferred briefly with Roger Steadman; I told him that I would monitor progress of the ordinance and keep him informed of its status. If the ordinance was passed by the City Council and signed by the mayor, I would file a request for an emergency injunction.

After I left City Hall and was walking across the courtyard, I saw Eric Burns walking rapidly in my direction to try to intercept me. I hadn't spoken to Burns since last summer and I didn't particularly want to talk to him now, but it was clear that he was intent on saying something to me, so I slowed down to allow him to catch up with me.

"I see that you still insist on making a nuisance of yourself," Burns sneered.

"I try my best," I said.

"Well, congratulations on a total shambles. I hope that you enjoy banging your head against the wall because that's all that's going to come of your efforts. You're engaged in an exercise in futility."

"It wouldn't be the first time."

"By the way, if your client is interested, my offer to buy the Chimera Gallery still stands."

"She's not interested. I'm sure you heard that the gallery had a very successful reopening the other night."

"Yeah, I also heard that it was interrupted by an ugly incident," he gloated. "I hope that there aren't any more such incidents. Running a gallery may prove a lot harder than she thinks. After awhile, she may be glad to take my offer. See you around." With that he abruptly turned and headed on his way.

I was a bit taken aback by Burns' comments, which sounded vaguely like a threat. I wondered if it was possible that Burns could have had something to do with the banner being hung from the water tower. No, I decided that the idea was too far fetched and dismissed it from my mind.

I spent the rest of the day working at the office. Late in the afternoon, I went onto the Surf Report website to check wave conditions. The site reported that there was a three-to-four-foot swell at the 21st Street beach break, where I often surfed along with a group of other surfers. I decided I'd take the evening off and hit the surf. It would do me good to relax and clear my head a bit now that the hearing was over. After knocking off work, I walked to my cottage and grabbed a quick bite to eat, and then changed into my boardshorts, grabbed my surfboard, and headed for the beach.

I arrived at the boardwalk and 21st Street, in the early evening, the most pleasant time of day on the beach - the sun was past it peak, the intense heat of the day had faded, and there was a nice offshore breeze. The hordes of tourists who crowd the beach during the day had largely departed. A few stragglers still were packing up their beach towels, coolers, and sand chairs before calling it a day. A smattering of other people remained on the beach flying kites in the breeze, tossing around frisbees, or walking along the water's edge.

A few surfers were out in the water, bobbing on their boards in the lineup. Terry Mannering was stationed on the beach by the water's edge, operating a video camera mounted on a tripod. Recording videos was part of Terry's coaching regime for Wendy Stevens and the other young surfers who he was helping to prepare for the Oceanic Park Surf Tournament. Terry would videotape their rides and, later, he would review the videos with them, critique their rides, and give them feedback on how to improve their performance.

I went down the ramp to the beach, walked across the sand, and greeted Terry.

"Hey, good to see you," Terry responded.

"How's the training going?"

"Not bad. Everyone should be in pretty good shape for the tournament next week."

I knelt down to wax my board and watched the waves coming in, trying to gauge their size and strength and get a feel for the conditions before I headed out. As I was watching, Wendy called out for a wave and then paddled into it. When the wave caught her board and propelled it forward, she moved into a crouching position with one smooth motion.

"Here she goes," Terry said and started following her with the video camera.

Wendy tore down the face of the wave, hit the bottom, and then cut back into the wave. She shot out of the top of the wave and was totally airborne. Gripping the upper rail of her board with her right hand, she reversed course in mid-air and shot back into the wave. When she reentered the wave, however, the impact caused her to lose her balance and fall off the board.

"Almost made it," Terry said. "She leaned a little too far forward and didn't keep her left hand extended over the rail of the board. But she's getting there."

I greeted Wendy as she came into the shallow water to retrieve her board.

"Hey, that looked really good," I said. "You've almost got it down."

"I don't know," she said, shaking her head in frustration. "I've got to get to the point where I nail that every time, if I want to have any chance of winning the tournament."

She flopped on top of her board and paddled back out into the lineup and I followed her out. I greeted everyone and took a spot in the lineup. Most of the usual crew were there - in addition to Wendy, there was Barry Pendleton, Wendy's boyfriend and a lifeguard with the Oceanic Park Beach Patrol; Alison Lee, also a lifeguard with the Oceanic Park Beach Patrol; Larry Donaldson, proprietor of the Boardwalk Cycle Shop; and Doc Cavanaugh, a retired doctor and long-time surfer.

We passed a pleasant evening surfing. The waves were in the three-to-four-foot range, which provided good conditions for practicing maneuvers. I managed to catch a few pretty good rides. Between rides, people chatted about the upcoming surf tournament, speculating about what sort of surf conditions would prevail and what the competition would be like. Doc Cavanaugh had been tapped to serve as a judge for the tournament. People also talked about the Sonny Burgess concert that was scheduled to take place the following night at the Crow's Nest, a local club. It looked to be one of the big musical events of the summer and everyone was looking forward to it.

As the evening progressed, the sun sank below the town's skyline and the sky began to grow dark. The lights in the businesses along the boardwalk came on and, as the boardwalk began to fill with people, the sound of music, conversation, and laughter drifted from the boardwalk out across the water. When visibility became poor, we called it a night.

Chapter 5. Saturday, July 23, 2005

The next morning, there was an article by Gary Rockwell about the hearing before the City Council on the front page of the *Oceanic Park Press*. Not surprisingly, the article was dominated by coverage of Belinda Restivo and her dog, Winston:

> REALITY TV STAR DEMANDS APOLGY FOR TREATMENT OF DOG. Reality t.v. star Belinda Restivo demanded a public apology from City Council President Kevin Sullivan for his treatment of her dog at a hearing on a proposed ordinance to regulate artists and performers on the boardwalk. After Sullivan cut short Restivo's testimony, her dog, Winston, ran across the hearing room and sank its teeth into Sullivan's pants leg. Restivo claimed that, in his efforts to dislodge Winston from his pants leg, Sullivan had severely shaken Winston. "Winston is extremely sensitive and was badly traumatized by the experience," Restivo stated. "That man needs to apologize for his treatment of Winston."
>
> "Her dog attacked *me*," Sullivan responded. "She's the one who should apologize for failing to control a vicious dog. That dog had no business being in the hearing room."
>
> A cellphone video of the incident posted on the internet shortly after the hearing has gone viral and subjected Sullivan to widespread ridicule. The

incident capped a contentious hearing at which supporters and opponents of the proposed ordinance offered starkly different interpretations of the effect that the ordinance would have on Oceanic Park.

Notwithstanding the drama of the hearing, it appears likely that the City Council will adopt the ordinance. Council President Sullivan indicated that he plans to vote in favor of the ordinance, stating that nothing that he had heard at the hearing changed his mind about the need for the ordinance. The other members of the City Council also indicated that they plan to vote in favor of the ordinance.

"I see that your star witness made a hash of things," Wendy commented, when she brought my breakfast to my table.

"I thought that she did rather well," I responded.

"Ha! She generated a lot of publicity for her t.v. show, you mean."

"I saw that video of her dog attacking Kevin Sullivan," Karen chimed in from behind the counter. "That was hysterical. He'll never live that down. It's going to put an end to his political career."

"Well, at least the hearing accomplished something worthwhile," I said.

As I was leaving, Java Joe called out to me from behind the counter and asked if I was attending the Sonny Burgess concert that evening at the Crow's Nest.

"Oh, yeah, I wouldn't miss that," I responded.

I spent the rest of the day running errands, cutting the grass, and working in the yard. At twilight, I made my way through the streets of Old Town toward the Crow's Nest for the Sonny Burgess concert. Burgess was a contemporary of Elvis and one of the original generation of rockabilly performers. He grew up on a farm near Newport, Arkansas, listened to country music on the Grand Ole Opry, and played in a country band called the Rocky Road Ramblers.

After a stint in the Army during which he was stationed in Germany, Burgess returned to Arkansas and, with some former members of the Rocky Road Ramblers, formed a new band called the Moonlighters. The band took their name from the Silver Moon Club, a local venue where they often played. Their repertoire consisted of country, western swing, and, eventually, rockabilly.

On October 24, 1955, a then up-and-coming Elvis Presley played at the Silver Moon Club and the Moonlighters opened the show for him. Elvis' current single at the time, a cover of Junior Parker's "Mystery Train," was his biggest hit so far. It would be his last record for the Sun label before he left Sun for RCA and broke through to national fame.

Inspired by their encounter with Elvis, the Moonlighters headed across the Mississippi River to Memphis to audition for Sun Records. After adding some new members and changing their name to the Pacers, the band began to record for Sun.

Their first record, "Red Headed Woman" / "We Wanna Boogie," was released in August 1956. Led by Burgess' shouted vocals and hard-driving guitar, the recording is one of the rawest and wildest rockabilly records ever made. The Pacers went on to record a few more records for the Sun label, including "Ain't Got a Thing," "My Bucket's Got a Hole in It," and "Sadie's Back in Town." While the Pacers achieved some local popularity, none of their records made the national charts.

After stints playing in Conway Twitty's band and a group called the King's IV, Burgess largely dropped out of the music business and worked as a sales person, although he continued to record sporadically during the '60s, '70s, and '80s for small independent labels.

During the rockabilly revival of the '80s, Burgess began to receive some increased attention. He began playing with the Sun Rhythm Section, an aggregation of lesser-known rockabilly veterans from the Memphis area, many of whom had recorded for the Sun label. The recordings he made with the Pacers for Sun were reissued on CD. Recently, he had made a couple of excellent new albums that were well received. Late in life, Burgess belatedly was receiving a modest amount of recognition for his work.

The Crow's Nest is housed in a strip mall that was built during the '50s and is located a few blocks north of the inlet. The club was founded as a jazz venue back in the fifties by Maurice Bellini, a local jazz aficionado and record collector. Bellini ran the club as a labor of love, featured live music seven nights a week, and presented many of the biggest names in jazz. During the seventies, however, the club began to struggle, with the waning audience for jazz. In the late seventies, Bellini sold the club to Andy Balham, its present owner. Balham broadened the booking policy to include blues bands and rock bands as well as jazz artists. These days the club generally has live music only on weekends with an occasional concert during the week. The club no longer features big names, but still has an interesting mix of performers, ranging from up-and-coming new artists to semi-well-known veterans like Sonny Burgess.

After paying the cover charge to the bouncer, I paused to look at the schedule of upcoming events that was posted by the door. Sophia Ambrosetti was listed as appearing at the club on Thursday, August 4 through Sunday August 7, less than a week and a half away. So, it appeared that she really was returning to Oceanic Park. I still wasn't sure how to handle the situation. Should I go and see her play and try to talk to her, or leave it up to her to make the first move? Time was running out and I couldn't put off deciding for much longer.

I entered the club, walking along a wall that was covered with black-and-white publicity photos of jazz artists who had played the club in its heyday and captured the glamour and romance of a bygone era. I paused and surveyed the room. There was a pretty good turnout - most of the tables surrounding the dance floor in front of the stage were occupied, and there was a crowd of people standing at the bar in the back. There were quite a few people dressed in '50s rockabilly style - men with ducktail haircuts and black leather jackets and women with poodle skirts and saddle shoes. This sort of event brought rockabilly fans out of the woodwork.

I spotted Java Joe, Lee Ellison, Roger Steadman, and a bunch of the surfers from the 21st Street beach break among the crowd standing by the bar and made my way back to join them.

The opening act was a local favorite, Allen Boudreaux, an African-American singer and piano player, who had been playing around the East Coast since back in the '70s. He played boogie-woogie and rock 'n' roll piano and specialized in covers of rock 'n' roll and rhythm and blues songs from the '50s. He and his band and turned in a high-energy set that included numbers such as Little Richard's "Keep a Knockin'," Jerry Lee Lewis' "High School Confidential," and Fats Domino's "I'm Ready." As their set progressed, more and more people ventured out onto the dance floor. Boudreaux and his band concluded their set with Bo Diddley's "Road Runner." They earned an encore from the crowd and returned to the stage and performed Jackie Brenston and the Delta Cats' "Rocket 88."

The roadies then took to the stage to clear away Boudreaux and his band's gear and get the stage ready for Sonny Burgess. When the stage was set, Andy Balham, the owner of the Crow's Nest, walked out onto the stage and went to the microphone.

"Ladies and gentlemen," Balham announced. "Tonight we have a very special event for you. A true pioneer and one of the first generation of rock 'n' roll performers. Please welcome Sonny Burgess!"

Sonny Burgess walked out onto stage wearing a black baseball cap with "Sun Records" in gold letters on the front, sunglasses, a western-style denim shirt with some colorful stitching on it, and black jeans. His hair and goatee were snow white, but he looked youthfully trim and fit. He had a blond Fender Esquire with an imitation pearl pick guard strapped across his chest, and was accompanied by a pianist, bass player, and drummer.

The audience greeted Burgess with enthusiastic applause and cheers, abandoned the tables, and crowded onto the dance floor in front of the stage. Burgess launched into "Red Headed Woman," belting out the song in a still-raw-and-powerful voice and unleashing a fiery guitar solo in the middle of the song. His set included songs from his early days at Sun such as "Ain't Got a Thing," "My Bucket's Got a Hole in It," and "Sadie's Back in Town," some old country, rockabilly, and rhythm and blues classics, and some material from his recent albums such as "Tennessee Border" and "Tiger Rose." In spite of the passage of time, Burgess' energy and enthusiasm appeared undiminished. He performed with the same kind of wild abandon that he had demonstrated back in the '50s. He exited the stage to wild applause and cheers, before coming back and performing "We Wanna Boogie" as an encore.

When I got home, I climbed the spiral staircase that leads to the turret on top of my cottage. The turret was one of the features that had attracted me to the cottage. It has windows on all sides and gives a panoramic view of the island and surrounding water. Turrets were a common feature on old fisherman's cottages. They allowed fishermen to observe approaching storm systems and allowed wives and other family members to watch for the return of the fisherman's boat. I've converted the turret into a small study with a desk, a chair with a reading lamp, and shelves filled with books and CDs.

I put Martin Denny's *Exotica* album on the CD player, picked up a copy of Raymond Chandler's *Farewell, My Lovely*, and settled down in a chair to read. I got lost in the familiar story of Philip Marlowe's encounter with Moose Malloy and search for the mysterious Velma and, at some point, drifted off to sleep.

The next thing I knew I was jolted awake by a loud wailing sound and I sat bolt upright with a start. The book that I had been reading clattered off my lap onto the floor. For a moment I was disoriented until I realized that I had been awakened by the siren of a police car as it went down the street. As I got up to look out the window, another police car sped past with a wailing siren and flashing blue light. My first thought was that perhaps the police were pursuing someone who had been posting anti-immigrant flyers. I saw that the police cars had stopped at the end of the block, where Adriatic Avenue dead-ends into the bay at the Angler's Haven Marina. The police cars' lights still were flashing, sending strobes of blue light pulsing through the night.

I glanced at my watch - it was 4:35 a.m. Shaking off my drowsiness, I hurried down two flights of stairs and out to the street. When I got to the marina, I saw that the police officers were standing in front of a large metal fish rack at the head of the marina's main pier. The rack was used to display prize marlins and tunas only now a woman's body was hanging from the rack by a noose. The woman had long black hair and was wearing a multi-colored, patterned shirt, tan cargo pants, and sandals. Her body hung lifelessly, like a rag doll, her head to one side at an unnatural angle. There was a piece of paper pinned to the front of her shirt. Even from a distance, I recognized it as one of the anti-immigrant flyers that had been posted by the Oceanic Park Vigilantes.

By that point, people from the nearby houses were starting to come out to see what was going on. William Price came down the street wrapped in a bathrobe and wearing bedroom slippers.

"Oh, my God!" he exclaimed when he saw the woman's body hanging from the fish rack. "A lynching!"

"Is Amanda with you?" I asked, looking around for her.

"No, thank God. She's still back at the cottage. We were asleep when we heard the sirens. I said that I'd come down and find out what's going on. I'm glad that she didn't see this, but I dread having to go back and tell her about it."

I tried to think of something reassuring to say, but there didn't seem to be anything appropriate.

"Will everyone please move back?" The request came from Sergeant Bartlett, who was among the officers who had arrived in the two police cars. He herded people away from the fish rack to the far side of the marina's parking lot, while another officer roped off the area around the fish rack with yellow crime-scene tape. An ambulance from the nearby volunteer fire station arrived, and the paramedics erected a screen in front of the fish rack to shield the body from public view. William and the other people who had gathered to see what was going on began to drift away. I was about to head back to my cottage when Gary Rockwell from the *Oceanic Park Press* arrived looking disheveled and harried, with a notepad in one hand and a computer case slung over his shoulder.

"Hey, what's going on?" he asked. "Someone called our hotline and said that there had been a lynching."

I filled Rockwell in on what I had seen and then he went over to talk to Sergeant Bartlett.

"He's not at liberty to say anything," Rockwell reported back after speaking to Sergeant Bartlett. "He said that their communications office will issue a statement in the morning. It doesn't look like we're going to learn anything more tonight."

With that, I decided to call it a night and trudged back down the street to my cottage.

Back in the turret, I sat and brooded over things. The anti-immigrant campaign had taken a decidedly brutal and vicious turn. Posting flyers and hanging a banner were one thing, but killing a person was another. The anti-immigrant campaign could no longer be dismissed as the work of cranks or thrill-seeking kids. It had become deadly serious. And the killing had been done in a way calculated to attract attention and terrorize the immigrant community.

Chapter 6. Sunday, July 24, 2005

It was nearly dawn by the time I got to bed, so I shut off my alarm and allowed myself to sleep late in the morning. It was almost lunchtime by the time I made my way over to Java Joe's. Everyone was in a state of shock over the killing and the mood in the cafe was somber. Gary Rockwell had managed to put together an article in time to make the late edition of the *Oceanic Park Press*:

BODY OF WOMAN FOUND AT MARINA. In the early hours of this morning, the body of an unidentified woman was found hanging by a noose from a fish rack at the Angler's Haven Marina in the Old Town neighborhood of Oceanic Park. The body was discovered by Les Connelly, a charter boat captain, who was headed to his boat to prepare for an early-morning charter. An anti-immigrant flyer bearing the name of the Oceanic Park Vigilantes was pinned to the front of the woman's shirt. The flyer was identical to flyers that have been posted in the Old Town neighborhood on three occasions this summer.

Shirley Logan, Communications Director for the Oceanic Park Police Department, said that the woman had been killed by a gunshot wound to the chest and not by hanging. Logan further stated that forensic evidence indicated that the woman was killed at another location and then her body was transported to the Angler's Haven Marina. She said that the police are pursuing several lines of inquiry into the killing.

Oceanic Park Police are asking the public for assistance in identifying the body. The woman is described as a middle-aged Latina woman with medium-length black hair and brown eyes, 5 feet 2 inches in height, with a tattoo of three teardrops on her left cheek and a tattoo of a cross entwined with a rose on her right bicep. If you have any information about the identity of the body, please call the Oceanic Park Police Department at 410-276-8913.

When the lunchtime rush had subsided a bit, Java Joe came out from the kitchen and took a seat across the table from me.

"Did you see or hear anything last night?" he asked.

"No. When I got home after the concert, everything was quiet. I didn't notice anything out of the ordinary. I read a bit and then fell asleep. The police cars woke me up when they went past my place on their way to the marina with their sirens blaring. Then I walked down to the marina to see what was going on."

"What do you make of it?"

"I don't know what to make of it," I replied. "It's hard to believe that any of these anti-immigrant crackpots would go so far as to commit a murder like this."

"Their flyers warned that they would do something like this and some of them are really crazy and fanatical."

"Yeah, I guess so. It's difficult to make much sense of the killing without knowing anything about the victim. Once she's identified, that may give us a better idea of the motive for the killing."

I spent the afternoon working at my desk in the turret of my cottage, sorting through mail that had accumulated during the week, writing checks to pay bills, and doing paperwork. As I was working, I noticed Sergeant Bartlett, dressed in his police uniform, working his way door to door down the opposite side of the street. I figured he was canvassing residents to see if they had seen or heard anything the previous night. When he finished the opposite side of the street, he crossed over to my side of the street and eventually worked his way to my cottage.

When I saw him heading up my front sidewalk, I went down to the porch to greet him.

After exchanging greetings, we took seats on the porch.

"I'm talking to everyone in the neighborhood to see if anyone saw anything last night," Sergeant Bartlett said.

"I'm afraid I didn't see anything," I said. "I got home fairly late, around 2:30. The Bay View Restaurant had closed by that point; the marina was quiet and deserted."

"If the body had been hanging from the fish rack at that time, would you have seen it?"

"I think so. The fish rack is visible from the sidewalk in front of my house. If the body had been hanging there then, I'm pretty sure that I would have noticed it."

"Did you see anyone else around?"

"No, no one."

"What about vehicles?"

"No, I didn't see any vehicles either."

"Well, at least that helps to narrow down the time frame a little bit. The body must have been left at the marina sometime between 2:30, when you got home, and 4:30, when Les Connelly discovered the body."

"Have you identified the body yet?"

"No, not yet, but we're hoping to get a response from the appeal that we put in the paper this morning. Somebody out there must know her and be missing her."

"Do you have any idea where she was killed?"

"No, not at this point. Once we identify her, we'll try to trace her movements during the time leading up to the killing."

"I take it that there weren't any fingerprints on the flyer."

"We should be so lucky."

"This must be causing a lot of concern among migrant workers."

"It is. We've been hearing from them and from migrant rights activists. We're going to do outreach to companies that employ migrant workers and issue guidelines for common-sense steps that people can take to keep themselves safe. We'll also step up foot patrols in the areas where migrant workers are employed and housed. But our resources always are stretched thin during the summer and there's only so much that we can do."

"I know that you've got a lot on your plate, but there's something else that I wanted to mention to you. I was going to bring it up at the community meeting the other night, but I didn't get the chance. I was talking to Buffalo Smith the other day and he told me that the police have been hassling homeless people about panhandling. That issue was supposed to have been resolved when the ordinance prohibiting panhandling was struck down."

"I know, but we still get a lot of complaints about panhandling. People come on vacation to get away from that sort of stuff. The mayor, the City Council, and the Merchants Association are always putting a lot of pressure on us to do something about it."

"Perhaps the mayor and City Council should do something to address the homeless problem instead."

"I don't disagree with you, but that's not my department. I'll remind the foot patrol officers in Old Town about the status of the law, but, as you say, I've got a lot of other things on my plate at the moment."

"I appreciate that," I said. "Good luck with the investigation."

In the evening, I walked down the block to the Bay View Restaurant, which is part of the Angler's Haven Marina complex. Activity at the marina was winding down for the day - the last of the fishing boats were coming in and tying up at the dock for the night, people who had been out fishing were unloading their catches, and charter boat captains and their crews were stowing gear and hosing down the decks of their boats. I noticed that the fish rack, where the woman's body had been hung, was covered with a tarpaulin.

The interior of the Bay View Restaurant has a nautical decor; its wood-paneled walls are draped with fishnets and adorned with stuffed fish and ship's implements, including a large ship's steering wheel, crossed oars, and ship's lanterns. Along one wall, large windows overlook the marina and a sliding glass door leads to an outdoor deck directly on the water.

It was dinner time and the restaurant was busy. I walked to the bar that occupies a wall at one end of the eating area, greeted Peter Fleming, the bartender, and ordered a carryout dinner. While I waited for the dinner to be prepared, I hung out at the bar and talked to Peter.

"Did anyone here know the woman who was killed?" I asked.

"No," Peter responded. "No one here knew her. As far as I can tell, she didn't have any connection to the marina. Apparently the body was left here just because they wanted to make use of the fish rack to send a message."

"I see that the fish rack's been covered with a tarp."

"Yeah. During the day, people were coming and taking pictures of themselves standing in front of the fish rack. It was really ghoulish. Hunter Phillips, the manager of the charter office, had a tarpaulin put over the it until he can have it taken down."

"The killing doesn't seem to have hurt business any."

"No, I thought we'd get a bunch of cancellations for dinner tonight, but we didn't. It seems like people are curious to see where the body was found."

After collecting my carry-out dinner and returning to the cottage, I ate, cleaned up, and then set out on my evening walk along the bay front. I couldn't see any evidence that the killing had dampened vacationers' holiday spirit. The sound of a typical crowd on the boardwalk drifted back from the beach front. Bond's Amusement Park was in full swing, crowded with people waiting in line to go on the various thrill rides. At the inlet, the Oceanic Park Princess was making its way out to the ocean for an evening cruise up the coast, packed with revelers. Since the threat of violence was directed at immigrants, I guessed that most vacationers weren't unduly concerned about it.

As I walked along the sea wall at the inlet, I noticed a man who appeared to be either drunk or sick, leaning over the railing and vomiting onto the sea-splashed rocks below. People walking along the sea wall were giving him as wide of a berth as the narrow wall allowed. As a I got closer to the man, I realized that it was Stuart Nichols, my old law school classmate who I had run into at the reopening of the Chimera Gallery and then seen on the yacht that crashed into the drawbridge.

"Hey, are you alright?" I asked as I approached him.

Nichols turned and looked at me with a blank expression on his face. He was bleary-eyed and disheveled and clung to the railing to steady himself on his feet. One of his eyes was blackened and swollen and he was missing one of his front teeth. Eventually recognition began to dawn on his face.

"Oh, it's you!" Nichols declared, with a hint of a sneer in his voice. "I've been reading about you in the paper."

"Oh, yeah?" I inched back a bit to try to escape the alcohol fumes that he was emitting.

"Yeah. What are you doing representing those losers on the boardwalk? You'll never get ahead doing that."

"I guess not."

"You really need to get a better class of client."

"Uh-huh."

"You should've attended the meeting of the Economic Freedom Foundation. You could've done some networking and scored some important business opportunities. I met Clifton Safir, the CEO of the Rubicon Consortium. He's the greatest economic mind of the new century. We discussed some business opportunities and he invited me to a party on his yacht."

"Is that when he got drunk and crashed his yacht into the drawbridge?"

"That wasn't his fault. The drawbridge is outdated and not designed to handle modern-day super yachts. This town needs to come into the 21st century and build a new bridge that can accommodate modern yachts. It's outrageous that they arrested him and charged him with operating a vessel while intoxicated. Do you know what that yacht cost? Fifteen million dollars! You can't treat a person with a fifteen-million-dollar yacht that way."

"I read in the paper that you were something of a hero."

"That's right. A woman got knocked overboard and I had to dive in and rescue her. If it hadn't been for me, she would have drowned."

I didn't mention the fact that I had been on the fishing pier and had seen what had actually happened.

"What are you doing down here at the inlet?" I asked.

"I was at the amusement park." Nichols nodded his head toward the bright lights of Bond's Amusement Park. "I went on the Himalayan Toboggan Ride - it made me so dizzy that I threw up in the car. They accused me of being drunk and threw me out. Can you believe that?"

"Shocking."

"It's an outrageous way to treat a guest who's in town for an important meeting. I've a good mind to sue the bastards."

"Uh-huh."

"Hey!" he said, as if he had just remembered something. "Can you lend me $2,500?"

"What?" I said, not quite sure that I could believe what I had just heard.

"Can you lend me $2,500?"

"What for?"

"I've maxed out my credit card and I need to pay my hotel bill."

"No, I'm afraid that I can't."

"What do you mean, you can't?" he said in a belligerent tone and took a step closer to me, as if preparing to assault me. "What sort of person are you?"

"I'm sorry, but I don't have that sort of money."

"No, of course not," he sneered. "You're a sad, pathetic loser, just like your clients. You'll never amount to anything. You're going to be stuck in this backwater town for the rest of your life. You're going to...Uh...excuse me, I think I'm going to be sick again."

Chapter 7. Monday, July 25, 2005

The next morning, the news broke that the body of the woman found at the marina had been identified. I read Gary Rockwell's article about it on the front page of the at my usual table at Java Joe's:

WOMAN FOUND AT MARINA IDENTIFIED. Yesterday evening, police announced that they have identified the woman whose body was found at the Angler's Haven Marina as Silvia Viejo, a migrant worker from Mexico. Viejo worked as a crab meat picker at the seafood processing plant owned by Bounty of the Bay Seafood Company and located in West Oceanic Park.

Curtis Hancock, the owner of Bounty of the Bay, contacted the police after seeing the description of the murdered woman in the paper. Hancock said that this was the seventh year that Viejo had come to Oceanic Park to work for his company under the guest worker visa program.

"Our employees have been really shaken by this," Hancock said.

Police stated that they are seeking a man who was seen loitering outside the Bounty of the Bay seafood processing plant and taking photos of the plant with a cell phone. The man is described as a White male in his late teens or early twenties with buzz-cut brown hair and tattoos on both of his arms.

A police artist has produced a sketch of the man based on the description of witnesses. If anyone can identify the man in the sketch, please call the Oceanic Park Police Department at 410-276-8913.

In the wake of the murder of Silvia Viejo, Walter Braddock, host of the "Rude Awakening" talk show on WDSF Business Talk Radio has come under intense criticism for inflaming anti-immigrant passions and is facing calls for him to resign or be fired. In an interview, Braddock denied that he bore any responsibility for the death of Silvia Viejo. "I have never said anything derogatory about migrant workers," Braddock said. "That is misinformation that is being spread by the left-wing media who want to silence me." When played an excerpt of one of his broadcasts in which he referred to migrant workers as "drug dealers, rapists, and murderers" and said that they "are bringing degenerate third-world culture to Oceanic Park," Braddock declined to comment further. Howard Denman, the general manager of WDSF, said that the station stands behind Braddock, whose morning drive-time show is the station's top-rated show

The story was accompanied by a computer-generated sketch of the suspect - a young man with a buzz cut, pork chop sideburns, a thin nose overtop of a broad mouth and pointed chin.

I sat back in my chair and thought things over. Knowing the identity of the victim didn't seem to clarify things much. It confirmed that she actually was a migrant worker, but lots of questions remained. Had the victim been targeted for a specific reason? Or had she been chosen at random simply because she was a migrant worker and the killer or killers wanted to send a message?

I looked at the sketch of the suspect again. It was hard to discern anything about his personality from the sketch. At least the police finally had a clue as to the identity of one of the members of the Oceanic Park Vigilantes.

"Oh, no!" Heather Kaylin exclaimed from a nearby table. "This is really awful." She was staring at the screen of a laptop with an expression of disbelief and horror on her face.

"What's that?" I asked.

"T-Shirt City is selling a t-shirt with a photo of the dead woman hanging from the fish rack on it. The t-shirt has a caption under the photo that reads 'The only good immigrant is a dead immigrant.' An ad for it just popped up on the news site that I was looking at."

"That is really awful," I agreed, looking over her shoulder at the picture on the screen.

"I heard about that t-shirt," Karen Cardenay chimed in from behind the counter. "They're advertising it on Walter Braddock's radio show."

"Who on earth would wear a t-shirt like that?" Heather asked. "It's sickening.

"I'm afraid that there probably are quite a few people who would wear it," I said.

I spent the day at the office, interviewing clients, drafting documents, and responding to emails and phone calls. Around the middle of the afternoon, we got word that the ordinance regulating artists and performers on the boardwalk had been adopted by the City Council and signed by the mayor. They were proposing to hold the first lottery to award spaces on the boardwalk on Monday of the following week. In anticipation of that outcome, I already had prepared a request for an emergency injunction and a supporting memorandum of law. I signed and dated the documents and Phoebe made copies. Then she went to the Circuit Court building and filed copies with the Clerk of the Court's office and went to City Hall and delivered copies to Adam Pulman, as attorney for the City Council.

In the early evening, I decided to knock off work and hit the surf. When I got to the 21st Street beach break, the usual gang was there. The Oceanic Park Surf Tournament started in a couple of days, and the people who were participating in the tournament were getting in their final practice sessions, trying to perfect their maneuvers.

At one point, an airplane flew up the beach pulling a banner that read: "The Endless Summer - Tuesday Night at Convention Center." Each summer, the Oceanic Park Surf Club organized a screening of Bruce Brown's classic surf film, *The Endless Summer*, in conjunction with the Oceanic Park Surf Tournament. The showing of the film on Tuesday night would kick off a week of events related to the tournament. Going to see the movie was an annual ritual among surfers in Oceanic Park.

"I can still remember the first time that I saw it," said Doc Cavanaugh, who had been surfing longer than any of us. "It was July 1964, when the film was shown on the East Coast for the first time. This was back before the film had a distributor and was shown in theaters. Bruce Brown took the film on a tour of the East Coast. He traveled in a big RV, with a crew and some surfers. During the day they would put on a surfing exhibition and in the evening they would show the film in surf shops and high school auditoriums. They were trying to prove to distributors that there was an audience for the film.

"They started out at the beginning of July in Gilgo Beach, Long Island. Then they worked their way down the East Coast. I had just started surfing a couple of summers before, and I was really stoked when I heard that they were coming to Oceanic Park. They pulled up to the Wavedancer Surf Shop in their big RV. Every surfer in town came out to greet them. They had some of the greatest surfers in the world with them - Corky Carroll, Hobie Alter, Phil Edwards, Mike Hynson, and Joey Cabell. The surfers put on a surfing exhibition right here at 21st Street. They were the best surfers we had ever seen. Then, in the evening, they showed the film in the school auditorium. The film didn't have a soundtrack yet at that point. Bruce Brown narrated it over the auditorium's PA system. Seeing that film was amazing. After that, a lot more people took up surfing. It really helped to bolster the surfing scene here in Oceanic Park."

The evening passed pleasantly. We sat in the lineup chatting and took turns catching waves. I managed to get a few good rides. It felt good to be out in the surf again and get away from all of the cares and concerns of the world for a little while.

Chapter 8. Tuesday, July 26, 2005

The next morning, I was seated at my usual table at Java Joe's, perusing the *Oceanic Park Press*. In Iraq, at least seven people were killed in a pair suicide bomb attacks on police checkpoints in central Baghdad...In Egypt, the official death toll rose to 64 in three coordinated bomb attacks that had taken place in the resort town of Sharm el-Shiek on the Red Sea...In London, police released the names of two fugitives wanted in connection with the attempt to bomb London's transit system the previous week. In local news, there was an article about the Oceanic Park Surf Tournament:

> OCEANIC PARK SURF TOURNAMENT BEGINS TODAY. The Oceanic Park Surf Tournament begins today and continues throughout the week. The event is being organized by the Oceanic Park Surf Club and sponsored by a number of local businesses.
>
> The event kicks off this evening with a showing of the surfing documentary *The Endless Summer* at the convention center. The competition gets underway tomorrow, with the first round of qualifying heats. The men's competition will take place in the morning and women's in the afternoon. A second round of qualifying heats will be held on Thursday. The main event begins on Friday, when winners of the qualifying heats compete against the top finishers from last year's tournament. The semi-final and final rounds of competitions will be held on Saturday. The

tournament will conclude on Sunday evening, with a trophy presentation ceremony, followed by a concert by Dick Dale, the "King of the Surf Guitar."

The winners of the tournament will advance to the Mid-Atlantic Regional Surf Contest, which will be held over Labor Day weekend in Atlantic City.

With all of the bad things that had been happening, the start of the surf tournament was a welcome bit of good news. I hoped that it would restore a bit of normalcy to the town's life.

As I was reading the paper, Keith Threlkeld entered the cafe, said "hello" to everyone, and took a seat at a table near mine. Keith worked as a bridge keeper on the drawbridge, holding down the 4:00 p.m. to midnight shift.

"How's it going?" I asked him.

"Oh, not so great," he sighed. "The Department of Public Works is conducting an investigation into that incident where a boat collided with the bridge while I was on duty."

"That was hardly your fault."

"Yeah, but the guy who was piloting the boat claims that it was, and is trying to get me fired. He's furious because I notified the police and caused him to get arrested and charged with operating a boat while intoxicated. He's a big shot with some investment company. The town government is eager to please him because they don't want to lose convention business."

"What's the guy saying?"

"He's saying that I was asleep on the job and failed to signal to warn him that he was off course."

"But you did signal him. You were leaning out or the window waving your arms and yelling. He was so entangled with the woman who was standing next to him that he wasn't paying attention to what he was doing."

"You saw it?"

"Yeah, I was on the fishing pier. The Prices were there as well."

"Would you be willing to talk to the investigators and tell them that?"

"Yes, of course. I'm sure that the Prices will be as well."

"That would really help me out a lot."

"Reverend Haycroft called," Phoebe informed me when I got into the office. "He wants to know if he can stop by and talk to you this morning."

"Yes, of course," I said. "Did he say what it's about?"

"No, he didn't say."

Reverend Haycroft arrived around the middle of the morning and I went out to the reception area to greet him.

"I don't know whether you've heard, but Larry Nolan, the proprietor of T-Shirt City, is selling a t-shirt with an image of the murdered woman hanging from the fish rack and a caption underneath that says 'the only good immigrant is a dead immigrant,'" Reverend Haycroft said, after he was seated in one of the seats facing my desk.

"Yeah, people were talking about that at Java Joe's yesterday morning," I said.

"A number of my parishioners have complained to me about it. They find it very offensive and upsetting and asked if there is anything that we can do about it. It's appalling that this man is profiting from that poor woman's death. I wondered if there is any sort of legal recourse that we can pursue."

"No, I don't think that there's anything that you can do about it. It's possible that the family or estate of the deceased woman would have a cause of action for appropriation of her image without consent. But you wouldn't have standing to bring a legal action because you don't have a direct interest in the matter and haven't suffered a direct injury as a result of it."

"What about the harm that it's causing to the community?"

"That's not specific enough. To bring a cause of action based on speech, the speech would have to be aimed at you and cause you a direct injury."

"I know that speech is generally is protected by the First Amendment, but isn't there an exception for speech that incites violence?"

"Yes, but it's a very narrow exception. The speech has to meet a two-part test. First you have to prove that the speech was intended to incite violence, and, second, that the speech was likely to actually incite violence. Making a statement that advocates violence at some indefinite point in the future isn't sufficient. You pretty much have to make a statement inciting violence in front of an angry mob that is poised to take immediate action. Printing a statement like this on a t-shirt doesn't even come close to meeting the standard."

"I was afraid of that. Well, it looks like I'll have to appeal to Nolan's sense of civic responsibility."

"I'm afraid that civic responsibility is largely a thing of the past."

"Oh, I don't know. Sometimes people will be reasonable, if you talk to them. I wonder if you would be willing to go along with me. The presence of an attorney might add some weight to our request."

"I doubt that my presence will add any weight, but I'll be glad to go along with you, if you like."

"Oh, no!" Reverend Haycroft exclaimed, when we arrived at T-Shirt City. "He's got the shirt displayed in the window!"

The shirt was indeed prominently displayed in the center of the store's large plate-glass window next to a sign that exclaimed "NOW IN STOCK! ONLY $12.99!" in bold, black letters on a fluorescent pink background.

Shaking his head in disbelief, Reverend Haycroft entered the store and approached a man standing behind a counter, next to a cash register. I followed him into the store.

"I'd like to speak to Larry Nolan," Reverend Haycroft said.

"You're talking to him," the man behind the counter responded. Nolan had longish hair and a three-day stubble streaked with grey and was wearing an unbuttoned Hawaiian shirt over a white t-shirt.

"I'm Reverend Haycroft from the Oceanic Park United Methodist Church. And this is Ned Johnston, a local attorney."

"Yeah?" Nolan sneered, letting us know that he was unimpressed.

"We've come to ask you, on behalf of the community, if you will stop selling those t-shirts with the picture of the murdered woman on them."

"You've got to be kidding me!" Nolan exclaimed. "Those shirts are my best seller!"

"They are causing a lot of concern in the community. People find them disturbing and offensive. The murder of this woman already has traumatized the community, capitalizing on it by selling this shirt is just making it worse."

"Well, that's just too bad, isn't it?"

"Can't you please have some consideration for the woman who was killed and for her family and friends. She deserves some dignity and respect."

"Do you represent her family?"

"Well, no, I can't speak for her family, but they deserve some consideration."

"What about consideration of my family? How can I support my family if I stop selling the shirt? You'd be taking food out of the mouths of my children."

"Surely you don't need to sell that shirt to support your family."

"Alright, I'll tell you what I'll do. I'll stop selling the t-shirt if you pay me $100,000 to make up for the revenue that I'll lose if I stop selling the shirt."

"A hundred thousand dollars? You know that's not possible."

"Then it's not possible for me to stop selling the shirt."

"If you won't stop selling the shirt, will you at least stop displaying it in your window? There are a lot of families with small children walking up and down the boardwalk. This is not the sort of thing that children should be exposed to."

"You must be out of your mind! How are people going to know about it, if I don't display it? A business opportunity like this comes along once in a blue moon, I've got to take advantage of it while I can."

The conversation was interrupted by an elderly woman who entered the store and approached the counter. She had grey hair, was bent over and walking with a cane, and looked like the stereotypical little old lady.

"Give me three of that shirt in the window," the woman told Nolan.

"What size?"

"Small. I need to take some presents home to my grandchildren."

Nolan turned to retrieve the shirts from the rows of shelves behind the counter. Reverend Haycroft appeared horrified by her request.

"Are you sure that that's an appropriate gift for your grandchildren?" he asked.

"Who the hell are you?!" the woman demanded.

"I'm Reverend Haycroft from the Oceanic Park United Methodist Church."

"Well, keep your nose out of my business!" She waved her cane menacingly in Reverend Haycroft's face.

"I'm sure that you don't want to encourage violence against immigrants," Reverend Haycroft said.

"It's about time that someone stood up for real Americans," the woman responded.

Nolan lay the three t-shirts on the counter for the woman to inspect. She glanced at them and then nodded her approval to Nolan who bagged them and rang them up on the cash register. The woman paid, collected her bag, and left the store.

Nolan then reached under the counter and picked up a large chrome-plated revolver, which he lay on the counter.

"I keep this close at hand in case anyone tries to rob the store," Nolan said. "If you two don't get the hell out of my store and stop interfering with my business, I'm going to use it on you."

Reverend Haycroft and I glanced at each other. There didn't seem to be anything else that we could say or do, so we left the store.

"That was an abysmal failure," Reverend Haycroft said, as we walked down the boardwalk. "Sometimes I just can't reach people."

"You did everything that you could to reason with him," I said. "Perhaps you should consider some other type of action, like organizing a boycott or picketing the store."

"Yeah, I'll talk to Helen Marwood and see if the United Human Rights Coalition is interested in doing something like that. She's good at organizing those sort of things."

I spent the rest of the day working at the office and then headed back to my cottage. After eating dinner and cleaning up, I left for the Convention Center to see *The Endless Summer*.

Twilight was falling as I made my way north along the boardwalk and the evening was shifting into gear - lights were coming on in the businesses along the boardwalk, throngs of people were turning out for the evening, and a palpable sense of anticipation and excitement was in the air. I walked past hotels ranging from shingled Victorian palaces, which dated from the early days of Oceanic Park, to contemporary high-rise monstrosities, which were increasingly altering the character of the boardwalk; past t-shirt and souvenir shops with their gaudy window displays featuring signs that screamed things such as "Two for One Sale!" "50% Off!" and "Buy One Get One Free!"; past amusement arcades with their blaring music, clanging bells, and flashing lights; and past food counters where the smell of pizza, french fries, caramel popcorn, and cotton candy mingled with the salty sea air and often overwhelmed it.

Artists and performers were out in force on the boardwalk as well. I walked past a sketch artist who drew caricatures of tourists on the spot; a man seated on a bench holding a sign that read "Free Advice"; a woman seated behind a folding table that displayed jewelry made from sea shells; and a puppet show being conducted in the window of a portable, booth-like puppet theater. I wondered how much longer they would be able to work on the boardwalk. If a judge didn't grant a preliminary injunction, the new ordinance would take effect the following week. One thing was for sure, the boardwalk certainly wouldn't be the same without the artists and performers.

Before long, the illuminated marquee of the convention center came into view, with "THE ENDLESS SUMMER" spelled out in large black letters. The convention center is located on a pier that extends from the boardwalk out over the beach and the ocean. The building has an art-deco-style facade with an arcade-type entrance that is topped by the marquee.

When I arrived, a few members of our gang of surfers - Doc Cavanaugh, Alison Lee, and Terry Mannering - already were there, hanging around outside the entrance to the convention center. Wendy Stevens, Barry Pendleton, and Larry Donaldson arrived shortly thereafter and we made our way into the auditorium.

When the lights in the auditorium went down, a cheer went up from the crowd. Then the classic opening shots of the film filled the screen - the surfers Robert August and Mike Hynson standing with their surfboards, silhouetted against the sun; waves breaking with the sun shimmering on the surface of the water; August and Hynson strapping their surfboards to the top of a car; the car driving away into the sunset; and the sun sinking below the horizon and sending shimmering light darting across the surface of the water. The images were accompanied by the theme music by the Sandals - strummed acoustic guitar chords, twanging electric guitar, and that haunting melody played on a melodica.

Like many of the people attending, I had seen the movie numerous times. I knew every scene by heart and could practically recite the narration from memory. But somehow, I never got tired of watching it.

After a brief overview of the surfing scene in Hawaii and California, we were off with Robert August and Mike Hynson on the familiar journey, following summer around the world in search of the perfect wave. As we followed the surfers, they crossed the country from California to New York; crossed the Atlantic Ocean to Africa; worked their way down the west coast of Africa from Senegal to Ghana, to Nigeria, to South Africa; crossed the Indian Ocean to Australia; crossed the Tasman Sea to New Zealand; and then crossed the Pacific Ocean to Tahiti and Hawaii. The movie ended with a final shot of a huge orange sun sinking below the horizon.

Chapter 9. Wednesday, July 27, 2005

On Wednesday morning, news broke that the police had arrested a man for the murder of the woman whose body had been found at the marina. When I got to Java Joe's, everyone was talking about the news. There was an article about it by Gary Rockwell on the front page of the *Oceanic Park Press.* After putting some music on the jukebox, I settled down at my usual table to read the article.

MAN ARRESTED FOR MURDER OF WOMAN FOUND AT MARINA. Police announced that they have arrested Bradley Cawthorne for the murder of Silvia Viejo, whose body was found at the Angler's Haven Marina in the early hours of Sunday morning. Cawthorne, age 19, lives with his mother in the Old Town neighborhood of Oceanic Park. He recently was fired from his job at Novello's Crab House after getting into an argument with a family of customers who were speaking Spanish. Cawthorne was identified by former co-workers at Novello's Crab House as matching the description of a suspect that the police had circulated earlier.

Police spokesperson Shirley Logan stated that, following the arrest, police had searched Cawthorne's computer and found the template for the anti-immigrant flyers that have been posted in the Old Town neighborhood of Oceanic Park by a group calling itself the Oceanic Park Vigilantes. In addition,

Logan stated that police had found that Cawthorne had made numerous postings to a White supremacist website called Storm Warning in which Cawthorne complained about immigrants in Oceanic Park and had threatened to take action against them in order to trigger a race war. Logan declined to comment when asked whether Cawthorne acted alone and whether any further arrests would be made.

Co-workers of Cawthorne at Novello's Crab House said that he frequently made derogatory comments about immigrants and threatened to take action against them. "We thought he was just shooting off his mouth," co-worker Cindy Michaels said. "We didn't take it seriously. We never thought that he would do anything like this."

Cawthorne is scheduled to appear at a bail hearing tomorrow morning in Bay County Circuit Court.

"Does anyone know if this Bradley Cawthorne is related to Sarah Cawthorne?" I asked.

"He's her son," Wendy responded as she maneuvered between tables to deliver an order.

Sarah Cawthorne was the proprietor of the Sea Breeze Bed and Breakfast, which was located in the northern part of Old Town. Sarah was well known and well liked in the Old Town community. As far as I could recall, I had never met her son.

"I feel really bad for Sarah," Karen said from behind the counter. "This is going to an awful experience for her. Her name's sure to get dragged into it and all of the publicity surrounding this will crush her."

"I've taken a couple of messages for you this morning," Phoebe informed me when I got to the office. "First, the request for an emergency injunction on the ordinance regulating artists and performers on the boardwalk has been assigned to Judge Willis. He's scheduled a pre-hearing conference for 10:00 o'clock tomorrow morning."

"O.k.," I said.

"Second, a woman named Sarah Cawthorne called. She's the mother of that guy who was arrested for killing the migrant worker. She wants to talk to you about representing her son. I wasn't sure whether you'd want to talk to her, so I told her that I'd have to get back to her."

"Sure, I'll talk to her," I said.

"You're not going to represent her son, are you?"

"I don't know. I'll decide after I talk to her. I've known Sarah for years - she runs the Sea Breeze bed and breakfast."

"But what her son did was so…awful."

"At this point, we don't know whether he actually did anything."

"But the State's Attorney's Office wouldn't charge him unless they had good grounds."

"The State's Attorney's Office charges people without good grounds all of the time. If you're going to work in law, you have to look at things critically and analytically. You can't assume that because the police or State's Attorney's Office says something, that it's true. I'm not saying that you should be cynical about everything, but you have to be skeptical. In any event, everyone is entitled to representation, regardless of what they've done. Our legal system wouldn't work if lawyers refused to represent defendants because they are unpopular."

"O.k., I'll call her back and schedule an appointment for this morning."

Around 10:30 a.m., Phoebe announced that Sarah Cawthorne had arrived, and I went out to the reception area to greet her. Sarah was in her late-forties, was rail-thin, and had a haggard appearance and a nervous demeanor. Her greying brown hair was pinned up with a clip, she had a pair of reading glasses hanging from a cord around her neck, and a was wearing flowered print dress.

I ushered her into my office and told her to have a seat in one of the chairs facing my desk, while I sat down behind the desk. She perched herself on the edge of the chair nearest the door and glanced about the office uncomfortably.

"It's about my son Brad," she began. "As you've probably heard by now, he was arrested last night for the murder of that woman whose body was found in the marina. I'd like to see if you'll represent him." She spoke in staccato bursts of speech with her hands in her lap, gripped together so tightly that the knuckles were turning white.

"Tell me what happened last night," I said.

"It was really horrible," she began. "Around 10 o'clock, I heard a lot of sirens. I thought that there must be a big fire someplace. I looked out of the window expecting to see a bunch of fire engines. Instead, there were five police vehicles pulling into our street with their sirens wailing and their lights flashing. A horde of police officers dressed like storm troopers got out of the vehicles and surrounded our place. They started banging on the door and yelling that if we didn't open the door immediately they would break it down. I was terrified, I thought they were going to kill us.

"I opened the door, the guy in front pushed me aside, and four or five of them charged into the house. Brad was in his bedroom up in the attic, working at his computer. They grabbed him, slammed him onto the floor, and handcuffed his hands behind his back. I asked them what was going on and they said that they had a warrant for Brad's arrest. They took him outside and put him in one of the police vehicles. Then they searched the house and seized Brad's computer and some notebooks.

"They did all of this right front of my guests and my neighbors. And there were news reporters and photographers there. The police must have alerted the press in advance, there's no other way they could have gotten there so fast. The police wanted to humiliate us in front of everyone. There was no need for any of that. If they had to arrest Brad, they could have done it quietly, but they wanted to put on a big show."

"They wanted to make sure that the arrest got plenty of press coverage to reassure tourists that the town is safe," I said.

"There's no justification for what they did," she responded. "A couple of my guests cut their stays short and checked out afterwards. Some other people who had reservations with me have cancelled them. Some of them are people who have stayed with me every summer for years."

"I'm sorry to hear that. According to the article that was in the paper this morning, the police found the template for the anti-immigrant flyers that have been posted in Old Town on your son's computer. Do you know if he's involved with this group, the Oceanic Park Vigilantes?"

"I don't know about that. We got hit with those flyers just like a lot of other businesses. It never occurred to me that Brad might be involved."

"The article also said he made postings to a White supremacist web site where he made anti-immigrant comments."

"He does spend a lot of time on the internet, and he's picked up some crazy ideas. He sometimes talks about how immigrants are invading the country, how our cultural heritage is being destroyed, and how the government is secretly controlled by the United Nations. All sorts of crazy stuff like that - I can't remember all of it. I'm afraid that I didn't take it very seriously. I thought that it was just a phase that he was going through and would grow out of it."

"Where is Brad now?"

"He's being held in the county jail. He has a bail hearing scheduled for tomorrow."

"O.k. I'll go over to the jail and talk to him this afternoon."

"Look, he may seem a bit angry and anti-social, but he's not a bad kid. He's just a bit aimless and mixed up and has come under the influence of these crazy ideas. Maybe he was involved with those flyers, but I can't believe that he killed that woman. He just wouldn't do that."

The Bay County jail is located in Old Town, down the street from the circuit court building, an arrangement that dates from the time when state law required the county jail to be within half a mile of the county courthouse. The jail was built around the turn of the century and is one of the few stone buildings in Oceanic Park. It is a rectangular-shaped, three-story building with a four-story entrance tower in the center. In the old days, the front part of the building housed the warden's living quarters, but that space now has been converted to administrative offices. The back part of the building houses the cell block, with an exercise yard behind it. During the forties, a garage was added to the west side of the building to provide a secure location for transferring prisoners to and from vehicles. The entire complex is surrounded by a chain-link fence topped with coils of barbed wire.

I checked in at the guard station by the visitor's gate and then walked up the drive toward the entrance tower. The entrance tower has imposing double wooden doors with a fan-shaped transom overtop, which give the entrance an almost elegant look. You might almost forget that they were the doors of a prison but for the bars over the transom. I went through the doors and down the hallway to the central lobby.

A handful of people were standing along the wall on the far side of the lobby by the stairway that leads to the cell block, waiting for their names to be called to go and visit friends or relatives.

I went to the reception window and asked the woman in the guard's uniform behind the window for a green card.

"Did you call ahead?" she asked.

"Yes, Ned Johnston to see Bradley Cawthorne."

She punched something into a computer keyboard and then checked the computer screen.

"Fill this out and return it to me," she said, handing me a green card.

I took the card to the counter and filled it out - I entered my name and contact information, the name of the prisoner I was there to visit, and the nature of the visit. When I was done, I returned the card to the woman behind the window.

"Do you have any ID?" she asked.

I handed her my bar association card. She glanced at it, handed it back to me along with the green card.

"O.k.," she said. "Wait until you hear your name called."

I walked across the lobby and joined the other visitors who were waiting along the wall by the stairway. My jacket, tie, and briefcase identified me as a lawyer and I sensed, or perhaps imagined, that the other visitors were eyeing me with a mixture of suspicion and resentment. If they had friends or relatives in jail, they probably had had enough experience with lawyers not to like or trust them.

After about fifteen minutes, my name was called, along with those of three other people. The four of us walked to the barred door at the foot of the short flight of stairs that led to the waiting room and visiting area on the first floor of the cell block. The door was rolled back and we went through. From the top of the stairs, a uniformed guard called down and instructed the visitors to put everything that they were carrying into one of the lockers at the foot of the stairs. Since I was there to meet with a client, I was allowed to take my briefcase into the meeting with me. While the other visitors were putting their things into lockers, I went up the stairs and through the metal detector. The guard opened another barred door and I entered the waiting room. I handed my green card to a uniformed guard who sat at a small desk looking through a window into the visiting area.

"Pick out a booth and let me know what number it is," he told me.

I opened the door and walked down the hallway toward the attorney's booths. I picked out the first empty booth, number seven, and tossed my briefcase onto the counter. Then I went back and told the guard the number of the booth. He got on the phone to have Bradley Cawthorne brought down to me. I returned to the booth and sat down in a wooden school-desk type chair at the worn-out linoleum counter in the center of the booth. A metal cage separated my side of the booth from the prisoner's side. The booth was lit by a fluorescent light in a fixture suspended from the ceiling. An old-fashioned brass foot rail ran along the base of the counter over the grimy tile floor. The prisoners' feeding schedule - replete with numerous spelling mistakes - was tacked to the wall. I got some work out of my briefcase to pass the time while I waited.

"Who are you?"

I looked up from the work I was doing at the sound of a gruff voice. Bradley Cawthorne had entered the other side of the booth and was glaring suspiciously at me. He looked a bit older than he was, had dark hair in a buzz cut, and tattoos on both of his forearms. He was dressed in a steel-blue prison jumpsuit and exuding barely suppressed hostility.

I introduced myself and explained to him that his mother had retained me to represent him.

"I don't need a lawyer, I'm going to defend myself," he said, sitting in the chair across the counter from me. "I told my mother that."

"She's concerned about you. She wants to make sure that you have proper representation."

"I don't need any representation, I'm perfectly capable of representing myself."

"What do you plan to present as a defense?"

"I don't have to present any defense. I'm a sovereign citizen. I don't recognize the authority of the federal or state government."

"That's not going to stop the court from exercising authority over you."

"The trial will give me a public platform. I'm going to use the trial to educate people about the issue of sovereign citizens and wake people up to what's really going on in the world. Did you know that Canada, Mexico, and the United States have a secret plan to merge into a North American Union that's modeled after the European Union? And that they're going to abolish private property and seize people's guns?"

"Uh...no, I didn't know that." I had decided that I wasn't going to waste time by arguing with him about crackpot conspiracy theories.

"You see?" he said triumphantly. "People need to wake up to what's going on, and I'm going to wake them up."

"A judge is not going to let you use the trial as a forum for making political speeches."

"They can't stop me."

"They can and will stop you. The judge will rule that sort of testimony irrelevant and inadmissible. He'll have the bailiffs physically restrain you if necessary."

"They can try to restrain me."

"Look, this isn't a game. Do you realize the seriousness of the charges that you're facing? You could get the death penalty or spend the rest of your life in prison."

"I don't need you to explain the charges to me, Mr. Lawyer," he sneered.

"If you want to get convicted, this is a good way to go about it."

"If I get convicted, it will trigger a civil war. People all over the country will rise up in rebellion."

"Why on earth do you want to trigger a civil war?"

"It's necessary. We have to cleanse the country and rid it of degenerate elements."

"I'm sorry, but you're deluding yourself. There's not going to be any civil war. If you get convicted, the only thing that's going to happen is that you're going to get the death penalty or spend the rest of your life in jail."

"No, you're the one who's deluded. You think that you're so smart, but you're just like all the rest. You're in for a big surprise."

I couldn't think of any response to that. How could you reason with someone who was living in an alternative reality and whose mind was impervious to facts and logic?

"Alright," I said. "It's your decision. But if you change your mind, just let me know."

"I won't be changing my mind, Mr. Lawyer," he smirked.

When I got back to the office, I phoned Sarah Cawthorne.

"I went to the jail and spoke to your son, but he wants to represent himself," I told her. "He intends to argue that he's a sovereign citizen and not subject to the authority of the federal or state government."

"Does that argument have any chance of success?" she asked.

"No, I'm afraid not."

"Isn't there anything that you can do?"

"I tried to reason with him, but his mind is made up."

"I'm so afraid of what is going to happen."

"Look, I have to be at the courthouse tomorrow morning for a pre-hearing conference. If I can, I'll stop by your son's bail hearing and see how it goes."

Chapter 10. Thursday, July 28, 2005

The next morning, I was seated alongside Adam Pulman on a couch in the outer room of Judge Willis' chambers, waiting for the judge to arrive. Margery Stein, Willis' long-suffering secretary, was seated behind her desk, working on her computer. Stein was a middle-aged woman with a frazzled appearance and an agitated and harried manner that made her appear to be suffering from shell shock. I supposed that having to endure the tyrannical presence of Judge Willis was enough to put anybody on edge.

"I see that they've arrested the guy who killed that migrant worker," Pulman said, by way of making conversation.

"Yes, he's scheduled for a bail hearing this morning," Margery Stein said.

"Who's handling bail hearings today?" I asked.

"Judge Hampton," Stein replied.

"I doubt that he'll get bail," Pulman said. "The State's Attorney's office will fight really hard to keep him locked up. The last thing that the town government wants is a headline in the *Oceanic Park Press* saying that the guy is out on bail."

As we were speaking, Judge Willis entered his chambers. Willis was a heavyset man in his late sixties. He had a shock of white hair combed back from his face, which had an unhealthy-looking, crimson-red complexion. He was wearing a polo shirt and khaki pants and had a case of golf clubs slung over his shoulder.

"Oh, no," Willis groaned when he saw Pulman and me sitting in his office. "It's the two of you again." Pulman and I had had a somewhat contentious pre-trial conference before Judge Willis the previous summer.

"I'm afraid so, you Honor," Pulman responded in a cheerful voice, trying to keep the mood light.

"Alright, give me a couple of minutes to get organized and then I'll be with you," Willis said.

As Willis was walking past us toward his office, he caught the tip of his shoe in a seam in the carpet, staggered forward a couple of steps, and then went sprawling face first onto the floor. The golf clubs shot out of the case on his back and ended up scattered on the floor around him.

"I've had it with this!" Willis yelled as he struggled to his feet. In a blind rage, he picked up one of his golf clubs and hurled it across the room. The club crashed into a vase of flowers on top of a bookcase. The vase shattered and the pieces cascaded to the floor, along with the flowers and water that had been in the vase. Margery Stein let out a horrified scream.

"Stop screaming, you stupid cow!" Willis yelled. "I've told you a thousand times to get that carpet fixed!"

"I've called General Services I don't know how many times," Margery Stein blurted desperately. "They keep saying that they're going to come and fix it but they never come."

"If that carpet isn't fixed by the end of the day, you're fired!" Willis yelled. "And pick up my golf clubs!" With that he went into his office and slammed the door behind him.

"I'll get the golf clubs," I said. I knelt down and started to pick up the golf clubs and put them back in the case. Pulman assisted me, while Margery Stein cleaned up the mess caused by the broken vase.

After picking up the golf clubs, Pulman and I returned to our seats on the couch to await our summons. We could hear Judge Willis in his office on the phone.

"I'm not going to your mother's," Judge Willis said in a loud, agitated voice. "I'm playing golf today."

"It sounds like he's talking to his wife," Margery Stein whispered to us.

"I'll play golf every day, if I want!" Willis yelled. "And I'll get home as late as I want!"

This was followed by a pause.

"I don't care if she's on her deathbed!" Willis yelled.

The conversation then came to an abrupt halt as if his wife had hung up on him. It was followed by several minutes of uncomfortable silence. I dreaded to think what sort of mood the Willis was going to be in when we finally got in to see him. Eventually, the phone of Margery Stein's desk rang. She picked up the receiver, listened for a few moments, and then replaced the receiver.

"He's ready for you now," she informed us.

When we entered the office, Willis was seated behind his desk in front of a wall covered with diplomas and citations. The other walls of his office were lined with bookshelves filled with state and federal law reports. Pulman and I took seats facing the judge's desk.

Willis appeared to have calmed down somewhat, although his face still was so red that it appeared to be glowing.

"Do you see the sort of conditions I have to work under?" he asked, apparently as a way of explaining his behavior. "I've been trying to get that carpet fixed for years."

"It's intolerable," Pulman said sympathetically, trying to score points with the judge.

I refrained from saying anything.

"Alright, let's make this fast," Willis commanded. "I have an early tee time at the Bay County Country Club. What are you two squabbling about now?"

"Your Honor, the City Council has adopted an emergency ordinance that severely limits the number of artists and performers allowed to display artwork or perform on the boardwalk," I said. "I represent a coalition of artists and performers who are challenging the ordinance. The ordinance violates the First Amendment rights of artists and performers by acting as a *de facto* ban on their right to free speech in a public forum. We are requesting that you issue an emergency injunction to prevent enforcement of the ordinance."

"The ordinance doesn't violate anybody's First Amendment rights," Pulman chimed in. "It simply imposes reasonable time, place, and manner restrictions."

"Alright, alright," Willis said. "What exactly does the ordinance do?"

Pulman provided a brief summary of the ordinance.

"What's your objection to it?" Willis asked me.

"While the ordinance doesn't expressly prohibit anyone from exercising their right to free speech, it is overly broad and will serve as a de facto prohibition on free speech. There will be a large number of artists and performers competing for the 25 spaces. The vast majority of them will get shut out each week. Because they have to reapply to the lottery every week, they don't know, from week to week, whether they will be able to work. If they don't work every week, it is not financially viable for them to continue to perform."

"Why a weekly lottery?" Judge Willis asked.

"It's due to the number of artists and performers," Pulman said. "If we awarded each of the 25 spaces to a single artist or performer for the entire season, a lot of artists and performers would be shut out completely. Awarding spaces on a weekly basis, will result in a weekly rotation of artists and performers on the boardwalk. During the course of the season, everyone will get a chance to appear. That way we don't we don't prohibit anyone from exercising their right to free speech."

"You do prohibit them from exercising their right to free speech on the weeks that they don't win the lottery, which will be most weeks of the season," I responded. "A person's right to free speech shouldn't be dependent on winning a lottery. There are other ways to ensure that everyone gets a chance to appear that are much less restrictive. As you know, your Honor, time, place, and manner restrictions are required to be narrowly tailored and must serve an important governmental interest. In this case, the restrictions are broad and sweeping and the City Council has not demonstrated that they serve an important governmental interest."

"Why has this ordinance been adopted now?" Judge Willis asked. "I've lived in Oceanic Park my entire life, and there have been people performing on the boardwalk as long as I can remember. When I was a little kid there was a blind guy who played a banjo and was led by a seeing-eye dog. He had a tin cup attached to the end of his banjo and I used to drop a nickel in it. Why has it become a problem all of a sudden?"

"It's true that people have been performing on the boardwalk for a long time, but the situation has gotten out of hand recently," Pulman responded, appearing alarmed at Willis waxing nostalgic about performers on the boardwalk. "It has become a health and safety hazard. The artists and performers are impeding pedestrian traffic and blocking egress and ingress of law enforcement officers and emergency responders."

"The City Council has made that assertion, but they haven't provided any evidence to support it," I said. "If you review the transcript of the hearing and the materials that were submitted by the City Council, you see that they have failed to provide documentation of any health or safety incidents caused by artists or performers on the boardwalk."

Judge Willis opened a thick file on the desk in front of him and started to leaf through it.

"I see that that actress appeared at the hearing," Judge Willis said.

"Belinda Restivo?" I asked.

"Yes, that's her," Willis said. "I really like that show that she's in."

"She was a strong advocate against the ordinance," I said. "As an artist, she understands the importance of protecting First Amendment rights"

"I would really like to have seen her testify," Willis said. "She's really hot."

"But your Honor, she's not even from Oceanic Park!" Pulman exclaimed, becoming more alarmed at the course that the discussion was taking. "She doesn't know anything about the situation here. She was so confused that she didn't know whether she was opposing the ordinance or supporting it. And then her dog attacked the President of the City Council."

"Her dog attacked Kevin Sullivan?" Willis asked.

"Yes, that's right," Pulman said, indignantly.

Willis threw his head back and burst out laughing with a giant guffaw.

"I would like to have seen that too!" Willis declared.

"You Honor, you can't…" Pulman started to protest, but Willis waved him into silence.

"I've heard all that I need to hear in order to make a preliminary decision," Willis stated. "I have to agree with counsel for the plaintiffs that this ordinance is overly broad and will prohibit people from exercising their 1st Amendment rights. It is my considered opinion that the plaintiffs in this case have a high probability of succeeding when this case goes to a hearing. Therefore, I am granting their request for a preliminary injunction to enjoin enforcement of the ordinance until a final decision can be made. I will instruct the clerk of the court to schedule the case for a hearing as soon as possible. And now, where are my golf clubs?"

"Well, your little publicity stunt really paid off," Pulman said bitterly. We were standing in the hallway outside of Judge Willis' chambers.

"I'm sure that Judge Willis' feelings for Belinda Restivo didn't influence his decision," I said. "I think that he exercised very sound and well-reasoned judgment."

"Yeah, right," Pulman scoffed. "Willis is getting crazier and crazier every day. It's a disgrace that he's allowed to remain on the bench."

"On the contrary, I thought that he acted with acumen and gravitas befitting a judge," I said.

"Don't give me that," Pulman groaned and rolled his eyes.

"If you're so unhappy with him, why don't you run against him at the next election?" I asked.

"Do you know how hard it is to unseat a sitting judge?" Pulman responded. "Once they get on the bench, they're there for life, no matter how crazy and senile they get."

After parting company with Pulman, I made my way to Judge Martha Hampton's courtroom on the second floor of the courthouse. Judge Hampton's courtroom, like all of the courtrooms in the Bay County Circuit Court building, is a traditional-style courtroom of the sort that they don't build anymore because the materials have become prohibitively expensive. The central focus of the courtroom is an imposing judge's bench of dark mahogany with recessed panels at the front of the room. An embossed bronze railing runs across the courtroom in front of the judge's bench to separate it from the rest of the room. To the left of the judge's bench, is a jury box of the same dark mahogany and, to the right of the judge's bench, a modest, utilitarian desk for the court clerk. Two trial tables with chairs for the parties to litigation face the judge's bench. Another bronze railing runs behind the trial tables and separates the front of the courtroom from the rows of pews in the spectators' gallery.

The bail hearings already were underway when I arrived at the courtroom. Judge Hampton was seated behind the bench, surveying the courtroom. Hampton is a Black woman in her thirties. Her hair was braided into cornrows, and she wearing wire-rim glasses and a black judge's robe. She is one of the better judges on the circuit court bench and runs her courtroom in a no-nonsense, businesslike manner.

Vivienne Marcus, an assistant state's attorney, was seated at the prosecution table with a thick stack of files on the table in front of her. Marcus' red hair was tied in a partially unraveled bun and she was wearing a nondescript blue business suit. She is a veteran prosecutor who is known for her no-holds-barred, scorched-earth approach. Her win-at-any-cost tactics have earned her a couple of reprimands from the Bar Council, but that only seems to enhance her standing within the State's Attorney's Office.

The jury box was being used as a holding pen for the prisoners who were in court for their bail hearings. I spotted Bradley Cawthorne among the eight or nine prisoners in the box. The box was flanked on each side by a Department of Corrections officer, keeping watch over the prisoners.

After a person has been arrested and processed by the police, the person goes before a Commissioner. The Commissioner informs the person of the charges against them, explains the possible penalties, and advises them of their rights. The Commissioner then gives the person their charging papers, which contain a list of charges, a statement of facts written by a police officer, and a checklist of their rights. In addition, the Commissioner sets or denies preliminary bail. At the next available session, the person goes before a judge for bail review. On a typical day, very few people have any interest in bail review hearings. A few family members or friends might show up, but that would be about it. Today, however, there was a large media presence concentrated in the first few rows of the spectators gallery. I spotted Gary Rockwell among the reporters. A few other spectators were scattered about the rows of pews in the gallery. I spotted Sarah Cawthorne on a pew about two-thirds of the way back and slid onto the pew next to her.

"Has your son's case been called yet?" I asked.

"No, not yet," she responded.

"Next up is case number 173-B7936, the State versus Franklin Jarvis," announced the court clerk in a loud, authoritative voice.

One of the prisoners in the jury box stood up and started walking across the courtroom to the trial table on the left side of the courtroom. He was middle-aged, unshaven, dressed in a steel-blue prison jumpsuit and leg irons, with a manila folder tucked under an arm.

A man in a business suit got up from the first row of the spectator gallery carrying a stack of folders and joined Jarvis at the defense table. I recognized him as Lester Enright, a lawyer I occasionally ran into around the courthouse.

"Lester Enright from the law offices of Enright and Kaslin on behalf of Franklin Jarvis," Enright announced to the court, putting his appearance on the record.

At the prosecution table, Vivienne Marcus stood to address the court.

"Vivienne Marcus on behalf of the Bay County State's Attorney's Office," she announced. Marcus consulted a file that she was holding open in front of her. "The defendant in this case, Franklin Jarvis, is charged with robbery and assault and battery. As you will see from the file, your Honor, the Commissioner denied preliminary bail in this case. We concur with the Commissioner's decision and request that bail be denied. This is a particularly serious case, involving a robbery as well as assault and battery. On the night of July 9th, the defendant broke into a motel room and stole a laptop, a mobile phone, and other items. As the defendant was leaving the motel property, a security guard sought to stop and challenge him. The defendant assaulted the security guard and severely beat him with the butt of a gun, resulting in serious injury.

"The defendant has two previous convictions for crimes involving violence. In 1987, he was convicted of assault and battery in connection with a fight in a bar. In 1993, he was convicted of armed robbery of a hardware store. During the course of the robbery, the defendant used an industrial stapler to staple the store clerk's hand to the counter to prevent him from calling for help. The clerk subsequently developed an infection in his hand and had to have it amputated.

"Given the defendant's history of violence, we believe that the defendant poses an immediate risk of danger and that it is not safe to release him into the community. Therefore, we request that bail be denied."

"Mr. Enright." Judge Hampton said. "How do you respond?"

"Your Honor, this is a case of mistaken identity," Enright said, rising to address the court. "On the evening on July 9th, Mr. Jarvis was attending a Barracudas minor league baseball game at Bay

County Stadium in Bellwether Hill. We will produce three witnesses who saw him at the game."

Judge Hampton briefly consulted the laptop that was sitting on the judge's bench in front of her.

"According to the schedule on the Barracudas website, there was no game scheduled at Bay County Stadium on the evening of July 9th," she said. "If you are going to offer a false alibi, you should at least get the date straight. Bail is denied."

Enright turned to Franklin Jarvis and began talking at him in a hoarse whisper. I couldn't make out what he was saying, but I gathered he was admonishing his client for making him look like an idiot in front of the court. Jarvis extracted a document from his file and handed it to Enright. He unfolded it, looked at it, and then threw it disgustedly down on the table.

"That's last year's schedule!" Enright hissed. He grabbed his stack of files, jammed them into a briefcase, and stalked out of the courtroom while the guards led Jarvis back to the jury box.

"Up next is case number 173-B6386, the State vs. Bradley Cawthorne," announced the court clerk.

At the sound of his name, Bradley Cawthorne rose from his seat in the jury box and made his way to the defense table. Like Jarvis, Cawthorne was wearing a steel-blue prison jumpsuit, his legs were shackled, and he was carrying a manila folder tucked under one arm.

Vivienne Marcus again stood to address Judge Hampton.

"The defendant in this case, Bradley Cawthorne, is charged with first degree murder," she stated. "We also are planning to bring additional charges. The Commissioner denied preliminary bail in this case and we concur with the Commissioner's decision. Accordingly, we are requesting that your honor deny bail.

"The murder victim is a migrant worker from Mexico who was working as a crab picker for Bounty of the Bay Seafood Company. As I'm sure your Honor is aware, a group called the Oceanic Park Vigilantes has been carrying out an anti-immigrant flyer campaign in the Old Town neighborhood. One of the flyers was pinned to the shirt of the murder victim. The police found the template for the flyer on the defendant's computer.

"The defendant has a history of expressing virulent anti-immigrant views. He has posted numerous comments on Storm Warning, a White supremacist website. I won't read the comments now, but copies are attached to our submission. In addition, the defendant recently was fired from his job at Novello's Crab House after he berated some customers for speaking Spanish. After being fired, the defendant declared that immigrants 'would get what's coming to them.'.

"In addition to all of this, we have evidence directly linking the defendant with the murder victim. The defendant had numerous photos of the Bounty of the Bay Seafood Company and the Ranch House Motel on his cell phone. The Ranch House Motel is an old motel that has been converted into housing for migrant workers and the murder victim was living there. The photos showed workers, including the murder victim, coming and going from the seafood company and the motel. It appears that the defendant was stalking the workers, studying their habits, and looking for an opportunity to get one of them alone and kill her."

"The court also should note that the defendant has a prior criminal record. In 2003, he was convicted for possession of methamphetamine, a Schedule I controlled dangerous substance.

"In summary, your Honor, this was a particularly cold and calculated murder. It was planned and premeditated. The surveillance photos on the defendant's cell phone show that he stalked the murder victim and studied her habits before killing her. In light of the defendant's past conduct, we believe that, if released, he would pose a danger to the community. Given the overwhelming evidence against him, we also believe that he may pose a flight risk to avoid trial. We are requesting that bail be denied."

"Thank you, counsel," Judge Hampton said. "We will now hear from the defendant."

Bradley Cawthorne rose to address the judge.

"Are you represented by counsel?" Judge Hampton asked.

"I'm representing myself."

"You are entitled to be represented by counsel. If you can't afford a lawyer, the court will appoint someone to represent you."

"I understand. I prefer to represent myself."

"I should think carefully about that if I was you. In the legal profession we have a saying - a person who represents himself has a fool for a client. It can be very difficult to navigate the complexities of the legal system without a lawyer."

"I understand. I have made my decision."

"Very well. Please proceed with your application for bail."

"I am a sovereign citizen and this court does not have any jurisdiction over me. I will not be tried by a member of the globalist new world order who is under the control of the United Nations. Under the Constitution of the United States, individual citizens are entitled to..."

"I asked you to explain why bail should be granted, not give me your theories about the new world order," Judge Hampton snapped, cutting off Cawthorne.

"I am a sovereign citizen and this court does not have any jurisdiction over me. ..."

"Do you have any reasons why bail should be granted?" Judge Hampton interrupted.

"I am a sovereign citizen and this court..."

"Bail is denied," Judge Hampton exclaimed, bringing her gavel down on the bench with a loud bang. "You may return to your seat."

"But I am a sovereign citizen!" Cawthorne shouted, showing no sign of moving. "You can't do this to me!" The two Department of Correction guards stepped forward and each grabbed one of Cawthorne's arms.

"You have no right to do this!" Cawthorne shouted as the guards struggled to lead him back to the jury box. "You are a dupe of the new world order!"

"Please remove the defendant from the courtroom," Judge Hampton ordered.

The two guards wrestled Cawthorne out of the side door of the courtroom. They probably would take him to the holding cell on the first floor of the courthouse until it was time to transport him back to the jail.

"Oh, my God," Sarah Cawthorne exclaimed, burying her face in her hands. "That was awful. If the trial goes like this, he's sure to be convicted."

"I'm afraid so."

"I'll talk to him again; maybe now he'll reconsider his decision to represent himself."

When I got back to the office, I called Roger Steadman and left a message for him, informing him that Judge Willis had granted a temporary injunction against the ordinance regulating artists and performers on the boardwalk. I spent the remainder of the day working at the office. Late in the afternoon, I received a call from Sarah Cawthorne.

"I've just spoken to Brad again," she said. "He's agreed to allow you to represent him after what happened this morning."

"O.k.," I said. "I'll make an appointment and go and talk to him tomorrow."

Chapter 11. Friday, July 29, 2005

The next morning, I was back in one of the attorney's booths at the city jail. I perused the *Oceanic Park Press* while I waited for Bradley Cawthorne to be brought down from the cell block. Five people had been killed in a suicide bomb attack outside of a hospital in Baghdad...The two Algerian diplomats who had been kidnapped the previous week in Baghdad had been killed...The three remaining suspects in the attempted bombing of the London transportation system had been arrested. In the local section, there was an article about Judge Willis' issuance of an emergency injunction against the ordinance regulating artists and performers on the boardwalk:

> JUDGE ISSUES EMERGENCY INJUNCTION AGAINST ORDINANCE. Yesterday, Bay County Circuit Court Judge Charles Willis issued an emergency injunction to prohibit the city from enforcing a recently-adopted ordinance regulating artists and performers on the boardwalk. The injunction was requested by a group of artists and performers calling themselves the Coalition to Save the Boardwalk who claimed that the ordinance abridged their First Amendment right to free speech in a public forum. The group was represented by local attorney Ned Johnston.
>
> In granting the emergency injunction, Judge Willis stated that he found it "highly probable" that

the group would succeed in its First Amendment claim.

Roger Steadman, an Elvis impersonator who performs on the boardwalk under the moniker, "Boardwalk Elvis," praised the judge's decision. "This is an important victory for free speech rights," Steadman said.

At a hastily-organized press conference, Kevin Sullivan, President of the Oceanic Park City Council, denounced Judge Willis' decision. "The ordinance is necessary to maintain order and protect brick and mortar businesses on the boardwalk," Sullivan stated. "Since when is the right to free speech more important than the right to do business?"

Sullivan cut the press conference short and ran from the room after being repeatedly interrupted and asked if he would apologize for his treatment of a dog belonging to reality t.v. star Belinda Restivo, with which Sullivan had become involved in an altercation at a hearing on the ordinance last week.

When Bradley Cawthorne was led down to the booth, he glared at me with resentment, furious that he had been forced into a position of having to accept my help. Gaining his confidence and trust was going to be difficult.

"I understand that you were at that bail hearing yesterday," he muttered as he took a seat at the counter, on the other side of the metal cage.

"Yes, that's right," I said.

"That was a perfect example of what's wrong with this country," he exclaimed, pointing a finger accusingly at me. "That judge wouldn't even let me speak. She's a dupe of the globalist new world order. She's part of a system that is trying to replace our American values with globalist values."

I listened patiently while he aired his grievances and ranted about injustice in order to allow him to let off steam and try to build up some rapport with him.

"Look," I said after awhile, "I'd be the first to tell you that our justice system is far from perfect, but it's a far better system than you will find in other countries."

"I don't recognize the justice system," he insisted.

"Be that as it may, we need to prepare for your trial. Do you have your charging papers?"

He opened the manila folder that he had brought with him, extracted some papers that were stapled together, and slid them through the narrow opening where the metal cage met the counter.

"Bradley Edward Cawthorne," I said, reading his name off the top of the charging papers. "Is that your correct name?"

"Yeah."

I wrote the name down on my legal pad. I proceeded to verify the rest of the routine information - address, phone number, age, etc.

"At the bail hearing, the Assistant State's Attorney said that you had a previous conviction for possession of a Schedule I controlled dangerous substance," I said. "Is that correct?"

"Yeah," he muttered grudgingly.

"Give me a minute to read the statement of facts," I said, flipping through the charging papers.

The statement of facts contained the same basic information that Vivienne Marcus had presented at the bail hearing: the police had found the anti-immigrant flyer posted by the Oceanic Park Vigilantes on Bradley Cawthorne's computer; he had posted anti-immigrant messages on the Storm Warning website; and he had surveillance photos of the Bounty of the Bay Seafood Company's processing plant and the Ranch House Motel on his cell phone.

"According to this, the police found the flyer that was posted by the Oceanic Park Vigilantes on your computer," I said. "Is that correct?"

"I guess so," he muttered.

"Is it correct or not?"

"Yes, it's correct," he hissed through clenched teeth.

"I take it that you're a member of the Oceanic Park Vigilantes."

He shrugged noncommittally.

"Are you a member or aren't you?" I asked.

"Alright, yes," he hissed.

"How did you get involved with the group?"

"I came across this website called Storm Warning when I was surfing the internet. I started reading things that were posted there and realized that they made a lot of sense. They helped to explain what was going on in the world. I found out what it means to be a sovereign citizen and how the U.S. government is secretly controlled by the globalist new world order and the United Nations. I realized that there were other people out there who felt the same way about things that I did. After awhile, I started posting things myself.

"Over time I got to know some of the other people who were posting comments on the website. Eventually, I made contact with some other people who live in the area. We started getting together occasionally. We would meet at the Lost Oasis and talk about what was happening in the world. We decided to start our own organization and take action at the local level."

"Who else belongs to the organization?"

"I can't talk about that. Our membership is secret."

"O.k. What about the flyers? I take it that you posted them."

"Yeah, but only the first time. The other two times, it was done by someone else."

"Wait a second. You're telling me you only posted the flyers the first time?"

"That's what I said."

"Look, if I'm going to defend you, you have to be honest with me and tell me the truth."

"That is the truth," he said, the volume of his voice rising with anger. "I've admitted that we posted the flyers the first time. If we had posted them the other two times, I would admit that too. I don't have any reason to lie about it."

"Alright. Do you have any idea who posted the flyers the other two times?"

"No, I don't know. Anybody could have taken one of the flyers and made photocopies of it."

"Did you tell the police that you only posted the flyers the first time?"

"No, I didn't tell them anything."

"What about the banner on the water tower? Did you do that?"

"No, we didn't do that either."

"What was the purpose of taking photos of workers coming and going from the Bounty of the Bay Seafood Company and the Ranch House Motel?" I asked.

"We were really infuriated when someone else started posting our flyers and using our name. We felt like someone was stealing our thunder. We wanted to take back the initiative, do something that would get people's attention. But we weren't going to kill anybody, we were just going spray paint some slogans on the walls of the Bounty of the Bay Seafood Company and the Ranch House Motel."

"Why were you monitoring people coming and going from the seafood company and the motel?"

"We wanted to know when the shifts changed, so we could pick a time when no one was around and we wouldn't get caught."

"Why did you target the Bounty of the Bay Seafood Company rather than some other company that employs migrant workers?"

"I knew about Bounty of the Bay because they supplied seafood to Novello's Crab House when I worked there. The Bounty of the Bay truck used to make deliveries there every day. I knew that Bounty of the Bay employed a lot of migrant workers and I knew that they housed them in the Ranch House Motel. It's just a coincidence that the woman who was killed happened to work for them."

"Do you have any way to prove that you just were planning to spray paint the seafood company and motel?"

"We bought the spray paint at Conner's Hardware Store."

"Did you pay with a credit card?"

"No, we paid cash. We didn't want anyone to be able to trace the purchase back to us."

"Do you still have the receipt?"

"I don't, but John...I mean, someone else may have the receipt."

"What's this person's name?"

"I can't tell you that. I'll check with them and let you know if they have the receipt."

"Where were you between 10:00 p.m. on Saturday night and 4:30 a.m. on Sunday morning?"

"I was at the Lost Oasis until about midnight and then I came home and went to bed."

"Can anyone confirm that you were at the Lost Oasis?"

"Frank, the bartender. He knows me pretty well, he should remember that I was there."

"Can your mother confirm what time you got home?"

"I don't know. I didn't see her when I got back. She probably had gone to bed already. I'm not sure whether she heard me come in or not."

"Alright, I think I have all of the information that I need for now. Make sure that you check on the receipt for the spray paint. That could be important."

After leaving the jail, I checked in briefly at the office and then set out to follow up on some of the information that Bradley Cawthorne had provided during our interview. My first stop was the Lost Oasis, which is located on a somewhat seedy side street in Old Town in the same block as a bail bond agency and a tattoo parlor. The bar is housed in a nondescript storefront with a small neon sign projecting out over the door and the bottom two-thirds of the display window blacked out. The place had been there as long as I could remember - I'd walked past it many times, but never had been inside of it.

There were a couple of customized motorcycles parked in the street in front of the Lost Oasis. Inside, it was cool and dimly lit. A scarred wooden bar ran along one wall with a row of battered barstools in front of it. The other three walls were lined with pinball machines, electronic games, and a jukebox. In the center of the room were two pool tables with fluorescent light fixtures suspended from the ceiling over top of them.

There was no one behind the bar. A couple of bikers were shooting pool at one of the tables, but they ignored me and continued with their game. "Long Train Runnin'" by the Doobie Brothers was playing on the jukebox. I glanced over the contents of the jukebox to see if there was anything worth playing, but it was a lot of arena rock from the '70s and '80s.

"Can I help you?" a deep, raspy voice asked. A man had emerged from a doorway behind the bar. He was middle-aged, had a lined face framed by black hair and a beard partway down his chest, and was wearing a tank top that showed off the tattoos on his arms.

"I'm looking for Frank," I said.

"You've found him," the man replied.

I introduced myself and explained that I was representing Bradley Cawthorne.

"I understand that you know Brad," I said.

"Yeah, he's a regular here."

"Do you remember if he was here on Saturday night?"

"If he says he was here, then he was here."

"I'm asking if you can verify that he was here."

"Sure, I can verify it."

"Do you remember what time he was here?"

"Whatever time he says that he was here, he was here."

"I really need to get your own independent recollection."

"Look, if Brad needs an alibi, I'll be glad to provide him with one. Just let me know what you want me to say."

"I'm afraid that it doesn't work that way. I have to know the truth - I need to have information that will stand up to scrutiny in court."

"What you need to do, is get Brad off on the charges, not get hung up on a bunch of legal technicalities."

I noticed that the clicking of pool balls had stopped. I glanced back over my shoulder and saw that the two bikers had paused in their game and were listening to our conversation.

"I will do everything that I can to get Brad off," I said, "but I have to do it in accordance with the law."

"Don't talk to me about the law," Frank responded. "This country is going to the dogs. We're being overrun by third-world scum. And what does the law do? Nothing. But when a person tries to stand up for real Americans, he gets charged with a crime. What kind of system is that?"

"The case involves something more than standing up for Americans. A woman has been killed. The charges against Brad are very serious."

"Let me tell you something." Frank pointed a finger accusingly at me. "This country is on the verge of a civil war. It is like a powder keg that is about to explode. All it needs is one little spark to set it off. If Brad get convicted, that will provide the spark. It will result in a violent uprising and reprisals. And one of the first casualties of those reprisals will be you. So, if you value your life, you had better make sure that Brad doesn't get convicted."

My next stop was Novello's Crab House, which is located on the bay front, off Oceanic Highway, about half a mile north of Old Town. The restaurant advertises its presence with a large sign by the highway, illustrated with a giant picture of a crab waving one of its claws at passersby: "Novello's Crab House and Raw Bar - Fresh Steamed Crabs - Oysters - Happy Hour Every Day 3 - 7 - Arrive by Land or Water - Free Parking and Boat Slips."

The crab house is set back from the highway behind a gravel-covered parking lot and housed in a large frame building topped by an aqua blue roof with a copula on it. A flagstone walk leads from the parking lot through a small garden with a miniature waterfall and pond to a glassed-enclosed entryway.

I was greeted by the maitre 'd behind the reception desk. She was a young woman with sun-streaked blond hair pulled back into a pony tail and sunburnt skin peeling from the bridge of her nose. I explained who I was and asked to speak to the manager.

The maitre 'd picked up a phone on the desk, punched in a few numbers, and spoke to someone in a hushed voice.

"He can see you now," she said. "Come with me."

She escorted me through the dining area, which was decorated with enlarged, vintage photos of local watermen at work - there were photos of watermen dredging for oysters, checking crab pots, and pulling in nets filled with tuna. There was a bar against one wall and the back of the dining area opened onto a covered deck overlooking the bay. A handful of early diners were getting a jump on the lunch rush.

The maitre 'd led me past the bar to a door in a corner of the room and knocked a couple of times.

"Come in," a voice called from the other side of the door.

The maitre 'd opened the door and escorted me into a small office, where a thirty-something man was sitting behind a desk working at a computer. He had a baseball cap tilted back on his head and was dressed casually in a Hawaiian shirt and khaki cargo shorts.

"This is Harry Novello," the maitre 'd told me and exited the office, closing the door behind her.

I introduced myself and explained that I was representing Bradley Cawthorne.

"I read in the paper that Brad had been arrested," Novello said. "It was a bit of a shock. I'm not quite sure what to think. I know he was a mixed-up kid, but I never believed he'd do something like that."

"According to the police, he was fired due to an incident that occurred here a few weeks ago," I said. "The prosecutors are using that incident as circumstantial evidence against him, to demonstrate his attitude toward immigrants. I'd like to find out more about what happened."

"Sure, but I have to tell you that I already have spoken to the police. A couple of police officers came here and asked me about Brad, trying to get background information on him. I didn't want to get him in trouble, but, under the circumstances, I felt like I had to tell them what happened."

"I understand. What sort of employee was he?"

"Not bad. He wasn't exactly the greatest worker in the world, but he showed up and he did the job. After he had been here awhile, though, I started to get some complaints about him. A couple of other employees complained to me that he was making derogatory remarks about Black and Hispanic customers. I had a talk with him and stressed that he couldn't make those sort of remarks in the workplace. Maybe I should have fired him at that point, but I hate to fire anyone, so I let him off with a warning."

"I take it that there was a more serious incident."

"Yeah, a few weeks ago, a family was in here eating and they were speaking Spanish. Brad heard them and demanded to know where they were from and if they were in the country legally. He said that if they didn't give him proof that they were in the country legally, he was going to report them to ICE. The family was here on vacation and they were extremely upset. After that, I had no choice but to fire him. I can't have that sort of thing happening in the restaurant."

"I understand that he made threats after you fired him."

"That's right. He said he was tired of living in a country that was being overrun by criminal elements from the third world. He said that it was time for Americans to start fighting back and that immigrants were going to get what was coming to them. I thought that he was just shooting off his mouth. It never occurred to me that he might actually do anything."

"The woman who was killed worked for Bounty of the Bay Seafood Company. Do you do business with them?"

"Sure, they're one of our primary suppliers. Their truck was just here making a delivery this morning. You don't think that she was killed because Bounty of the Bay does business with us, do you?"

"No, I don't have any reason to think that, I'm just trying to connect all of the pieces."

I decided that my next stop would be the Bounty of the Bay Seafood Company to see if I could learn any information about the woman who had been murdered. Bounty of the Bay's crab picking plant is located across the bay on the mainland in West Oceanic Park, the blue-collar neighbor of Oceanic Park and home to the area's commercial fishing fleet. I made my way back through Old Town and headed across the drawbridge toward the mainland

The drawbridge was built in 1948 and consists of a series of concrete spans with a steel draw span over the boating channel about a third of the way across the bridge. The bridge has a four-lane asphalt road bed with a sidewalk on each side of the bridge.

Prior to construction of the drawbridge, Oceanic Park could be reached only by ferry or train. Construction of the drawbridge made Oceanic Park more easily accessible and greatly boosted its popularity as a vacation spot. In the '70s, people began to complain that raising the draw span to allow boats to pass through was tying up traffic and started pushing to replace the drawbridge with a humpbacked bridge that was high enough to allow large boats to pass underneath. Local residents and historic preservationists pushed back and sought to preserve the drawbridge. A compromise of sorts was reached when a second bridge - a humpbacked bridge - was built several miles further north. Recently, however, people had again begun calling to replace the drawbridge with a more modern humpbacked bridge. When Clifton Safir's yacht collided with the drawbridge the other night, it had brought renewed attention to the issue. People now were complaining that the drawbridge wasn't big enough to accommodate modern "super yachts," which businesses were hoping to attract to Oceanic Park.

I walked along the sidewalk on the north side of the bridge. The sidewalk was bordered on the road side by a chain link fence and on the water side by a waist-high concrete wall topped by a metal railing. Cars and SUVs filled with vacationers and loaded down with luggage and beach gear zipped past in the opposite direction, on their way into Oceanic Park. A few people were fishing from the bridge, their rods propped against the concrete wall and the lines dangling into the water. Seagulls were squawking and circling overhead. As I walked past the bridge keeper's booth adjacent to the drawspan, I waved hello to Lou Gellart, the bridge keeper.

When I reached the mainland, I walked north along the bay front past the Smuggler's Cove Bar and Grill; the Land's End Marina, where Buddy Emerson kept his boat docked; and the old crab-picking plant of the Mid-Atlantic Seafood Company, now converted into artists' studios.

The Bounty of the Bay crab picking plant is housed in a large wooden building that resembles a warehouse and is topped with a tin roof. The company's name and logo are painted on the side of the building. A work boat was tied up at the dock alongside the crab picking plant and a couple of men were unloading bushels of crabs.

I went through the door of the crab-picking plant and paused for a few moments in the entryway while my eyes adjusted to the indoor light after the bright sunlight outside. There were no windows in the plant and it was lit by fluorescent lights in fixtures suspended from the ceiling. The pungent smell of crab meat permeated the air.

The crab pickers - all women - stood at long stainless-steel tables piled high with crabs. Each of the crab pickers was wearing a white hair net, a baseball cap with the company's logo on it, and a large apron. They would crack the shell of a crab with a wooden hammer and then use their knives to extract the meat from the shell. Extracting all of the meat out of a crab shell is difficult, tedious, and time-consuming work. After extracting the meat, the workers would place the meat in one of the plastic containers on the table in front of them. There were different containers for different categories of crab meat - backfin, claw, and lump. Each container had the worker's number on it. In addition to their base pay, the workers received money based on how much crab meat that they picked.

"Can I help you?" I was approached by a middle-aged woman who appeared to be a supervisor and spoke with a Spanish accent.

I introduced myself and said that I would like to speak to the manager.

"His office is back this way," she said, leading me to a door in the back corner of the plant.

The door of the manager's office was open, allowing him to keep an eye on operations on the plant floor. He was sorting through some papers on his desk, but looked up as we approached his office. He was middle-aged, wearing tortoiseshell glasses, a loosened tie, and a short-sleeved shirt. The office was nothing fancy, strictly utilitarian. It had plain wooden walls with work schedules and other documents tacked to them. Unlike the plant, however, he had a window overlooking the bay.

I introduced myself and explained that I represented Bradley Cawthorne and was investigating the death of Silvia Viejo.

"I'm not sure how I can help you," he replied warily, taking off his glasses and rubbing his eyes. He looked me over, weighing whether he should talk to me.

"I'm trying to get some background information about Silvia Viejo."

"I don't know much about her background," he said with a shrug.

"According to the article that was in the paper, this was the seventh year that she had worked here. Is that correct?"

"Yes, that's correct," he grudgingly admitted.

"How did you hire her?"

"We use a recruitment agency in Mexico. They recruit workers for us, help the workers to obtain visas, and arrange for transportation."

"Are you aware of anyone who would want to do her harm?"

"Why are you asking me that? The police have arrested the person who killed her."

"The fact that he's been arrested doesn't mean that he killed her. That has yet to be proved."

"Who else could it have done it? She didn't know anyone around here, no one would have any reason to harm her. It had to be one of those anti-immigrant fanatics."

"Did Silvia Viejo have any friends among the other workers? Do you mind if I talk to them?"

"Look, I don't want you bothering the workers. They're very busy and this matter has upset them really badly. They've already had to talk to the police. I don't want you bothering them with any more questions. I'm sorry, but I'm very busy." With that, he returned his attention to the papers in front of him, indicating that the conversation was over.

I thanked Hancock and made my way out through the crab picking plant. If I wanted to talk to the workers, I would have to try to do it in the evening, after they had gotten off work and were back at their lodgings at the Ranch House Motel.

I started making my way back along the bay front toward the drawbridge. As I was walking past the Land's End Marina, I noticed a group of people gathered around the marina's fish rack, admiring a large white marlin that was hanging from the rack. As I got closer, I saw that Captain Dan and Buddy Emerson were among the group of people. Emerson works out of the Land's End Marina, which primarily caters to commercial fishermen, after having been blacklisted by the more upscale marinas in Oceanic Park, which cater to charter boat captains.

I headed toward the fish rack to see what was happening.

"Hey, what are you doing here?" Captain Dan asked when he saw me.

"I just happened to be passing by," I said.

"Take a look at this," he said proudly, gesturing toward the white marlin.

"You caught it?"

"Damn right. One hundred and twenty one pounds."

"Not bad," I said. It was somewhat short of the state record of 135 pounds, but, given that marlins typically are in the 45-to-50-pound range, it was an impressive catch.

"We need to take a photo to document the catch," Captain Dan said. He rummaged through a carry-all bag sitting on the dock by his feet, pulled out a camera, and handed it to me.

"You can do the honors," he instructed me. "Get a couple of shots."

Captain Dan and Emerson posed, each standing on one side of the fish, and I snapped a couple of photos. I was reminded uncomfortably of the woman's body hanging on the fish rack, but I pushed that image from my mind.

"We're going over to the Smuggler's Cove Bar and Grill to have a few drinks and celebrate," Captain Dan said. "Why don't you come along?"

I agreed that it sounded like a good idea.

The Smuggler's Cove Bar and Grill is housed in a weathered frame building on the bay front. Inside, it has a bar on one level and, a few steps down, a dining area that opens onto a wooden deck overlooking the bay and the drawbridge. The wood-paneled walls of the bar and dining area are decorated with advertising posters for various brands of beer and colored lights are strung overhead among the exposed rafters.

A baseball game was playing on a large widescreen t.v. mounted overtop of the bar. A few people were seated at the bar, boisterously shouting encouragement or insults at the screen. We walked past the bar, through the dining room, and out onto the deck, where we sat at a wooden picnic table. In addition to Captain Dan and Buddy Emerson, there was Kent Gannon, the manager of the Land's End Marina, and a couple of boat captains, Joel Kastner and Ted Ventrella.

A fierce late-afternoon sun sent glints of silver darting across the surface of the bay. A few people were paddle boarding in the shallow water near the edge of the bay. Farther out in the channel, fishing boats of various sizes were coming and going. A steady stream of traffic was headed across the drawbridge into Oceanic Park.

A waitress came and took our order for drinks and food. Captain Dan proceeded to give us a blow-by-blow account of his epic struggle with the white marlin.

I heard a buzzing sound and looked up to watch a jet ski heading up the bay toward the inlet. A man was piloting the jet ski with a woman seated behind him, her arms around the man's waist, her hair blowing in the wind.

"I hate those things," Emerson snarled. "The people who ride on them are a menace."

"Oh, they look like they're having fun," I said.

"Nah, Buddy's right, the people who ride those things are a menace," Ted Ventrella said. "Some clowns on a jet ski nearly collided with my boat the other night in the dark, when I was coming back late."

"Wait a second," I said. "What night was this?"

"I don't know, sometime last week."

"It wouldn't have been Tuesday night, would it?"

"Let me see." He frowned in concentration. "Yeah, now that I think about it, it was Tuesday night."

"What exactly happened?"

"I was coming back late. I had just gone through the drawbridge and was heading up the bay toward the marina when this jet ski came tearing out of nowhere. It seemed like it was on the verge of going out of control, and nearly ran into my boat. They just barely missed me, and then turned and headed up the bay."

"I don't suppose you got the registration number."

"No, but I recognized where it was from - Blue Water Boat Rentals. Their jet skis are painted a distinctive lime green color, they're easy to recognize, even in the dark. Why?"

"I think the people on the jet ski may have been the ones who hung the banner from the water tower on Tuesday night."

By the time we left the Smuggler's Cove Bar and Grill, evening was coming on and a fiery red sun was making its way toward the western horizon. Fireflies were beginning to flicker in the descending twilight and insects were chirping in the shrubbery. The crab pickers at the Bounty of the Bay Seafood Company should have completed their shift and returned to the Ranch House Motel for the evening. I decided to walk back along the bay front to the motel and try to talk to some of the crab pickers.

The motel had seen better days. It is a one-story building in a semicircle around a courtyard with a swimming pool in the center. It had been built in the '50s and was designed to look like a western ranch house.

At a casual glance, the place looked derelict and deserted. The neon sign was unlit, there were no cars in the parking lot, and no one was lounging about the swimming pool. If you looked closer, however, there were a few signs of life - laundry was hanging from a clothes line in the yard beside the motel, lights had gone on in some of the rooms, and a Mexican flag was flying from a holder affixed to the wall of the building.

I walked up the driveway, across the parking lot, and past the swimming pool. The chain link fence around the pool was rusted and the pool was empty except for a puddle of rainwater in the deep end. The aqua blue paint on the interior of the pool was faded and peeling and there was a large crack in bottom of the pool with weeds growing up through it.

I heard the faint sound of a t.v. coming from one of the rooms. I went and knocked on the door. A young woman dressed in a t-shirt, cut-offs, and sandals answered the door.

I introduced myself and explained that I was investigating the death of Silvia Viejo. A look of incomprehension and panic crossed her face.

She turned, called for another woman, and retreated into the room.

I could see that there were three bunk beds in the room, which meant that six women were living in a room designed for two. One wall had been decorated with a crucifix and family photos. Women were sitting on the edge of a bed watching a Spanish-language show on an old t.v. on top of a small cabinet.

Another woman approached the door. It was the supervisor who I had encountered at the crab picking plant. She recognized me and did not seem pleased to see me.

"What can I do for you?" she asked in a stern voice that suggested that she had no intention of doing anything for me.

I introduced myself again, explained that I was investigating the death of Silvia Viejo, and asked if she would be willing to talk to me.

"You're that lawyer," she said. "Mr. Hancock said that you might be coming around. He told us not to talk to you."

"Don't you want to help find out who killed Silvia Viejo?"

"I'm sorry, I can't help you," she said, stepped back into the room, and shut the door in my face.

I turned away and headed back to the drawbridge.

Chapter 12. Saturday, July 30, 2005

The next morning, I was back at my usual table at Java Joe's, perusing the *Oceanic Park Press*. In Iraq, a suicide bomber had killed 25 people who were gathered at an army recruiting center in the village of Rabia, near the northern city of Mosul...Senate Democrats considering the nomination of Judge John Roberts to the Supreme Court had requested that the White House turn over memos written by Roberts when he was deputy solicitor general under President George H.W. Bush, including memos relating to the case of *Rust v. Sullivan*, in which Roberts had argued that the Supreme Court should overturn *Roe v. Wade*...In local news, there was an article about the Oceanic Park Surf Tournament:

> FINAL DAY OF COMPETITION IN OCEANIC PARK SURF TOURNAMENT. The final day of competition in the Oceanic Park Surf Tournament will begin today at 10:00 a.m. on the beach at 21st Street. Yesterday, the eight top finishers from the qualifying trials held on Wednesday and Thursday competed in one-on-one heats against the eight top finishers from last year's tournament. Today, the four winners of the second round of yesterday's competition will advance to the semi-finals, with the two winners of the semi-finals advancing to the finals. The men's competition will be held in the morning and the women's in the afternoon.

The tournament will conclude on Sunday evening, with a trophy presentation ceremony, followed by a concert by Dick Dale, the "King of the Surf Guitar." The winners of the tournament will advance to the Mid-Atlantic Regional Surf Contest, which will be held over Labor Day weekend in Atlantic City.

The article was followed by a listing of the individual results - Wendy had advanced through the first two rounds of the main event to the semi-final round that afternoon. She was off from work to give her time to prepare for the competition.

"Hey, we missed you at the surf tournament yesterday." Java Joe had emerged from the kitchen and was taking a seat across the table from me.

"Sorry, I got tied up with a case that I'm working on," I said. "I see that Wendy advanced to the semi-finals."

"Yeah, she surfed really well. All the training that she's been doing has paid off."

"How was the competition?"

"Pretty strong. The level of performance was very high. There was a new, young surfer named Jessica Mayfield who was very impressive. And Virginia Hartnett advanced to the semi-finals as well." Hartnett was the winner of last year's tournament and would be the person to beat.

"Will you be there this afternoon?" Java Joe asked.

"Yeah. I've got a few things that I need to check out this morning, but I'll definitely be there this afternoon."

Shortly after leaving Java Joe's, I was headed north on the Oceanic Highway on the bright red Vespa LX 150 scooter that I maintained for those occasions when I had to venture outside my Old Town stomping grounds. I had left Old Town and what used to be known as Northern Oceanic Park behind, and was passing through Condo City. To my right, on the ocean side, the highway was lined with a seemingly endless row of high-rise condos with people packed into them like ants in an ant colony. To my left, on the bay side, the highway was lined with large shopping malls and smaller condo complexes built around canals that led back to the bay.

When I was a kid growing up in Oceanic Park during the sixties and seventies, the town had ended at 64th Street. Beyond that, there was nothing but miles of sand dunes, sea grass, and scrub pines all the way to the state line. My friends and I used to ride our bikes up to the sand dunes beyond 64th Street to surf and avoid the crowds. At first the development of this area was gradual - a few hotels and vacation cottages appeared here and there among the dunes. In the late seventies, however, there was a building boom in the northern part of the island. Seemingly overnight, the sand dunes were paved over and replaced with a row of densely-packed, high-rise monstrosities, built in the then-fashionable "brutalist" style.

The cozy relationship between the City Council and the property developers ensured that the developers had free rein. The developers were able to ignore the "set-back" requirement in a zoning ordinance that prohibited them from building too close to the beach and, instead, built the condos right on the edge of the beach. They also bulldozed a protective sand dune barrier that had been built by Army Corps of Engineers after a hurricane in 1961 because it would have blocked the view from the lower floors of the condos. As a result, they had exacerbated problems with beach erosion caused by the natural westward drift of a barrier island.

Up ahead on my left, I spotted a large sign for Blue Water Boat Rentals:

Blue Water Boat Rentals & Water Sports
Catamarans, Jet Skis, Kayaks, Pontoon Boats, Skiffs, Paddleboards
Safe and Easy Boarding from Our Sandy Beach
Free Parking
Walkups Welcome

I turned off the highway and onto a road that made its way past a large shopping complex and back to the bay, where Blue Water Boat Rentals was hidden from view of the highway. I parked in a lot covered with crushed oyster shells. At the far end of the parking lot was a seawall with stairs that led down to a small sandy beach. Alongside the stairs was a wooden hut with a large sign on its roof that read "Blue Water Boat Rentals." There was a rack of kayaks and a rack of paddleboards alongside the hut, while catamarans, jet skis, pontoon boats, and skiffs were lined up on the beach. I walked over and leaned on the counter of the hut. The attendant was down on the beach helping a young couple who were renting paddleboards. After getting the couple successfully launched on their paddleboards, he headed back to the hut.

The attendant, who appeared to be in his late teens or early twenties, entered the other side of the hut. He had peroxided blond hair, zinc oxide on his nose, and was wearing a t-shirt with a tropical design printed on it and baggy boardshorts.

"What can I do for you?" he asked in a sullen voice, which made it sound like whatever I wanted would be considered be an imposition.

I introduced myself and explained that I was investigating the murder of the woman whose body had been found in the Angler's Haven Marina.

"On the night of Tuesday the 19th, you rented a jet ski to someone. I need to find out who that was."

"You're mistaken," he fired back instantly. "We don't rent gear at night. We close at 5:00 p.m. and all rentals are required to be returned by that time." His response was so quick and precise, it sounded like he had been anticipating the question and had prepared his answer in advance.

"I'm not mistaken. One of your jet skis was seen in the bay at around 9:00 p.m. on Tuesday the 19th."

"Seen by whom?"

"A fishing boat captain. The jet ski nearly collided with his boat."

"That's not possible. All of our rentals were returned and accounted for by 5:00 p.m."

"Can you check your records?"

"I don't need to check our records. I know for certain that we didn't rent a jet ski at that time."

"Look, I haven't told the police about this, but, if you don't tell me who was operating the jet ski, I'm going to have to tell the police, and then you can answer their questions."

Some uncertainty began to creep into the determined look on his face. It was starting to dawn on him that it wasn't going to be as easy to bluff his way out of this as he had hoped.

"I can assure you that I'm a lot easier to deal with than the police," I said.

"If I answer your question, will you promise not to report this to the police?"

"I can't promise that, but I won't tell the police anything if I can possibly avoid it."

"Alright. I rented the jet ski to a guy I know. He told me that he needed a jet ski for that evening. I told him that we didn't rent jet skis at night. He said that he really needed one; he and another guy wanted to pull a surprise on a friend of theirs. He offered to pay extra for it. So, I agreed to do it off the books."

"What happened that evening?"

"The guy came here, along with a friend of his. The two of them got on the jet ski and took off. They said that they would be back within the hour and they were. That's all there was to it."

"In what direction did they go?"

"South, toward the drawbridge."

"Were either of them carrying anything?"

"The guy I know was carrying something that looked like a rolled-up bed sheet," he responded, shifting uncomfortably.

"When you heard about the banner that was hung on the water tower, you must have suspected that they were responsible."

"Look, I had nothing to do with that!" the attendant declared, throwing his hands up in the air. "I had no idea what they were going to do; they told me that they wanted to play a surprise on a friend of theirs. All I did was let them use the jet ski."

"What's the name of this friend of yours?"

"He's not really a friend, just somebody I know."

"I still need to know his name."

"Is that really necessary?" he groaned.

"I'm going to have to talk to him."

"His name is Aaron Trafford."

"What about the other guy with him?"

"I don't know him at all. I'd never seen him before."

"Where does Aaron Trafford live?"

"I don't know where he lives, but he's a skateboarder. He hangs out around the skate bowl, that's where I know him from. You should be able to find him there."

"Alright, thanks."

"Listen, you won't tell anyone else about this, will you? If the owner of the company found out that I'd rented something off the books, I'd lose my job."

"I can't make any promises, but I'll keep you out of it if I possibly can."

Back in Old Town, I stashed my scooter in the shed behind my cottage and walked to the skate bowl in the city recreation area. The skate bowl is a large concrete bowl with a wooden stairway that leads to a platform at the top of the bowl where skateboarders launch themselves into action. The skate bowl is surrounded by a chain-link fence and flanked by wooden bleachers for spectators to sit and watch the skateboarders perform.

When I arrived at the skate bowl, skateboarders were lined up on the stairs, waiting for their turn to take off from the platform at the top of the skate bowl. Some spectators, along with a handful of skateboarders taking a break, were sitting on the bleachers alongside the skate bowl.

I sat down on the bleachers and watched a few skateboarders take off from the platform and perform their maneuvers. After awhile, I turned to one of the skateboarders sitting on the bleachers.

"Excuse me," I said. "Do you know Aaron Trafford?"

"That's him," the guy said gesturing toward the skateboarders lined up on the stairs. "The second from the top."

"Thanks," I said. Like the other skateboarders, the one standing second from the top was wearing a helmet and knee pads and clutching his skateboard under his arm. There was something familiar about him, but I couldn't place him at first. Then it came to me. I had encountered him the previous summer when I was investigating the death of Count Rupert. We hadn't exactly gotten on, so I didn't think that he would be too pleased to see me.

I watched Aaron Trafford take off from the platform, tear down the wall, across the bottom of the bowl, and up the embankment on the other side. He shot up into the air, balancing himself with one hand on the rim of the skate bowl, reversed course in mid-air, and smoothly ran down the wall again and up the wall on the other side to the platform. After he had completed his run, he went to the back of the line at the bottom of the stairs, to wait another turn.

After making several more runs at the skate bowl, Aaron Trafford took a break, left the skate bowl, and walked out onto the sidewalk. I walked over to intercept him.

"Oh, no, not you again," he said when he saw me. "What do you want now?"

"I need to talk to you for a minute."

"I'm listening," he said, with an exasperated sigh.

"I understand that you rented a jet ski Tuesday night of last week."

"Get lost," he said and turned to walk away.

"Maybe you'd rather talk to the police," I said.

He turned around and glared at me.

"If you don't talk to me, I'm going to have to give the information that I have to the police. And then, you'll have to talk to them."

"What information do you have?" he demanded.

"I know that you rented a jet ski from Blue Water Boat Rentals on Tuesday night of last week. And that you were involved in hanging the anti-immigrant banner from the water tower."

"You don't know any of that. You're just guessing."

"Fine. I'll talk to the police."

"Alright, alright," he muttered resignedly.

"Are you a member of the Oceanic Park Vigilantes?"

"Hell, no!" he declared. "I don't know anything about them."

"Then how did you get involved with hanging the banner?"

"A guy came around here one day and asked a few of us if we'd like to make some money. We asked him what we had to do. He told us he'd pay us fifty bucks each to post some flyers in Old Town during the middle of the night. We said o.k. It sounded like easy money. We thought that they were going to be some sort of advertising flyers."

"Then what happened?"

"The guy came back a couple of days later and gave us a box of flyers. When we looked at them, they weren't advertising flyers, they were those Oceanic Park Vigilantes flyers."

"But you still went ahead and posted them anyway."

"Hey, for fifty bucks each, we didn't care what the flyers said."

"What instructions did this guy give you about posting the flyers?"

"He just said to post the flyers in Old Town. The only specific instruction that he gave us was to make sure that we got plenty of the flyers on the Chimera Gallery."

"He specifically asked you to target the Chimera Gallery?"

"Yeah, that's right."

"So, what happened after you posted the flyers?"

"The guy came back the next day. He told as that we'd done a good job and paid us the fifty bucks."

"How did he pay you?"

"In cash."

"I take it that he came back a couple of weeks later and asked you to post the flyers a second time?"

"Yeah."

"What about the banner?"

"When the guy came back and asked us to post the flyers a second time, he also asked us if we would hang a banner from the water tower. He said that the Chimera Gallery was having this big reopening and he wanted us to disrupt it by hanging the banner from the water tower."

"Did he tell you his name?"

"He said that we could call him 'Mr. Smith.'"

"Great. Did he give you a phone number or any way to get in contact with him?"

"No."

"What did he look like?"

"He looked like he was in his thirties, had dark hair and a mustache, and was wearing aviator sunglasses. He was dressed like a businessman."

"O.k., thank you. This is information is really helpful."

"Hey, you're not going to go to the police, are you?"

"No, I don't have any reason to at the moment. But my client is on trial for murder and it's possible that I may need to use this information at some point as part of his defense."

Back at my cottage I grabbed a quick bite to eat and then headed to the 21st Street beach break to catch the surf tournament. A stage had been erected on the beach in front of the boardwalk, with a large banner overtop that read "Oceanic Park Surf Tournament." To one side of the stage, was a large electronic scoreboard and, to the other side, an elevated judge's platform. The five judges were seated on chairs on the platform with laptops open on a shelf in front of them and beach umbrellas attached to the railing behind them to give them some shade. The judges did their scoring on the laptops and, at the end of each ride, the results were shown on the electronic scoreboard. I waved hello to Doc Cavanaugh, who was seated on the judge's platform.

There was a fairly good crowd of spectators scattered about the beach, some standing, some seated on sand chairs, and some sprawled on beach blankets. A number of the spectators had binoculars or spotting scopes so that they could follow the action more closely. Down by the water's edge, some photographers with cameras mounted on tripods were set to take pictures. A large tent with open sides had been set up for the competitors who were waiting for their heat to start or unwinding after a heat.

I spotted a group of people I knew among the spectators on the beach - Java Joe and Karen Cardenay were there, along with Barry Pendleton, Alison Lee, and a few other surfers from the 21st Street beach break. I walked over and joined them.

They filled me in on the results of the men's competition, which had taken place during the morning. The winner had been Ross Layman, the defending champion from last year. Barry Pendleton had finished third, a very good showing.

"Good afternoon, and welcome to the final day of competition in the Oceanic Park Surf Tournament." A loud voice reverberated through the sound system from the stage. "I'm Lee Ellison from WVOP radio, the voice of Oceanic Park, and I'll be serving as MC today." Lee Ellison had taken the stage, dressed in in his usual WVOP baseball cap, Hawaiian shirt, and boardshorts. "This afternoon, we have the women's semi-final and final heats. The winner of today's final heat will proceed to the Mid-Atlantic Regional Surf Tournament in Atlantic City over the Labor Day weekend.

"I'd like to explain the rules for this afternoon's competition. Competitors will surf in 45-minute heats. The start of a heat will be announced by a double horn blast, a five-minute warning will be given by a single horn blast, and the end of the heat will be announced by another double horn blast.

"Surfers are allowed to catch up to 15 waves per heat. For each wave that a surfer catches, the five-judge panel will score the surfer based on the number of successful maneuvers that the surfer performs, the skill with which the surfer performs the maneuvers, and the difficulty of the maneuvers. Scoring will be done on a ten-point system, with quarter point increments. From the total number of waves that a surfer catches during the heat, the six best scores will be averaged together to determine the surfer's final score for the heat.

"A coin will be tossed before the start of each heat to determine which surfer has the right to choose the first wave. After the contestant who has won the coin toss rides a wave, the other contestant gets to choose the next wave. After that, the surfer who paddles around the priority buoy gets priority in choosing the next wave. A surfer loses priority by riding a wave or paddling for and missing a wave. A surfer also loses priority if a surfer fails to catch a wave within three minutes after taking priority.

"We will now proceed to the first semi-final heat, which features Natalie Bankhead against Wendy Stevens. Will the competitors please proceed to the front of the judge's stand for the coin toss."

Clutching their surfboards under their arms, Wendy and Natalie Bankhead were met by an official in front of the judge's stand for the coin toss. The official spoke to them and then tossed a coin in the air and let it fall into the sand. After kneeling down and picking up the coin, the official called out to Lee Ellison on the stage.

"The winner of the coin toss is Natalie Bankhead, giving her first choice of waves," Lee Ellison announced.

The two surfers proceeded to position themselves at the water's edge to await the starting horn. At the double blast of the horn, they ran into the surf, dove atop their boards, and paddled out to assume positions in the lineup. They each were wearing a brightly-colored vest - Wendy's was blue and Natalie Bankhead's was red - so that the judges could easily identify them at a distance.

Sitting on her board in the lineup, Bankhead scanned the horizon for a good wave. Wave selection is an important part of competition - surfers want to choose a wave that has adequate size, strength, and duration to allow them to perform a sufficient number of maneuvers to make a good score.

A large, well-formed swell approached the lineup and Bankhead started readying herself to catch it. As the wave got closer, she began to paddle to get her speed equal to that of the wave. When the wave caught her board and began to lift it, she moved into a crouching position. She rode down the face of the wave to the bottom, did a bottom turn, and rode back up to the top of the wave. At the top, she did an off-the-lip reentry and then cut back into the wave to extend the length of her ride. She performed a whitewater rebound off the top of the wave, but by then the wave was petering out and she hopped off her board in the shallow water.

It was a solid performance to start the heat with and the judges gave her a score of 7.75.

Wendy now had choice of the next wave. When she saw one that suited her, she took off on it. She started off with the same basic combination of maneuvers that Bankhead had used - a bottom turn, an off-the-lip reentry followed by a cutback. She then performed a whitewater rebound and another bottom turn. She raced back to the top of the wave and performed a second off-the-lip reentry. She then rollercoasted over the whitewater as the wave dissipated in shallow water.

It was a very strong performance. Compared with Bankhead, Wendy had attacked the wave more aggressively, achieved greater speed, and managed to pack more maneuvers into her ride. The judges rewarded her with a score of 8.25.

As the two surfers swapped rides, the pattern established by their first rides continued - Bankhead surfed skillfully, but Wendy consistently surfed better and scored higher. Once Wendy had six strong rides under her belt and a solid lead, she could afford to cut loose and try some riskier and higher-scoring maneuvers. On her next ride she, executed an arial reentry - she shot out of the top of the wave becoming totally airborne, reversed direction in mid-air, and smoothly reentered the wave. That ride received a 9.0, increasing Wendy's lead. Trying to keep up, Bankhead attempted an arial reentry on her next ride, but slipped off her board as she reentered the wave and wiped out. After that, Wendy was all but uncatchable. She ended up winning the heat by a final score of 8.83 to 8.0.

The second heat of the semi-final pitted Virginia Hartnett, the top-seeded surfer and last year's champion, against Jessica Mayfield, a young newcomer who had qualified through the trials.

Virginia Hartnett won the toss. On her first wave, she skillfully ran through a repertoire of maneuvers that included bottom turns, cutbacks, and off-the-lip reentries and scored an 8.5. She appeared to be off to a solid start. Jessica Mayfield then surprised everyone - rather than following the conventional strategy of playing it relatively safe until she had six solid rides under her belt, she cut loose on her first wave and successfully pulled off an arial reentry, earning her a score of 9.25. Mayfield's strong performance on her first wave did not cause Hartnett to alter her strategy. On her second wave, Hartnett stuck to her plan of getting six strong rides under her belt before she attempted riskier maneuvers; she turned in another solid ride for a score of 8.75. Hartnett probably figured that Mayfield's performance on her first wave was a fluke and that she wouldn't be able to continue to perform risky maneuvers without making errors. That, however, didn't prove to be the case. On her next ride, Mayfield again pulled out all of the stops, this time successfully completing a 360 spinner and scoring a 9.5. Mayfield now had a significant lead. Hartnett seemed to realize that she was in trouble and was going to have to abandon her original strategy and perform some more difficult maneuvers sooner rather than later. On her next wave, she attempted an arial reentry, but lost her balance and pitched headfirst into the wave, her board shooting into the air without her. The wipeout, combined with Mayfield's aggressive strategy, seemed to rattle Hartnett and throw her off balance. She never really regained her stride after that. Mayfield continued to surf spectacularly and Hartnett simply could not catch up with her. When the double horn blast announced the end of the of the heat, Mayfield had scored a tremendous upset with a score of 9.21 to 8.96.

The members of our little group of spectators all exchanged apprehensive glances and exclamations of astonishment at Mayfield's performance. It was apparent that Wendy was going to have unexpectedly tough competition in the final. I looked over at the competitors' tent and saw Wendy getting some last-minute advice from Terry Mannering.

Wendy won the toss, giving her first choice of waves. Wendy had the advantage of having seen Mayfield's approach during the semi-final heat and Wendy knew that she was going to have to alter her own strategy in order to beat Mayfield. Wendy came out strong with her first ride, pulling out all of the stops, including performing an arial reentry. She earned a score of 9.25. Mayfield responded with a strong ride, earning a score of 9.0. As the two surfers exchanged rides during the heat, they remained neck and neck, the lead going back and forth by a slim margin.

Barry Pendleton was keeping track of the average of each surfer's six best rides on the calculator function on his phone. As they approached the five-minute warning, he calculated that Mayfield was ahead of Wendy by 9.25 to 9.17. Wendy currently had priority. She was sitting on her board, scanning the horizon for a wave. As the five-minute warning sounded, she took off on a wave, earning a score of 9.0. With the 9.0 replacing the lowest of her top-six scores - an 8.75 - Wendy's average score increased to 9.21. She was now only slightly behind. Another ride with a good score could put her ahead, but it was unclear if she would get the chance.

Mayfield now had priority with about four and a half minutes remaining. If she got a good score on her next wave, she could increase her lead and possibly put herself out of reach. She also could run down the clock by taking as much of her three minutes as possible to catch a wave. Mayfield sat on her board in the lineup, alternating between scanning the horizon for waves and glancing at her watch to keep track of the three-minute limit. She passed up a couple of good waves in order to run down the clock. That, however, turned out to be a mistake. As the three-minute limit neared, there were no good waves on the horizon. Mayfield had to settle for what she could get - a small, choppy wave that closed out prematurely. She was unable to perform many maneuvers on the wave and scored only a 7.5. Since the score was not among her top six, it would be discarded and did not affect her average score.

Wendy now had a small opening. She had priority, but there was only a minute and a half remaining. She would have to take the first wave that looked halfway decent. As she sat in the lineup, a nicely-shaped three-and-a-half-foot wave headed toward her. Wendy caught the wave and pulled out all of the stops, putting on a dazzling display of maneuvers that concluded with a 360 spinner in the shallow water. We waited for the judges' scores to appear on the scoreboard. When they did, the judges had rewarded her with a score of 9.5, making the final score 9.29 to 9.25 in Wendy's favor.

"The winner of the women's competition is Wendy Stevens with a score of 9.29 to 9.25," Lee Ellison announced, making it official. "The tournament will conclude tomorrow night with an awards ceremony and a concert by Dick Dale on the beach at 9th Street.

A cheer went up from the crowd and we rushed down to the water's edge to congratulate Wendy on her victory.

Chapter 13. Sunday, July 31, 2005

The next morning, when I arrived back at my cottage after breakfast, I was surprised to see someone sitting in one of the chairs on the front porch. It was a young Latina woman with dark hair, wearing a brightly-colored striped shirt, jeans, and sandals. When she saw me approaching, she stood up apprehensively, tightly clutching a macrame bag that was slung over her shoulder.

"I hope that you don't mind, but I had to talk to you," she said as I came up the stairs of the porch. She spoke haltingly with a heavy Spanish accent.

"It's perfectly o.k.," I said. "Please sit down."

She sat back down in the deck chair and I sat in another one.

She introduced herself as Maria Castellon.

"I understand that you're investigating the death of Silvia Viejo," she said.

"Yes, that's right."

"I saw you when you came to the Ranch House Motel on Friday. I wanted to talk to you then, but I couldn't talk in front of the other people. I have information that someone should know about. I don't want to go to the authorities, but I thought maybe I could tell you. You have to promise that you won't tell anyone where you got the information." She appeared extremely uncomfortable, often pausing to try to find the right word. She was gripping her macrame bag so tightly that her knuckles were turning white.

"Yes, of course," I assured her.

"I worked with Silvia at the Bounty of the Bay crab-picking plant. One day, our boss, Mr. Hancock, asked to speak to Silvia and

174

me after our shift was over. He told us that we were his two best crab pickers and asked us if we'd like to make some extra money by working an extra shift on Sunday, which is our day off. We said that we would. He told us to come to the plant that Sunday at 10:00 a.m. and not to tell any of the other workers about it. He said that he didn't want to other workers to know that he was giving us extra work.

"That Sunday, Silvia and I went to the plant. The place was deserted except for the two of us and Mr. Hancock. He had received a shipment of crab meat from Venezuela. It was packed in plastic containers labeled 'Venezuelan Crab Meat.' He told Silvia and me to take the crab meat out of the containers that it had been shipped in and pack the crab meat in the containers that we normally use - the ones that have the Bounty of the Bay name and logo on them and say that it is local crab meat. We were really shocked at the request, but we went ahead and did it. We didn't know what else to do.

"Afterward, Silvia was really angry. She said that Mr. Hancock was taking advantage of us - that he was using us in a scam because we were in a position where we couldn't refuse his request or do anything about it. That he had made us accessories in his scheme. She said that we should report Mr. Hancock to the authorities. I pleaded with her not to. I told her that if she reported him, we would lose our jobs. I said that that crab meat is crab meat, that people can't tell the difference between Venezuelan crab meat and local crab meat from the bay. People will enjoy the crab meat just the same. In the end she agreed not to report it, but I could see that it still was bothering her.

"Then, at the end of the day on Saturday, when we were getting ready to walk back to the Ranch House, Silvia said that she wanted to stay behind to talk to Mr. Hancock. And that was the last I ever saw of her - she didn't return to the Ranch House that evening and the next day we learned that she had been killed."

"Do you think that she may have said something to Hancock about the Venezuelan crab meat, perhaps threatened to report him to the authorities?"

"I'm afraid that she may have. She was really upset about it."

"Do you think that he may have killed her to prevent her from reporting him?"

"I don't know," she said and threw her arms up in the air in despair. "I just don't know. I can't believe that he would do that, but I'm very bothered about the whole thing. I thought that someone should know about it. I had to get it off my chest."

"You did the right thing," I tried to reassure her. "Were you and Silvia friends?"

"Yes. The first year that I came here to work, it was very difficult for me. I had never been away from home before. I was really lonely and homesick. Silvia took me under her wing and showed me the ropes. She looked out for me."

"How long have you been coming here now?"

"This is my third year."

"Where are you from?"

"San Felipe de Ramos. It's a small village in central Mexico."

"How did you get the job?"

"A recruitment agent came to our village, trying to recruit crab pickers. I had been working in a corn-husking plant, but the pay and conditions were really bad. I realized I could make more money by becoming a crab picker. It seemed like the best option open to me. After I signed on, I took a bus to Monterey along with some other recruits from my village. In Monterey, we had to do interviews at the U.S. Consulate and fill out a lot of paperwork in order to get our visas. Then we took a bus into the U.S., across the southern part of the country and up the east coast to Oceanic Park."

"What is the work like?"

"It's difficult and really boring. You cut your fingers to shreds." She held out her hands showing that she had bandages on three of her fingers. "And there's the smell of crab meat; it permeates your clothes. You can't get the smell of crab meat out of your clothes no matter how many times you wash them. When I go home, my children say that I smell like crabs."

"You have children?"

"Yes, a boy and a girl. That's the hardest part, being separated from my family. But I'm able to send them money every month, so my children will have a better future. Anita Munoz, our supervisor has been coming here for 17 years. She's made enough money to put her daughter through college."

"Do you know if Silvia had any family?"

"No, she didn't have any family. She had a very difficult life. She wasn't from Mexico originally, she was from Honduras. Back in the eighties, she got arrested for taking part in a student demonstration. She was put in prison and tortured. They did unspeakable things to her. When they finally released her, she wasn't the same. She suffered from depression and had terrible headaches. That's why she had those three tears tattooed on her cheek - to mark the time she spent in prison. She couldn't stand to remain in Honduras, so she came to Mexico. She wanted to go back to school and finish her degree, but she was too traumatized from her experience. She never really recovered from what happened to her. She worked at a bunch of different jobs and finally ended up taking a job as a crab picker."

"Did she say what she was charged with when she was sent to prison?"

"Only that she had taken part in a demonstration against the Honduran government and that the government was cracking down on anyone who spoke out against them. She claimed that the CIA was behind it. She said that when she was in prison, an American CIA officer used to pay regular visits to the prison. The prison guards referred to him as 'Mr. Bob.' The prisoners would call out to him for help, but he ignored them. He saw what was going on there, but he didn't do anything to help them. She swore that if she ever found Mr. Bob, she would kill him."

"I understand that she had been coming here to work for seven years."

"Yes, that's right."

"Do you know if she had become acquainted with anyone in the area? Whether anyone would have had any reason to want to harm her?"

"No, we keep to ourselves. We don't mix with the locals."

"Do you know if Silvia had a computer or a cell phone?"

"She had a cell phone, but not a computer. She used the computer at the public library."

"The library branch on Dunstable Avenue?"

"Yes. She used to go there on Sunday, our day off. I went with her a few times."

After Maria Castellon had left, I climbed the spiral staircase to the turret. I sat at my desk, looked out over the rooftops, and thought over what I had just learned. Had Silvia Viejo confronted Curtis Hancock and threatened to expose his fraudulent sale of Venezuelan crab meat as local crab meat? And was that a sufficient motive for murder? If the restaurants that Hancock supplied found out that he was selling Venezuelan crab meat as local crab meat, his business would have been finished. Still, it didn't quite feel like a strong enough motive for murder.

I spent the remainder of the day catching up on paperwork and chores around the house and yard. At twilight, I made my way north along the boardwalk. As I approached 9th Street, the bandstand on the beach where the awards ceremony and the Dick Dale concert would take place came into view. Dale had almost single-handedly created instrumental surf music back in the late '50s and early '60s when he and his band, the Deltones, had a residency at the Rendezvous Ballroom by Newport Beach in Balboa, California. A surfer himself, Dale attracted a following of fellow surfers to the Rendezvous Ballroom who did a dance called the "surfer's stomp" to his music. Dale began trying to emulate the sound of the surf with his guitar and gave his instrumental numbers surf-related titles. On his early singles such as "Let's Go Trippin'," "Shake-N-Stomp," "Miserlou," and "Surf Beat," Dale established the hallmarks of surf instrumentals - staccato double-picking, glissandos on the bass strings, and heavy use of reverb.

Dale's first album, *Surfer's Choice*, was released on his own Del-Tone label in late 1962 and made a strong showing for an album on a small independent label. The success of the *Surfer's Choice* album attracted the attention of major labels, and Dale signed a deal with Capitol Records. Dale went on to record six albums for Capitol and appear in the Annette Funicello and Frankie Avalon movies *Beach Party* and *Muscle Beach Party.*

In the wake of Dale's success, teenagers began to form bands to play instrumental surf music in Dale's style. While Dale himself never scored a big national hit, some of the bands that followed him had big hits that helped to further popularize instrumental surf music. Songs such as "Wipe Out" by the Surfaris, "Out of Limits" by the Marketts, "Pipeline" by the Chantays, and "Penetration" by the Pyramids introduced surf music to a wider audience.

In the mid-sixties, surf music was eclipsed by the British Invasion and Dale was further sidelined by health problems. By the end of the seventies, Dale largely had retired from performing. In the early '80s, there was a revival of instrumental surf music spearheaded by new bands such as Jon & the Nightriders, the Surf Raiders, the Insect Surfers, the Halibuts, and the Wedge. This revival brought renewed attention to Dale and encouraged him to start performing again but surf music remained largely an underground phenomenon during this period.

In early 1993, Dale released *Tribal Thunder*, his first album of new material in more than 25 years. *Tribal Thunder* was very well received and brought Dale to the attention of a younger audience. Dale's loud, aggressive guitar style appealed to listeners who were into "alternative" and "grunge" music. Dale became more popular than ever, and, for the first time in his career, he began touring extensively outside of California.

At 9th Street, I went down the ramp to the beach and across the sand to the bandstand. Lee Ellison of WVOP Radio, who was serving as MC, was onstage spinning records until it was time for the show to start. "Gear" by Dave Myers and His Surf-Tones was blasting through the sound system.

A crowd of people had gathered on the sand in front of the bandstand, some on blankets, others on sand chairs. Many people had brought coolers and picnic baskets and were eating picnic dinners. Some people had set up grills and were grilling hot dogs and hamburgers. Boats were anchored offshore, beyond the breakers, waiting for the show to begin.

I spotted Java Joe, Wendy Stevens, Barry Pendleton, Terry Mannering, and a few other people standing off to the side of the stage and walked over to join them. After awhile, Lee Ellison stepped up to the microphone to get things underway.

"Good evening everyone and welcome to the grand finale of this year's Oceanic Park Surf Tournament. I'm Lee Ellison from WVOP, the voice of Oceanic Park. We have a really great lineup of events for you this evening. First up, we have the awards ceremony for the winners of this year's tournament."

Ellison proceeded to introduce Ron Hammond, president of the Oceanic Park Surf Club, who presented trophies to the winners and runners-up of the surf tournament. We all cheered for Wendy when she went onstage to accept her trophy as winner of the women's tournament.

"Alright, we have a really fantastic show tonight," Lee Ellison announced, resuming his duties as MC. "To get things started, please welcome our own surf-rock band, from right here in Oceanic Park, the Castaways!"

The members of the Castaways took the stage to polite applause from the audience. The Castaways had expanded to a five-piece band since I had seen them last summer - in addition to their longtime lineup of Clint Forte on guitar, Wayne Griffin on bass, and Jane Abrams on drums they had added a keyboard player and a saxophone player. The band opened their set with "Inertia," and proceeded to play a mixture of retro-sounding originals, well-known surf music standards like "Out of Limits," "Penetration," and "Pipeline" and lesser-known surf music numbers like "Bangalore," "Latin'ia," and "Squad Car." The addition of the new members allowed them to expand their repertoire to include numbers like "Theme from *The Endless Summer*" which showcased the keyboard player, and "Surfer's Stomp" which featured the sax player. As the set progressed, the band won over the crowd with their high-energy performance. They closed their set with an extended workout on "Wipeout," which earned them an enthusiastic response from the audience. The came back for an encore and performed "K-39."

Lee Ellison proceeded to spin some more records while the crew changed equipment and got the stage ready for Dick Dale. When the stage was set, Ellison stepped up to the microphone to introduce Dale.

"Ladies and gentlemen, tonight we are honored to have one of the true legends of rock 'n' roll" Ellison announced. "Please welcome the King of the Surf Guitar, Dick Dale!"

Dale took the stage accompanied by his drummer and bass player. Dale was dressed entirely in black - he sported a black headband over his greying hair, which hung in a ponytail down his back; a black t-shirt with a skull and crossed guitars emblazoned on the front; baggy black shorts; and black sneakers. His gold-metal-flake 1960 Fender Stratocaster dubbed "the Beast" was slung over his shoulder. Dale launched into "Shredded Heat" and unleashed a furious onslaught of rapid-fire picking, shrieking and rumbling glissandos, and heavy reverb. The music was so loud that you could feel it reverberate in the pit of your stomach. I suspected that people at the far end of the boardwalk, two-and-a-half miles away, probably could hear it as well. The set was a mixture of recent numbers like "Nitro," "The Trail of Tears," and "Calling Up Spirits" and old classics like "Miserlou," "The Wedge," and "Ghost Riders in the Sky." Dale threw in covers of Link Wray's "Rumble" and a surfified version of Jimi Hendrix's "Third Stone from the Sun." He closed his set with two old favorites. "Let's Go Trippin'" and "Shake 'n' Stomp" to an enthusiastic response from the crowd. When the cheering continued, he came back and performed the Latin-inflected "Esperanza."

After Dale left the stage, Lee Ellison resumed playing records over the PA system and the crowd began disburse, drifting toward the ramps that lead to the boardwalk. It still was fairly early and the boardwalk remained crowded, so I decided to walk back home along the beach. I walked along the water's edge where the sand was packed the hardest, occasionally having to dodge an incoming wave. A few other people were walking on the beach, singly or in pairs. Partway down the beach, I came across a group of people sitting in a ring around a bonfire and singing songs, accompanied by a guitar and bongo drums. I paused to listen; they were singing "Luau" and then went into "Come a Little Bit Closer," with everyone joining in on the refrain. I listened to a few more songs and then continued on my way.

When I spotted the Werner's confectionary store that is located at the corner of Adriatic Avenue and the boardwalk, I started cutting across the beach toward the boardwalk. I was about two-thirds of the way across the beach when I saw the familiar figure of a woman with long auburn hair walk beneath a streetlight, headed south on the boardwalk. For a moment, I had a clear view of her profile illuminated by the streetlight - it was Sophie.

I hesitated for a moment, unsure whether I wanted to confront her and what I would say. Then, without really thinking, I began running toward the boardwalk with my feet clumsily sinking into the sand. I raced up the ramp and down the boardwalk, darting between the tourists. After I had gone a few of blocks, I realized that I should have overtaken her if she was walking at a normal pace, but I hadn't. I doubled back and glanced into arcades and shops and down side streets, but there was no sign of her. It was as if she had vanished.

Eventually, I gave up and headed down Adriatic Avenue toward my cottage. As I walked, tried to recall exactly what I had seen. When I had seen the woman walking under the street light, I had been certain it was Sophie, but now I began to wonder. Maybe I had been mistaken. Sophie had been on my mind a lot lately because of her upcoming gig at the Crow's Nest, so perhaps I was letting my imagination was run away with me.

Chapter 14. Monday, August 1, 2005

The next morning, I was back at my usual table at Java Joe's, eating breakfast, listening to music, and perusing the *Oceanic Park Press*. As usual, there was bad news from Iraq. Seven people were killed in Baghdad when a car bomb exploded near the National Theater...Two British security contractors were killed when a roadside bomb exploded next to a British consulate convoy in Basra, in southern Iraq...With an August 15 deadline looming for completion of a new Iraqi constitution, leaders of the different factions still disagreed on fundamental issues, including what type of government Iraq should have. In local news there was an article about the radio talk-show host Walter Braddock:

> CALLS INCREASE TO FIRE RADIO TALK SHOW HOST. Calls for the firing of radio talk show host Walter Braddock increased following the revelation of comments that Braddock made in an appearance on the America First podcast, hosted by right-wing activist Bernie Estel, earlier this year. During a discussion of immigration on the podcast, Braddock referred to immigrants as "third-world scum" and said that immigrants who died while attempting to cross the Mexican border into the U.S. "got what they deserved."
>
> Among those calling for Braddock's firing is Helen Marwood, president of the local chapter of the United Human Rights Coalition. "While Braddock

may have a right to express his extreme views, WDSF should not provide a public platform for him to do so," Marwood said. Marwood called on sponsors to withdraw their support for Braddock's show.

Braddock released a statement saying that his comments were "taken out of context" and were being "distorted by the left-wing media." Howard Denman, the general manager of WDSF, reiterated the station's support for Braddock. "Braddock's show is our top-rated show," Denman stated, "and his ratings have only increased over the course of this summer. It is an insult to his many listeners to suggest that he should be fired."

"Will you be out this evening?" Wendy asked when she brought my breakfast to my table. She was back at work after her triumph in the surf tournament and now was training for the Mid-Atlantic Regional Surf Contest, which was held in Atlantic City over the Labor Day weekend.

"I'll try to make it out, if I can," I said.

"The conditions should be pretty good. Predictions are for a four to five foot swell."

When I got to the office, I brought Phoebe up to speed on what I had learned over the weekend. I recounted the conversations that I had had with the attendant at Blue Water Boat Rentals and the skateboarder, Aaron Trafford.

"So, Bradley Cawthorne told you the truth," Phoebe said. "The Oceanic Park Vigilantes really didn't post the flyers the second two times or hang the banner."

"That's right."

"Do you have any idea who hired the skateboarders to post the flyers and hang the banner?"

"I can't prove it, but I'm fairly certain that Eric Burns was behind it. The person who hired the skateboarders instructed them to target the Chimera Gallery. I think that Burns is trying to harass the Chimera Gallery and make it difficult for them to conduct business. He wants to drive the gallery out of business so he can buy the property and put up a condominium."

"Does this help with the murder charge?"

"No, not really. It's interesting, but it doesn't have any direct bearing on the murder case."

I went on to recount what I had learned from Maria Castellon - how Curtis Hancock of Bounty of the Bay Seafood Company had asked her and Silvia Viejo to repackage Venezuelan crab meat so that it could be passed off as local crab meat. "She thinks that Silvia Viejo may have confronted Hancock about it and threatened to report him to the authorities," I concluded.

"And he killed her to keep her quiet?"

"It's a possibility. It does seem kind of extreme under the circumstances, but if the restaurants and supermarkets that Hancock does business with found out that he was selling them Venezuelan crab meat as local crab meat, it would put him out of business. He would lose everything."

"So, what are our next steps?"

"Maria Castellon said that Silvia Viejo used the computers at the Oceanic Park branch of the Bay County Library. We need to get the court to issue a subpoena directing the library to produce a copy of her computer history - what searches she did, what websites she visited, any emails that she sent or received, and any documents that she created and stored in her account. I'm going to draft a request for a subpoena now. When I get it done, you can file it with the court. Then I'm going to talk to Curtis Hancock again."

I had to figure out some way of approaching Curtis Hancock without getting Maria Castellon in trouble. I wracked my brains and finally came up with an idea. I went to the supermarket and bought a plastic container of Venezuelan crab meat. I took it home, transferred the crab meat to another container, which I put in my refrigerator. Then I put the empty container in my briefcase.

It was late afternoon by the time I headed across the drawbridge toward West Oceanic Park. As I approached the mainland, I could see the crab pickers leaving the Bounty of the Bay Seafood processing plant and starting the walk back to the Ranch House Motel. I would have to hurry if I wanted to catch Curtis Hancock before he left as well.

When I got to the Bounty of the Bay Seafood processing plant, I found Curtis Hancock in his office, packing up his briefcase.

"What do you want?" he asked. "I was just getting ready to leave."

"I just have few more questions," I responded.

"You've got a lot of nerve coming back here asking questions, after you tried to talk to my employees when I told you not to."

"My client is on trial for murder. I have to follow every possible avenue that could provide information."

"I've already told the police everything that I know."

"Not quite everything."

"What do you mean?"

"I understand that Silvia Viejo stayed behind to talk to you after work on Saturday, the day that she was killed."

"She may have said a few words to me after work, nothing unusual about that."

"What did you talk about?"

"I don't remember."

"Perhaps this will refresh your memory." I took the empty container for Venezuelan crab meat out of my briefcase and placed it on his desk.

"Where did you get that?"

"From your dumpster."

"My dumpster?! What were you doing going through my dumpster?!"

"In the course of my investigation, I found that there are rumors going around town that you've been selling Venezuelan crab meat as local crab meat. I wondered whether I could find any evidence of it. And I did. That's what Silvia Viejo stayed behind on Saturday to talk to you about, isn't it?"

"Oh, my God," Hancock moaned. "How did I get into this situation?" He sank down into the chair behind his desk and buried his head in his hands. After awhile he looked up at me.

"Listen, you don't know what I've been going through," he said. "This is a really tough business. Look over there." He pointed through the window of his office at the skyline of Oceanic Park across the bay. "There's 300,000 people over there enjoying their summer vacation. They create a huge demand for local crab meat and it's becoming more and more difficult to meet. The crab population in the area is dwindling. There are regulations that restrict the number of crabs that can be caught. How am I supposed to meet the demand for crab meat? I try to avoid it, but sometimes the only way that I can meet demand is by importing crab meat. People can't tell the difference - it all tastes the same."

"The people who are paying a premium price for local crab meat might disagree."

"Are you telling me that people can tell the difference? What harm is there? The important thing is that people got the crab cakes that they want. Everybody's happy and no one knows the difference."

"If you say so."

"Listen, I catch flak from both sides. On one hand, people say 'why don't you hire Americans?' I'll tell you why - it's because they don't want to do this sort of work. Every spring I run ads for seasonal workers. I go to recruitment events at college campuses. I have notices posted in the employment offices. And what response do I get? None. Students don't want to sit at a table picking crab meat out of a shell eight hours a day. It's tough, tedious work. They'd rather take the fun jobs, working in an amusement park or crewing on a cruise boat. I'm competing for workers with businesses that can offer much more attractive positions.

"On the other hand," he continued, "migrant rights activists accuse me of exploiting the migrant workers, when, in fact, I'm helping them to get ahead. At the end of the season, they go back home with more money than they could earn in five years back home. It's a mutually beneficial situation."

"O.k., I understand the situation that you're in," I said. "What did Silvia Viejo talk to you about?"

"Uh…well…she…um…," he stammered. "She said that she needed a gun," he finally blurted out

"A gun?! What did she need a gun for?!"

"I don't know, she wouldn't tell me. She said that something had happened and that she was in fear for her life. I told that if she was worried about those flyers, to forget about it. It was just a bunch of cranks. She said that it wasn't the flyers that she was worried about. Something else had happened, but she wouldn't tell me what. I told her that I couldn't possibly give her a gun. She said, if I didn't, she would report that I had been selling Venezuelan crab meat as local crab meat. I told her if she did that she would be shooting herself in the foot - it would destroy the business and she would lose her job. She said that she didn't care, her life was as good as over anyway."

"What made her think that you would have a gun?"

"I do target shooting as a hobby. Everybody knows about it. I carry my gun case with me, because I sometimes go to the shooting range after work."

"You didn't actually give her a gun, did you?"

"I had to. What else could I do? She had me over a barrel."

"What kind of gun was it?"

"A Ruger P90."

"What caliber bullet does it use?"

"Forty-five."

"That's the same caliber of bullet that she was shot with."

"You think that I don't know that? I've been beating myself up over this every day since it happened. What a mess I've gotten myself into. I guess all of this is going to have to become public, isn't it?"

"It depends on how things go," I said. "If this case goes to trial, I may have to call you as a witness. But, if my investigation is successful, I may be able to get the charges dismissed before the case goes to trial, in which case the information may not have to come out.

One thing, though - if you take retaliatory action against any of your employees because this, I'll make sure that all of the restaurants and supermarkets that you supply crab with meat know that you've been supplying them with Venezuelan crab meat."

"I understand."

I left him looking miserable. I thought things over as I walked back toward the drawbridge. What could Silvia Viejo have been so worried about that she needed a gun? Had she received some sort of threat? Who would threaten her? As far as I could tell, she didn't know anyone in Oceanic Park. Perhaps the computer records from the library would hold some clue.

As I walked back across the drawbridge toward Oceanic Park, I looked out over the skyline of the southern end of the island and took in the familiar sights - the Bayview Restaurant and the Angler's Haven marina, located just south of the bridge; the municipal fishing pier; the yellow-brick Coast Guard station; the antennas and masts of boats docked at the Paradise Bay marina; and the old Breakers Hotel on a strip of land behind the seawall at the inlet. Rising above the skyline in the background, I could see the monorail and the tops of the ferris wheel and the roller coaster at Bond's Amusement Park.

As I walked, my attention was caught by a skull-and-crossbones flag flying on the mast of a sailboat in the Paradise Bay marina. The flag looked exactly like the one that Sophie flew from the mast of her sailboat, the Piranha. From my vantage point on the bridge, I could see only the boat's mast; I couldn't see the boat's hull or the name painted on it. The flag didn't necessarily mean anything; lots of people fly pirate flags on the masts of their boats, but I had to know.

After leaving the bridge, I walked along the bay front to the Paradise Bay marina. I spotted the mast with the pirate flag and walked out onto an adjacent pier where I could get a clear view of the boat. Sure enough, it was Sophie's boat, the Piranha.

So Sophie really was in town. I actually had seen her the previous evening and hadn't just imagined it. Apparently, she had arrived early for her gig at the Crow's Nest. I wondered how long her boat had been docked here and how many times I had walked past the marina without noticing it, while it was hidden in plain sight. I wondered if she were on board her boat and if I should attempt to speak to her. But then I thought better of it. So far, she had chosen not to contact me. Perhaps she had a good reason for not contacting me. I decided to leave it up to her. If she wanted to contact me, she would.

I arrived at the beach at 21st Street in the early evening. The usual crew of surfers were there. Terry Mannering was working to help Wendy perfect her maneuvers for the Mid-Atlantic Surf Contest. The rest of us took turns catching waves.

As we were sitting on our boards in the lineup, a plane flew up the coast trailing a banner that read "Rude Awakening - 6:00 a.m. to 9:00 a.m. - WDSF Business Talk Radio." A collective groan went up from everyone when they saw the banner. Not only was WDSF not heeding the calls to fire Braddock, they were doubling down on promoting his show.

As predicted, conditions were pretty good, and I caught a few good rides. Between waves, people talked about the just-completed surf tournament and about plans to travel to Atlantic City over the Labor Day weekend to lend support to Wendy when she competed in the Mid-Atlantic Regional Surf Tournament. We continued to surf until it got dark and we called it a day.

Chapter 15. Tuesday, August 2, 2005

The next morning, I perused the *Oceanic Park Press* while seated at my usual table at Java Joe's. President Bush had made a recess appointment of conservative activist John Bolton as U.S. Ambassador to the United Nations, bypassing the Senate confirmation process...Legal advocacy groups were scrutinizing the record of Supreme Court nominee John Robert's time in the Justice Department during the Reagan administration, where Roberts had led the Reagan administration's efforts to roll back civil rights protections. A headline in the local section caught my attention:

STATE'S ATTORNEY TO SEEK DEATH PENALTY IN MURDER OF MIGRANT WORKER. In a news conference yesterday, Bay County State's Attorney, Sandra Rappaport, announced that she will seek the death penalty in the case of Bradley Cawthorne, who is charged with the murder of migrant worker Silvia Viejo. Viejo's body was found hanging from a fish rack at the Angler's Haven Marina in the early morning hours of Sunday, July 24. An anti-immigrant flyer attributed to the Oceanic Park Vigilantes was pinned to her shirt. The template for the flyer was found on Cawthorne's computer. Police also found photos on Cawthorne's phone that indicated that he was conducting surveillance of Viejo's workplace and residence prior to the killing.

"This was an abhorrent crime," Rappaport said. "Under no circumstances will we offer a plea deal for a lesser sentence. My office intends to send a strong message that we will enforce the law to the maximum extent in Bay County."

I had been expecting this. Sandra Rappaport had run for office on a tough law-and-order platform, promising to seek the death penalty in every case in which the defendant was eligible for it. This was just the sort of case that Rappaport relished and she would milk it for all of the publicity that she could get out of it and use it to further her political ambitions.

Rappaport was a political figurehead and was not involved in the day-to-day running of the State's Attorney's office. She rarely came into the office and spent most of her time holding news conferences and giving speeches to civic and political groups and schoolchildren. The office actually was run by the Deputy State's Attorney, Glenn Dixon, a career prosecutor. He was a hack lawyer but a skilled bureaucratic infighter who had been able to claw his way up in the office. He was considered a shoo-in for appointment as a judge the next time there was a vacancy on the Bay County Circuit Court.

I glanced up from the paper and saw Lee Ellison, the WVOP disc jockey, enter the cafe. We exchanged greetings and he took a seat at a nearby table.

"Hey, I enjoyed your set of music before the Dick Dale concert Sunday night," I told him. "You played some really great stuff."

"Thanks," he responded. "I enjoyed doing it. It looks like this will be the last year that I do it, though."

"What do you mean?"

"Do you remember that I told you that WVOP is getting killed in the ratings by Walter Braddock on WDSF and that the management of WVOP is considering a change in formats? Well, the management has made a decision - at the end of the summer they're going to do away with music and switch to an all-talk-show format in order to compete with WDSF."

"You're kidding! That's awful. If the station changes formats, it would be a huge loss to the community."

"I'm afraid that not that many people share your opinion. Music's just not as important as it used to be, no one cares about it anymore. People would rather listen to demagogues like Braddock ranting and raving."

"I'm sure that a lot of people in the community will oppose any change in format," I said, trying to reassure him, although I wondered if it would be possible to rally much opposition to the change.

"Sarah Cawthorne called," Phoebe informed me as soon as I came through the door of the office. "She saw the article in the paper this morning saying that said that the State's Attorney is going to seek the death penalty for her son. She's really upset."

"O.k., I'll talk to her."

"Also, Judge Hampton's office called. She's issued the subpoena for Silvia Viejo's computer records from the library. I'm going to go over to the courthouse to pick it up and then I'll deliver it to the library."

"O.k., great."

At the desk in my office, I called Sarah Cawthorne.

"The State's Attorney's case against Brad is entirely circumstantial and not very strong," I told her. "They don't have any DNA evidence or other physical evidence linking Brad to the killing. Also, they don't know where the murder was committed and they haven't found the murder weapon."

I assured her that my investigation was making good progress and that, at this point, she shouldn't be unduly concerned about announcement from the State's Attorney's office that they were going to seek the death penalty.

"I have something that I want to check with you," I told her. "When I interviewed Brad at the jail he said that he was at the Lost Oasis on Saturday night, that he left a little after midnight, and then went home and went to bed. Can you confirm that he was at home on Saturday night?"

"No," she responded. "Brad comes and goes as he pleases. With guests staying at the house, there always are people going in and out. I don't really keep track of who is there and who isn't. I wish that I could confirm that Brad was home on Saturday night, but I'm afraid that I can't."

"That's alright," I said. "We have a few different leads that we're following up on. I'm confident that we'll find out what actually happened."

In the early afternoon, Phoebe announced that she had just received electronic copies of Silvia Viejo's computer history from the library in response to the subpoena that she had delivered that morning.

"Do they tell us anything?" I asked, going out to the reception area and looking over her shoulder at her computer screen.

"I'm going through her search history now," Phoebe said. "It looks like she was searching for information about the Economic Freedom Foundation."

"The Economic Freedom Foundation?"

"Yes. She visited their website several times. She also looked at news articles about their annual meeting at the Oceanic Park Plaza. And she was searching the website and the articles for the names 'Bob' and 'Robert.'"

"That's interesting. Maria Castellon said that, when Silvia Viejo was in prison in Honduras, the prison was visited regularly by a CIA officer who the guards referred to as 'Mr. Bob.'"

"Perhaps Silvia Viejo had some reason to think that Mr. Bob was attending the annual meeting of the Economic Freedom Foundation."

"That could be. That would explain why she wanted a gun. She told Maria Castellon that, if she ever found Mr. Bob, she would kill him."

"Maybe she went to the Oceanic Park Plaza, confronted him with the gun, and things went wrong, and she ended up getting killed instead."

"That must be what happened. I think that the key to this killing lies with things that happened to Silvia Viejo in Honduras back in the '80s. I need to get some background information so I can understand what was going on in the country at the time."

"Do you want me to try to do some research?"

"No, I'm going to go and talk to Helen Marwood. Her organization monitors human rights abuses in countries around the world. She's probably familiar with the situation or knows where to find information about it."

I found Helen Marwood at her desk in the law library at the courthouse. After we had exchanged greetings, I explained that I had been investigating the death of Silvia Viejo and that her death appeared to be related to events that had occurred in Honduras in the '80s. I recounted what Maria Castellon had told me about Silvia Viejo being arrested, imprisoned, and tortured for taking part in a student demonstration.

"That sounds like the work of Battalion 316," Helen said.

"Battalion 316? What's that?"

"Back in the '80s, the Reagan administration was using Honduras as a base for covert operations in El Salvador and Nicaragua. They wanted to make sure that Honduras remained reliable and politically stable, and didn't experience a left-wing insurgency like those in El Salvador and Nicaragua. So, the U.S. helped Honduras create a secret army intelligence unit known as Battalion 316, to root out any left-wing insurgency before it could occur. Battalion 316 targeted anyone they saw as having left-wing sympathies and being a threat to the government — student activists, labor union leaders, journalists, college professors. Battalion 316 kidnapped, tortured, and killed hundreds of Honduran citizens."

"Silvia Viejo said that a CIA officer regularly visited the prison where she was being held and tortured," I said. "The prison guards referred to him as 'Mr. Bob.' He saw what was going on in the prison, but didn't do anything to help her or the other prisoners."

"There's been a lot of debate about the extent of the CIA's involvement with Battalion 316," Helen explained. "We do know that the CIA was involved in training and equipping Battalion 316. The CIA provided training to members of Battalion 316 at a secret location in the United States and also at bases in Honduras. They maintain that that was the extent of their involvement. There have been allegations, however, that the CIA was more directly involved in Battalion 316's activities in Honduras. The Reagan administration whitewashed the entire matter. During the time that Battalion 316 was torturing and murdering people, the State Department released reports stating that Honduras had an excellent human rights record."

"Silvia Viejo said that, if she ever found Mr. Bob, she would kill him. She seemed to have some reason for thinking that he was attending the annual meeting of the Economic Freedom Foundation. She was searching the Economic Freedom Foundation website and news articles about the meeting for references to 'Bob' and 'Robert.'"

"I have a bunch of information that we compiled on the Economic Freedom Foundation when we were organizing the demonstration and boycott. We put together a list of people who were attending the meeting. Let me take a look at it." Helen removed a laptop from a knapsack in the floor behind her desk, laid the laptop on her desk and opened it. Then she started punching keys and scrolling through information.

"Three people named Robert attended the meeting," she announced. "There's Robert Dodd, a lobbyist for Accelerated Dynamics Corporation; Robert Oakley, a Republican congressman from Montana; and Robert Seville, a professor of economics at Fontaine College."

"Do you know anything about them?"

"No, but let me do a quick search on the internet. I should be able to find background information on them." She switched from the laptop to a computer on her desk and spent a few minutes punching keys and scrolling through screens.

"It's Robert Oakley," she announced. "According to the biography on his congressional website, he was stationed at the U.S.

embassy in Honduras as a trade representative from March 1982 to November 1987. That sort of position often is used as cover for CIA agents and he was in Honduras at the time that Battalion 316 was active and that Silvia Viejo was imprisoned."

After thanking Helen Marwood for her help, I headed back to the office. The pieces finally were starting to fall into place.

"So the person that Silvia Viejo went to the Plaza Hotel to confront was this Congressman, Robert Oakley," Phoebe summarized, after I had briefed her on what I had learned from Helen Marwood.

"Yes, it looks that way."

"I wonder what made her think that he was attending the annual meeting of the Economic Freedom Foundation."

"The meeting got a lot of media coverage. She probably saw his picture in the paper or in a news report on t.v. and recognized him as Mr. Bob. Then she did research on the internet to find out exactly who he was."

"Do you think that he could have transported the body to the marina and hung it on the fish rack by himself?"

"It's possible, but it would have been very difficult. I think that it's more likely that he had help."

"So there may be other people involved."

"Yes. And someone had a stroke of inspiration to pin one of those anti-immigrant flyers onto the victim's shirt as a way of deflecting suspicion away from Oakley and making it look like she had been killed by a member of the Oceanic Park Vigilantes. They provided a convenient scapegoat."

"How are we going to prove any of this?"

"I'm not sure. We need to place Silvia Viejo at the Plaza Hotel the night that she was killed."

"You know, the Plaza Hotel is supposed to have a state-of-the-art security system. If she went to the Plaza that night, they might have her on security video."

"Right, we'll have to request a subpoena requiring the hotel to produce security video for the night of the murder. I'll get to work on that first thing tomorrow."

After dinner, I took my usual walk along the bay front to the inlet and back again. As I walked past the Paradise Bay marina, I looked toward the docks and saw that the mast of the Piranha with the pirate flag flying from it still was there, but made no effort to stop and see if Sophie was on board.

I wandered out onto the municipal fishing pier and found the Prices sitting in their usual spot, with their fishing rods propped against the pier's railing.

"How's it going tonight?" I asked after we had exchanged greetings.

"Not bad," William responded. "We've actually gotten a few bites."

I looked in the plastic bucket next to them on the pier. There were three good-sized flounders flopping about in the water in the bucket.

"Not bad at all," I said.

"Our luck was due to change," William said. "The people attending that meeting have left town and taken their super yachts with them. We finally have some peace and quiet and can get some fishing done."

"Yeah, but there'll be more people with super yachts coming soon. That was just an advance look at what's in store."

"Be that as it may. At least we can enjoy some peace and quiet while it lasts."

No sooner had he spoken, than the night air was rent apart by an ear-shattering explosion and a fireball erupted to the south of us, lighting up the night sky. I felt a sharp impact on my left eardrum, which was facing the direction of the explosion, as if someone had smacked me on the side of the head. The concussive impact was followed by a wave of hot air.

"Oh, my God!" Amanda exclaimed, grabbing hold of the railing as if she was afraid of being blown away. "What on earth was that?!"

"It looks like it came from the Paradise Bay Marina," William said.

No, I thought, it can't be.

"I'm going to run down there and see what's going on," I said.

I raced along the bay front, past the Coast Guard station, to the Paradise Bay Marina. Sophie's boat, the Piranha, no longer was in the slip where it had been docked. The boat had been blown apart and splintered pieces of it were scattered over the dock, the surrounding boats, and the surface of the water. The mast had been snapped off and the top of it was protruding from the water and leaning against the dock. What was left of the cabin and the hull was in flames and rapidly sinking below the surface.

A man had emerged from a nearby boat and was standing on the dock staring at the slip where Sophie's boat had been. I ran down the dock to where the man was standing.

"What happened?" I asked.

"I don't know," he responded. "I was asleep and the explosion woke me up."

"Do you know if the owner was onboard?"

"I think so. I saw her onboard earlier."

I scanned the water for some sign of Sophie, but all I could see were debris floating in a wide arc on the surface. I called out Sophie's name but didn't get any response.

In the distance, I could hear the eerie wail of the siren at the volunteer fire station, calling the volunteers into action. Someone must have called 911.

I felt like I had to do something, so I yanked off my shoes and dove into the water. I swam around amidst the debris, diving underwater looking for some sign of Sophie, but it was an exercise in futility. It was pitch black under water and impossible to see anything. When I heard the approaching siren of a fire truck, I gave up, swam back to the dock, and pulled myself out of the water. By that time, several more people from neighboring boats had gathered on the dock.

A fire truck pulled up to the head of the dock and three firefighters disembarked and made their way down the dock.

"What happened?" the firefighter in the lead asked.

"The sailboat that was docked here exploded," the man from the nearby boat explained.

"Was there anyone on board?"

"I think that the woman who owned the boat was on board."

The firefighter shone a high-powered flashlight out over the water and the floating debris.

"We've been in contact with the police and they're sending a launch to search for survivors," the firefighter said. "That was an extremely powerful explosion, though. It's doubtful that anyone could have survived that."

After several minutes, the police launch approached from the south. It had a powerful spotlight mounted on the stern of the boat. The launch drifted among the wreckage, shining the spotlight on the debris and the over the surface of the surrounding water. After making a thorough reconnaissance, the police launch pulled to the end of the dock and one of the firefighters went over to confer with the police officers.

The firefighter came back down the dock.

"There is no sign of the woman who was on the boat," he reported. "I'm afraid there's nothing more we can do tonight. We'll rope off the area to preserve any evidence. We'll notify the Coast Guard. They can send divers down in the morning when it's light."

I trudged wearily back to the cottage, not quite able to believe what had just happened. What could have caused the boat to explode? A fuel leak from the auxiliary engine? A short in the wiring? I was starting to regret not having made an effort to talk to Sophie after I found out that she was in town and still had the chance. After changing into some dry clothes, I climbed the spiral staircase to the turret and sank down in the chair. I put an Henri Salvador disc in the

CD player and played "Syracuse" several times. Sophie had sung the song that first time that I had seen her perform at the Crow's Nest, and it always reminded me of her.

After awhile, someone started banging on the front door. The last thing I wanted to do was to talk to anyone, but I thought it might be someone from the fire department or the police department with news about Sophie. I got up and dragged myself down two flights of stairs. When I opened the front door, I was surprised to see that it was Buffalo Smith, one of the homeless people who hang out under the drawbridge.

"Come quick!" he commanded excitedly, waving his arm for me to come with him. "Come quick!"

"What's going on?" I asked.

"Someone needs your help!" he exclaimed. "Come quick!"

By then, Buffalo Smith already was halfway down the front sidewalk, so I shut the door and hurried after him. He turned toward the bay front and, shortly, it became apparent that he was headed toward the drawbridge. As we approached the drawbridge, I could see that a few people were sitting on the large rocks that formed a breakwater on one side of the small crescent beach under the bridge.

"This way," Buffalo Smith indicated. He climbed over the rocks and gestured toward a figure that was slumped on the beach with her head resting on a folded blanket.

It was Sophie. She was soaking wet, her hair was bedraggled, and she was dressed in a t-shirt and cut-offs. Her left eye was swollen shut and her face, arms, and legs were covered with cuts and scrapes.

"She drifted up under the bridge clinging to a piece of wood," Buffalo Smith explained. "We waded out and pulled her ashore. She said that she's a friend of yours."

I was so shocked by the sight of her, that I froze. Then I raced over and knelt down by her side.

"What happened?" I asked. "Are you alright? I thought you were dead."

"Not yet."

"You're hurt, though, you need to see a doctor."

"No, no doctor."

"Let me take you to the clinic."

"No, I'm not going to the clinic."

"Everyone thinks that you're dead. The Coast Guard is going to send divers down looking for your body as soon as it gets light. I'm going to have to let them know that you're alive."

"No!" She grabbed my arm and gripped it tightly. "Don't tell anyone that you've seen me. I want people to think that I'm dead."

"So...the explosion wasn't an accident?"

"No, I don't think so."

"What's going on? You think that someone is trying to kill you?"

"I'll explain later. Right now, I need you to do something for me."

"What?"

"I have a storage unit at Bay County Self Storage on 12th Street. There's a carry-all bag stored there. Could you get it and bring it to me?"

"Yes, of course."

"The access code to the building is *20457593!. My unit number is 2045 on the second floor. Here's the key to the padlock on my unit." She took a key on an elastic strap from around her ankle and handed it to me. "Be careful. Make sure that no one follows you."

I took a roundabout route to the storage facility, doubling back a few times to make sure that I wasn't being followed. I retrieved the carry-all bag from the storage unit without any problem. The bag was fairly heavy and its zipper was secured with a combination lock. On my way back to the drawbridge I again took a roundabout route. The precautions probably were unnecessary; there were very few people on the streets at that hour of the morning and no one was paying any attention to me. Still, in light of what had happened, it seemed better to play it safe.

When I got back to the drawbridge, I gave the carry-all bag to Sophie.

"What are you going to do now?" I asked.

"I need to find a place where I can lay low for awhile."

"You can stay in the guest room at my cottage."

"No, that's not safe. People know that we worked together. That's the first place that they would look for me. I need to find someplace where no one will look."

"I can help you find someplace."

"No, I can manage now."

"How can I get in touch with you?"

"I'll let you know, once I get settled someplace."

For the second time that night, I trudged wearily back to my cottage. My emotions had been on a roller coaster ride over the past few hours and I felt wrung out. I wondered whether Sophie actually would get in touch with me when she got settled someplace. Given her penchant for secrecy and double dealing, I doubted that I would hear from her.

When I got back to the cottage, I collapsed onto my bed and immediately fell into a deep sleep.

Chapter 16. Wednesday, August 3, 2005

It was the middle of the morning by the time I awakened. As soon as I did, the events of the previous night came flooding back into my mind. I tried to make sense of everything as I showered and got dressed.

Since I was running so late, I decided to skip my usual stop at Java Joe's. It was just as well since I didn't want to have to face people, answer a lot of questions about what had happened, and act as if I hadn't seen Sophie. I retrieved the newspaper from the porch where it had landed and perused it while I ate a few slices of toast for breakfast. There was an article by Gary Rockwell about the explosion on the front page.

> EXPLOSION AT PARADISE BAY MARINA.
> Last night, a sailboat named the Piranha was destroyed in a powerful explosion at the Paradise Bay Marina. The owner of the Piranha, Sophia Ambrosetti, was seen on board the boat shortly before the explosion occurred and has not been seen since. Police believe that she may have been killed in the explosion, although no trace of her body has been found.
>
> "We are working with the Fire Department to determine the cause of the explosion," said Police Department spokesperson Shirley Logan. Some nearby boats suffered minor damage from falling debris but no injuries were reported.

Ambrosetti, a singer and pianist, was scheduled to appear at the Crow's Nest in Old Town this coming weekend.

When I finished eating, I headed to the office.

"I read about the explosion of Sophie's boat in the paper this morning," Phoebe said when I arrived at the office. "Is there any news about her?"

"No, not as far as I know," I responded. "No one has heard from her." I felt vaguely guilty about deceiving Phoebe, but, under the circumstances, I had little choice.

"I'm really sorry. I know that you were very fond of her."

"Thanks. Are there any messages or anything?" I asked, to change the subject.

"No, it's been quiet this morning."

"O.k. I'm going to start working on the request for a subpoena for security video from the Plaza Hotel. If we can show that Silvia Viejo was at the Plaza Hotel the night that she was killed, that will undermine the case against Bradley Cawthorne."

In the early afternoon, I heard someone enter the reception area and then heard the familiar voice of Sergeant Bartlett greeting Phoebe and asking whether I was available.

"Let me check," Phoebe responded and stuck her head in my office. "Can you talk to Sergeant Bartlett?"

"Yes, of course," I said.

Sergeant Bartlett entered my office, dressed in his blue police uniform with his hat tucked under an arm. We exchanged greetings and shook hands and he sat down in one of the chairs facing my desk and placed his hat on the other chair.

"I wanted to touch base with you about the events of last night and bring you up to date on what's happening," he said. "The Coast Guard sent divers down at first light this morning. They didn't find any trace of Sophia Ambrosetti's body. The explosion was extremely powerful. If she was on the boat when it exploded, the chances are that she's dead. The problem is that we don't know for certain whether she was on the boat when it exploded. I take it that you haven't heard from her since the explosion."

"No, I haven't." I said it as casually as I could, trying to keep a blank expression on my face.

"We're a bit concerned about not being able to find the body."

"That must not be unusual in cases like this. It may have been carried out to sea by the tide."

"The thing is, though, the tide was coming in, rather than going out. Under those conditions, we would expect the body, or at least some parts of it, to wash up somewhere in the bay, not get carried out to sea."

"Well, I don't know. Certainly, if she were alive, she would have been in touch with someone by now."

"If she was able to get in touch, and if she wanted to."

"What do you mean?"

"Do you know what she was doing in Oceanic Park?"

"She had a gig at the Crow's Nest."

"I mean apart from that. Was she working on anything in her capacity as an investigator and researcher?"

"I don't know. Why do you ask?"

"It appears that the explosion wasn't an accident. The fire department investigators found the remains of an explosive device in the wreckage of the boat. We're trying to determine if someone had a motive for trying to kill her. We thought perhaps it was related to an investigation that she was conducting."

"I'm afraid I don't know whether she was working on anything."

"Well, if she hasn't been in touch with you by now, I don't suppose that there's much chance that she'll get in touch; but if she does, please let me know immediately."

"I will."

I finished the request for a subpoena for security footage from the Plaza Hotel late in the afternoon. Phoebe took it to the courthouse to file with the clerk's office. When Phoebe returned from the courthouse, she came into my office brandishing a postcard in her hand.

"When I got back from the courthouse, I found this postcard in the mailbox," she said, handing the postcard to me. "There's no stamp on it, it must have been delivered by hand."

"O.k., thanks," I said.

I looked at the image on the front of the postcard - it was a picture of the Monte Carlo Motel. I flipped the postcard over and looked at the back, but there was no message. Flipping the postcard back to the front, I looked at the picture more closely. The Monte Carlo Motel is a two-story, L-shaped building that is built around a swimming pool. I noticed that there was a small "x" on the door to the last room on the second floor, at the long end of the L-shaped building. I fed the card into the shredder.

At dusk, I set out for the Monte Carlo Motel. The motel is located north of Old Town, in what used to be called "Northern Oceanic Park" before the town's further northward expansion during the '70s. Once again, I took a roundabout route and doubled back several times to make sure that I wasn't being followed.

As I approached the motel, I paused to size up the situation. The Monte Carlo Motel was built in the '50s and designed in the Googie style of architecture that had been popular at the time. It was a time when architects were trying to incorporate the futuristic contours of jet planes and rocket ships into the design of buildings. The motel had a slanted roof with one end that appeared ready to take off into space. Jutting out from the roof at an angle like the wing of a jet was a fin-shaped projectile with "Monte Carlo Motel" spelled out in pink neon letters against an aqua-blue background.

A handful of people were making use of the swimming pool, which was illuminated by underwater lights, giving the water a ghostly aqua-colored glow. Otherwise, there didn't seem to be anyone around. Most people probably were at dinner or out for an evening on the boardwalk or one of the amusement parks. The windows of some of the motel rooms were dark, while others were illuminated. There was a dim light showing through the curtained window of the room that had been marked with an "x" on the postcard.

No one paid any attention as I approached the motel. I climbed the steps to the balcony that ran along the second floor, walked to the end, and knocked on door number nine, the one that had been marked with an "x" on the postcard. The door opened a crack on a chain and Sophie peered out cautiously before closing the door, undoing the chain, and opening the door further.

"Come on in," she said, grabbing my arm and pulling me inside, while she glanced over my shoulder to see if anyone was watching. She swiftly closed and locked the door.

"Are you sure that you weren't followed?" she asked.

"Yes, I was very careful."

Sophie lowered herself painfully into a chair and lay her head back wearily against the back of the chair. Her hair was pulled back into a pony tail and she had a gauze patch over her left eye and a large area around the eye was covered with an ugly purple bruise. She was wearing a baggy striped shirt and khaki shorts, and her bare arms and legs were covered with cuts, scrapes, and bruises.

"Are you alright?" I asked.

"Yeah, I'm o.k."

"What about your eye? Have you had a doctor look at that?"

"It'll be alright."

"You may lose the sight in it, if you don't take care of it."

"I'll worry about that later."

I sat down in another chair and glanced around the motel room. It was furnished with retro-fifties style furniture. I was amused to see that they had reproductions of a couple of Captain Dan's Tiki-style paintings on the walls. They must have gotten them from the gift shop at the Chimera Gallery.

"Listen," Sophie said. "I want to thank you for your help last night. It was really good of you to help me and not ask any questions. I wouldn't have imposed on you, but I had no one else to turn to."

"Forget it," I said.

"I suppose that you must have been surprised to see me after what happened last summer."

"Actually, I knew that you were in town. I thought I saw you on the boardwalk when I was walking home after the Dick Dale concert on Sunday night. And then I noticed that your boat was docked in the Paradise Bay Marina."

"I knew that there was a risk of running into you at the Dick Dale concert, but I couldn't resist going. I thought that there would be enough people there that I could hide in the crowd."

"What happened last night? How did you survive the explosion?"

"I was lucky. Before I turned in, I came out onto the deck to make sure that everything was secure for the night. So, I was on deck when the explosion occurred. I was thrown off the boat into the water by the force of the explosion. I got hit by the mast and a bunch of wooden fragments and was stunned, but I grabbed hold of a piece of wood and managed to stay afloat. I half drifted and half swam up the bay until I was underneath the drawbridge. I grabbed hold of one of the bridge's pilings and started trying to make it to the shore. Some of the homeless people under the bridge saw me and waded out to help me. If I had been below deck when the explosion occurred, I doubt I would've survived."

"You probably wouldn't have. The police said that it was a very powerful explosion."

"You've spoken to the police?"

"I had a visit from Sergeant Bartlett earlier today. The police aren't sure whether you're dead or not. The fact that they haven't found your body is bothering them."

"Why should that bother them? It easily could have been washed out to sea."

"I suggested that to Sergeant Bartlett. The problem is that the tide was coming in rather than going out. They think that your body should have washed up somewhere in the bay."

"Damnit, that was bad luck."

"They also know that the explosion wasn't an accident. The investigators from the fire department found the remains of an explosive device in the wreckage of the boat. The police are trying to determine who had a motive to kill you. Sergeant Bartlett suggested that perhaps it's related to an investigation that you've been conducting."

"That may be the case. I've been following up on the events of last summer. I started looking into the collapse of Atlas Investments and trying to see if I could trace where the money from the accounts in the Cayman Islands went. I thought if I could trace that money, perhaps some of it could be recovered and there would be a finder's fee. It might even lead us to the location of a certain individual." The collapse of Atlas Investments was a result of events that had occurred the previous summer following the burning of the Chimera Gallery and the death of Count Rupert.

"I found out that Atlas Investments had been working with someone named Vincent de Quircy," Sophie continued. "He's known as 'Dr. Q,' and he specializes in the formation of offshore business entities. He does a lot of work for Russian oligarchs and the Russian mafia; he helps them to get their money out of Russia, launder it, and hide it.

"Atlas Investments had been using Dr. Q to set up bank accounts and shell companies to hide assets. In the course of my investigation, I bought some information about Dr. Q from a broker who deals in black market data. A couple weeks after that, the broker's body washed up on a beach on the east coast of Cyprus. If Dr. Q had the broker killed and got hold of his records, Dr. Q may have found out that I bought information about him from the broker. He may want to eliminate me as well."

"This Dr. Q sounds like a nasty character. What are you going to do?"

"I'm not sure. I'm going to lay low here for a few days while I recover my strength and plan what to do next."

Chapter 17. Thursday, August 4, 2005

After breakfast at Java Joe's, I spent the next morning doing paperwork in my office. Late in the morning, Phoebe informed me that she had received notice that Judge Hampton had issued the subpoena for security video from the Plaza Hotel and that she was going to the courthouse to pick it up. When she returned, she came into my office with the subpoena.

"Do you want me to take it to the hotel?" she asked.

"No, I'll deliver it myself," I responded.

The Oceanic Park Plaza Hotel and Conference Center is a garish monstrosity that would look more at home on the boardwalk in Atlantic City or the strip in Las Vegas. I had driven past it a few times, but had never actually been inside of it. The hotel is fronted by a three-story glass atrium that serves as a lobby, with a twenty-seven story, glass-and-concrete tower rising behind it.

After parking in a multi-story garage alongside the hotel, I walked along a curving walkway to the entrance of the hotel. The walkway was lined with transplanted palm trees that would die when the weather turned cold and would have to be replaced every summer.

Inside, a large, modernistic chandelier hung from the ceiling of the atrium. A wide stairway with gleaming brass railings led to a balcony overlooking the atrium, where two glass-encased elevators waited to whisk vacationers to their rooms in the tower. In addition to serving as a lobby, the atrium housed a variety of upscale stores and restaurants.

I went to the reception desk, which was staffed by a young woman wearing a blue blazer with a brass nameplate pinned to it. I introduced myself, gave her my card, and asked to speak to the head of security. She picked up the phone, punched a button, and spoke to someone in hushed tones. Another woman, similarly uniformed in a blue blazer with a brass nameplate pinned to it, emerged from a door next to the reception desk. She took my card from the receptionist and instructed me to follow her.

I followed the woman into an office, where a stern-faced man in a jacket and tie was sitting behind a desk. A name plaque on his desk identified him as Ray Weston. On the wall to the right of his desk was a bank of video monitors that covered the various parts of the hotel - a couple of the monitors covered the lobby while others covered hallways, meeting rooms, the swimming pool, and the grounds of the hotel. From his desk, he could monitor activity in every part of the hotel. I wondered if the guests realized how closely they were being watched.

The woman handed Weston my card and then discreetly exited the office. Weston made an elaborate show of tossing my card into his trashcan without looking at it.

"How can I help you?" he asked without bothering to introduce himself, in a voice that made it clear that he had no intention of helping me.

"I'm investigating the death of Silvia Viejo, the migrant worker who was murdered," I explained. "I'm trying to find out if she was in the hotel the night of Saturday, July 23 and the morning of July 24. I have a subpoena requiring you to produce any video security footage from that evening." I took the subpoena from my briefcase and handed it to him. He glanced through it and then lay it on his desk.

"What makes you think that she was in the hotel that evening?" Weston asked.

"I have reason to believe that she came here to speak to someone who was attending the annual meeting of the Economic Freedom Foundation."

"Even if she was here, she may not have been picked up on video."

"You seem to have pretty thorough coverage," I said, nodding toward the bank of video monitors. "The chances are that she would have been picked up by one of the cameras."

He picked up the subpoena from his desk and read through it again.

"I'll have to consult with our attorney and get his advice on the matter before I can comply with this subpoena," he said. "We have to protect the confidentiality of our guests. I imagine that our attorney may want to challenge the subpoena in court. Let me talk to him, and I'll get back to you."

"Look, there's no point in stalling. We have probable cause to believe that Silvia Viejo was in the hotel on the night that she was killed. You're going to have to turn over the video sooner or later."

"I said that I'll consult with our attorney and get back to you."

At that moment, a door in the wall behind Weston opened and Eric Burns stepped into the office. He froze when he saw me.

"What are you doing here?!" he demanded.

"I'm serving a subpoena."

"A subpoena for what?

"Video from your security system."

"What do you want that for?"

"I'm investigating the death of Silvia Viejo, the migrant worker who was murdered. I have reason to believe that she was here the night that she was killed."

"What are you talking about? Let me see that subpoena!" Burns snatched the subpoena off of Weston's desk. Burns glanced over the subpoena and then tore it into pieces and threw them on the floor.

"There's your subpoena," he declared, pointing at the fragments of paper on the floor. "Pick up the pieces and get out of here."

"That's not going to do you any good," I responded. "If you don't comply with the subpoena, the court will hold you in contempt."

"No one's going to hold me in contempt. My lawyer will make mincemeat out of that subpoena. Now get out of here." He pointed toward the door. "I don't want to see you around here again and I don't want you talking to any of the hotel staff. If you're seen on the premises again, I'll have you arrested for trespassing."

"What are you so afraid of?" I asked.

"Not of you. Now get out of here."

There didn't seem to be anything to be gained by arguing further, so I got up and walked toward the door. When I got to the door, I paused and looked back at Burns and Weston.

"By the way," I said, "I wouldn't try to hire those skateboarders to post any more anti-immigrant flyers. I don't think that you're going to be able to get away with that again."

A look of surprise and panic flashed across Burns' face, but he quickly recovered his composure.

"I don't have any idea what you're talking about," he declared.

"No, of course not," I said, and left the office.

When I reached my scooter in the parking garage, I saw that a plain white envelope had been taped to the handlebar. I glanced around, but there was no one else in sight. I slipped the envelope into my jacket pocket and then took off.

Back at my cottage, I stowed the scooter in the storage shed, sat on the porch, and opened the envelope. It contained a single sheet of Plaza Hotel letterhead with a single sentence typed on it: "If you want information about the death of Silvia Viejo, meet me on the boardwalk at Aegean Avenue at 7:30 tonight." There was no signature.

I wasn't sure what to make of it. Was it a genuine offer of information or some sort of trick? I debated whether I should keep the proposed appointment or ignore it. After what had happened to Sophie, I was a bit apprehensive.

I didn't think it could be a trap, though. At 7:30 p.m., the boardwalk would be crowded with people. If someone wanted to eliminate me, they wouldn't do it front of all of those people. Rather, the selection of a crowded, public location suggested that the writer of the letter wanted to hold the meeting in a place that was safe for him or her. I decided that I would go ahead and keep the appointment.

At 7:30 that evening, I was sitting on a bench on the boardwalk at Aegean Avenue, looking out over the beach. Behind me the boardwalk was crowded with people and buzzing with activity. By contrast, the beach was largely deserted. A couple of kids were flying a kite and a handful of surfers were out, bobbing on their boards in the lineup. A formation of pelicans flew past, heading up the coast.

After I had been sitting there about ten minutes, I sensed the presence of someone standing behind me. I didn't turn around, but kept looking straight ahead, out over the beach.

"Are you Ned Johnston?" a man's voice asked.

"Yes," I responded.

"I understand that you're interested in information regarding the death of a certain woman."

"Yes, that's right."

"O.k. Let's talk out on the beach where no one will overhear us. I'm going to walk out onto the beach. Wait for a few minutes and then follow me out."

I sensed the person move from behind the bench and, a few moments later, I saw a man wearing a baseball cap, a Hawaiian shirt, and baggy shorts, walk down the ramp, cross the beach, and sit on the crest of the berm, looking out over the ocean.

I realized then why he had chosen this location for the meeting. The beach was at its widest point here. We would be in full view of people on the boardwalk, but, at the same time, would be too far away for anyone to actually recognize us.

After a few minutes had elapsed, I walked out onto the beach and sat down next to the man. He looked like he was in his thirties and had a gaunt, sunburned face.

"What's your name?" I asked.

"You can call me Matt," he responded.

"So, you have information about the death of Silvia Viejo?" I asked.

"No, not me," he said. "I'm here on behalf of another party, a woman who witnessed the killing. It would be worth your while to meet with her. If we can come to terms, I can arrange a meeting."

"Can you prove that the party you represent actually witnessed the killing?"

"The woman who was killed had a knapsack with her at the time of her death. The party I represent now has possession of that knapsack. This was in it." He reached into his shirt pocket, pulled out a Mexican passport, and handed it to me. I opened it to the ID page - it had a photo of Silvia Viejo alongside her address.

"O.k.," I said and handed the passport back to him. "What are you proposing?"

"Here's the deal," he said. "The party I represent will meet with you, tell you how the woman died and who killed her, and turn the knapsack and its contents over to you. In return, you will pay her $10,000."

"I'm afraid that my client doesn't have that kind of money."

"That's the price. The party I represent is in an extremely difficult position. Her life is in danger. She needs money in order to disappear."

"She ought to go to the police. They can protect her."

"No, she can't go to the police. That's out of the question."

"It's the best way to handle it. If she testifies about what happened, the police can get her into a witness protection program. They will relocate her and give her a new identity."

"No, going to the police is out of the question."

"Is she currently wanted for something?"

"Let's just say it is not possible for her to go to the police."

"Alright. Assuming that we can raise the $10,000, how do we know that the information is worth that much?"

"Oh, it's worth it alright. It will get your client off on the murder charge."

"I need to know specifically what the information she can provide."

"Fair enough. I can summarize what she will tell you when she speaks to you. Let me start by explaining the situation. I work as a VIP concierge at the Oceanic Park Plaza. The hotel has a lot of very important guests - CEOs, entertainers, politicians. They are a special class of people who aren't subject to the same laws as everyone else. My job is to provide these guests whatever they want, even if it's not strictly legal. I have certain connections and am able to procure certain goods and services that may not be available on the open market.

"As you probably know, the hotel hosted the annual meeting of the Economic Freedom Foundation. Before the meeting, the owner of the hotel, Eric Burns, informed us that he was bringing in an expert to oversee security for the meeting. He introduced this security expert to us and instructed us to cooperate with him, and do whatever he asked us to do. The security expert speaks with a heavy foreign accent - I think that he may be Russian. He started strutting around the hotel and giving orders as if he owned the place. I suspect that he may have some sort of hold over Burns.

"Anyway, the security guy told me that he wanted to run a sting operation against a person who would be attending the meeting. The person will have to remain nameless for now. I'll refer to him as 'Mr. X.' The security guy wanted to bug his suite with cameras and microphones and catch him in the act with a woman. He asked me if I could procure a woman for the job. I told him that I had connections with someone who might be willing to do that sort of job.

"I spoke to a woman I employ sometimes and she agreed to do it. She was instructed to target Mr. X, get him to take her back to his hotel suite, and engage in certain acts with him. She was successful in targeting him and getting him to take her back to his hotel suite. Before things could progress very far, however, they were interrupted by a knock on the door. Mr. X asked who was at the door. A woman replied that it was management. He opened the door and a woman came into the room with a gun aimed at him. The woman asked Mr. X whether he remembered her. He said he had never seen her before. She said that she had been held in a prison in some Latin American country. He had visited the prison and seen that she and other prisoners were being tortured, but he hadn't reported it or done anything about it. She told him that now he was going to get what he deserved.

"She cocked the trigger on the gun and, at that moment, Mr. X lunged at her and tried to grab the gun out of her hand. The gun went off and the shot hit him in the shoulder. They went down onto the floor, struggling over the gun. He got control of the gun and shot her. She appeared to be dead and he was down on the floor, bleeding badly from his shoulder. At that point, the party I represent grabbed the dead woman's knapsack and fled the room. She came running to me and asked for help.

"I felt responsible for putting her in that situation. I helped her get away from the hotel and I have her stashed temporarily in a place that I know. She can't stay there for long, though. The security guy is still here and he's looking for her. If he finds her, he'll kill her. If he finds out that I'm helping her, he'll kill me too. He doesn't want to leave any loose ends hanging. I have to get some money for her, so she can disappear. I would say that all of that information is worth $10,000 to you."

"Not really," I said. "You're not telling me anything that I don't already know. I know who Mr. X is and why he killed Silvia Viejo."

"You can't possibly know that," he said. He sat up straight with a look of alarm and panic on his face.

"But I do. Mr. X is Robert Oakley, a congressman from Montana. He was a CIA agent stationed in Honduras when Silvia Viejo was in prison there. It wasn't that hard to figure out his identity."

"O.k., you may have guessed the killer's identity, but you don't have any proof that he killed Silvia Viejo," Matt insisted. "You don't have an eyewitness account of the killing."

"No, but an eyewitness account isn't worth anything unless she's willing to make a statement to the police and repeat it in court," I said.

"That's out of the question."

"What about a video deposition?"

"No, no video. It would end up all over the internet. Everyone would know what she looks like and she'd have nowhere to hide. She'll give you the dead woman's knapsack and its contents. That should be sufficient to verify her story."

"Hardly. I'd have no way of proving who gave the knapsack to me or what she told me. Her story would just be hearsay. At the very least her statement would have to be witnessed by a third party and she'd have to sign a transcript of it and have it notarized."

"That's not workable. We can't go through a lot of time-consuming rigamarole."

"No, it's perfectly workable, there won't be any time-consuming rigamarole. I can bring my law clerk to the meeting along with a laptop and a portable printer. My law clerk is an exceptionally fast typist. She can witness the statement, type a transcript of it, and print it on the spot. The party you represent can sign it and my law clerk will notarize it. It won't take very long."

"Well…maybe that would work."

"If the party you represent is willing to do that, I might be able to get her a thousand dollars."

"A thousand dollars! You've got to be kidding. This information is worth a lot more than that."

"There's a very limited market for the information. Apart from me, no one is going to pay you for it. And my client has very limited means."

"You've got to make it two thousand, at least."

"I might be able to go to fifteen hundred."

"Alright," he said resignedly. "How soon can you get it?"

"I imagine that my client will need at least a day."

"You've got until 2:30 tomorrow afternoon."

"I don't know if my client can get the money together that quickly."

"If you don't have the money by then, the price will go up. I'll call you at your office at 2:30 tomorrow afternoon. If you have the money, I'll give you instructions for how to proceed to the meeting. It will be held in a location that I designate. You and your law clerk will come alone. You won't notify the police or anyone else. You won't carry cell phones with you or anything else that would allow someone to track your location. I'll be watching you on the approach to the rendezvous point and, if I see that you're being followed, the meeting is off." With that, he got up abruptly and began walking up the beach.

I waited until Matt was out of sight and then headed to the Sea Breeze Bed and Breakfast to talk to Sarah Cawthorne. The Sea Breeze is located in the northern part of Old Town and housed in a large, Victorian mansion with numerous gables, gingerbread trim, and a screened-in front porch that is filled with old-fashioned wooden rocking chairs. The house is set back behind a crab grass lawn with a mimosa tree in the center of it. There is a lush flower bed in front of the porch, filled with tiger lilies and sunflowers.

By the time I arrived at the Sea Breeze, dusk was falling and fireflies were blinking as they hovered about the lawn and the flower bed. An elderly couple were sitting in rocking chairs on the porch, sharing a bucket of caramel popcorn form Werner's confectionary store on the boardwalk. I exchanged greetings with them and then knocked on the front door.

Sarah Cawthorne answered the door, dressed casually in a baggy shirt over a pair of faded jeans.

"Oh, hello," she said. She seemed surprised to see me.

"Sorry to bother you at this time of the evening," I said, "but something has come up that I need to talk to you about."

She held the door open for me and then led me into a sitting room furnished with overstuffed antique furniture and reading lamps and adorned with nautical paintings on the walls. I sat on a sofa and she sat on one of the chairs. The house was quiet - apart from the couple on the porch, there didn't seem to be anyone around.

"What's happened?" Sarah asked apprehensively.

I explained about my meeting with Matt, the VIP concierge from the Plaza Hotel, the information that he was offering, and the deal that he was proposing.

"Do you think that this woman really has information about the killing?" she asked.

"It appears that she does," I responded. "She has the dead woman's passport. That supports her contention that she was present when the woman was killed. Also, her explanation of how the woman was killed is consistent with what we've learned through our investigation. I think that her statement, together with the other information that we've gathered, should be sufficient to get your son off on the murder charge."

"In that case, I'll get the money together."

"Do you think that you'll be able to do it by 2:30 tomorrow afternoon?"

"Yes, I have some savings bonds that I had set aside for retirement. I can redeem them at the bank tomorrow morning."

"O.k. Hopefully, this whole ordeal will be over shortly."

After leaving the Sea Breeze Bed and Breakfast, I decided to walk to the Monte Carlo Motel to check on Sophie. It seemed unlikely that I was being followed, but out of an abundance of caution, I went through my routine of doubling back a couple of times on my way to the motel, just to make sure that no one was tailing me.

I climbed the stairs to the second-floor balcony and knocked on her door. After a short pause, the door was opened a crack on a chain by a woman with short black hair. I was taken aback for a moment before I realized that Sophie had cut her hair short and dyed it black. She closed the door, undid the chain, and then opened the door further.

"Don't stand there looking shocked," she said. "Come on in." She stood aside to let me into the room and quickly closed the door behind me.

"I hardly recognized you," I said.

"That was the idea," she said.

We sat in a couple of chairs around a table that held a laptop, the remains of a carryout dinner, and a partially empty bottle of wine.

"Would you like some wine?" she said.

"Sure."

She retrieved a plastic cup from a grocery bag on a counter and poured me a cup of wine and handed it to me.

"What brings you by?"

"I was in the area and thought I'd stop by and see how you're doing."

"I'm much better today."

"Do you need anything? Food? Any sort of supplies?"

"No, I'm managing o.k. Have you heard anything further from the police?"

"No, nothing. What are your plans?"

"I'll be moving on in another day or two."

"Where will you go?"

"It's better that you don't know."

"Will I be able to get in touch with you?"

"I'll get in touch with you once I'm settled."

This was followed by an awkward silence.

"What about you?" she asked. "I saw in the paper that you're representing the guy who is charged with murdering that migrant worker."

"Yeah," I said. "His mother asked me to represent him. I've known her for years, she runs the Sea Breeze Bed and Breakfast in Old Town. I just stopped by there and met with her before I came here. We're working on a deal to get some information that will clear her son."

"So, you really think that he's innocent?"

"Yeah, at this point, I'm fairly certain of it. The killing had nothing to do with the Oceanic Park Vigilantes. It grew out of things that happened in Honduras back in the '80s."

I gave her a brief summary of what I had learned in the course of investigating the case, concluding with what I had learned earlier in the evening during my meeting with Matt, the VIP concierge from the Plaza Hotel.

"That's really interesting," Sophie said. "You know that Eric Burns lost a lot of money when Atlas Investments went belly up. I discovered that in the course of investigating the events of last summer."

"I knew that Burns had put money into Atlas Investments, but I didn't know how much he had lost."

"He took a really big hit. He already was in financial trouble. He had sunk everything into the Oceanic Park Plaza Hotel and he was struggling to complete it. The project was behind schedule and there were massive cost overruns. It looked like he was going to have to declare bankruptcy. But then a company stepped in and bailed him out in exchange for an ownership interest in the hotel."

"What company?"

"It's a company called Diversified Holdings, Limited. It's actually a shell company that was set up by Dr. Q and registered in Cyprus. I've traced ownership of it back through a series of shell companies to Dimitri Aleksashenko, a Russian oligarch with close ties to Vladimir Putin and the Russian intelligence services."

"So the money for the Plaza Hotel is coming from a Russian oligarch?"

"Yeah. Oligarchs want to launder their money and get it out of Russia. One way that they do that is by funneling the money through a series of bogus companies and then investing it in real estate."

"This all adds up. This guy, Matt, said that he thought that the security guy brought in for the meeting of the Economic Freedom Foundation is Russian."

"He probably is. The sting operation against Robert Oakley sounds like an FSB operation."

"You think that the security guy is an FSB agent?"

"It's likely. Think about it. It was the perfect setup - a meeting of the Economic Freedom Foundation at a hotel in which a close associate of the Vladimir Putin and the Russian intelligence services has an ownership interest. The FSB probably coerced Burns into allowing them to run sting operations against people attending the meeting in exchange for the financial bail-out. It provided a perfect opportunity for the FSB to get *kompromat* on Western politicians."

"Well, they certainly succeeded beyond their wildest dreams. They wanted to get video of Oakley committing a sex act with a prostitute, instead they got video of him killing someone. They probably couldn't believe their luck. If they were to get away with it, they'd be able to control him for the rest of his life."

"You don't think that they'll get away with it?"

"Not if we get the statement from the witness tomorrow. She saw Oakley kill the woman. With any luck, Oakely will end up getting charged with murder."

"So, what are the arrangements for getting the statement?"

"The concierge is going to call at 2:30 tomorrow afternoon to verify that we have the money. Then he'll give us instructions about the meeting."

"Are you going alone?"

"No, the plan is for Phoebe, my law clerk, to go with me. She'll transcribe the woman's statement and notarize it after the woman signs it. I haven't had a chance to talk to Phoebe about it yet, but I'll talk to her in the morning."

"What are your plans for back up?"

"Back up? I don't know. I haven't had time to think about it."

"You need to. Once you get to the location where the meeting's going to be held, what's to stop this guy from pulling a gun on you, taking the money, and not giving you any statement in return?"

"Well...I don't know."

"At the very least, you need someone to track you and see where you go. Someone who you can signal for help if you get into trouble."

"Well, I can make some arrangements tomorrow. There'll be time in the morning."

"There's no need. I'll do it."

"But you can't. You're hurt. And you need to say out of sight."

"I'm o.k. and I'll be staying out of sight. I'm starting to become intrigued by this. I wonder about this Russian security guy. If he's connected to Dimitri Aleksashenko, he's probably connected to Dr. Q as well."

"What? You think that he's the one who planted the explosive device on your boat?"

"The idea had crossed my mind. I thought that a specialist must have been brought in to do the job, and this guy fits the bill. And he was conveniently in town at the time of the explosion."

"Well…o.k.," I said.

"There's just one thing. No one else can know that I'm involved."

"But Phoebe will have to know…"

"No, there's no reason that she needs to know. I'll be watching your office at 2:30 tomorrow afternoon. When you leave the office to go to the meeting, I'll pick you up and tail you. It's actually better that your law clerk not know that you're being shadowed. If people know that they're being shadowed, they tend to look around and it gives things away. She'll act more normally if she doesn't know."

"Well…alright."

Chapter 18. Friday, August 5, 2005

At the office the next morning I filled in Phoebe on what I had learned from Matt, the VIP concierge at the Plaza Hotel, and explained the arrangements for the meeting with the witness. I told her that there could be some danger involved in the meeting, but she expressed a strong willingness to participate.

I spent the remainder of the morning trying to do some paperwork, but had trouble concentrating. All sorts of questions and concerns were buzzing through my mind. Was the Russian security guy really an FSB agent? Had I made a mistake by agreeing to let Sophie get involved?

In the late morning, Sarah Cawthorne arrived at the office with the money in one of those heavy cardboard accordion files with a string clasp on it. Phoebe gave her a receipt for the money and placed the accordion file in the office safe.

"What happens next?" Sarah asked.

"The concierge from the Plaza Hotel is supposed to contact us at the 2:30 this afternoon and give us instructions for the meeting. If things go o.k., we should have the witness statement by sometime this afternoon."

At almost exactly 2:30 p.m., the phone on my desk rang.

"This is Matt," a voice said. "Do you have the $1,5000?"

"Yes, I have it."

"O.k., listen carefully. I want you and your law clerk to walk across the drawbridge to West Oceanic Park. When you get there, turn right on Bayshore Avenue and walk north until you come to the intersection of Bayshore and May's Landing, next to the entrance to the parking lot for the Smuggler's Cove Bar & Grill. Stop there and wait. I'll meet you there. If I'm satisfied that you've complied with all of my instructions, we'll proceed to the meeting. Have you got that?"

"Yes, I've got it."

"And remember - you and your law clerk are to come alone. I'm going to be watching you. If I suspect that anyone is following you, the meeting is off. When we meet, I will check for cell phones and tracking devices and, if I find a cell phone or tracking device on either you or your law clerk, the meeting is off. Is that clear?"

"Yes, quite clear."

"Alright. I'll see you shortly. And remember, I'll be watching." With that he hung up.

"What do we do?" Phoebe asked.

"He wants us to walk across the drawbridge and meet him in West Oceanic Park."

We left the office with Phoebe carrying a laptop and me carrying a briefcase that contained the accordion file with the money in it and a case that contained a portable printer. I was tempted to look around for Sophie to make sure that she picked us up, but I resisted the temptation.

"Won't this evidence be challenged because we paid for it?" Phoebe asked, as we walked through Old Town toward the drawbridge.

"It will be, but the witness has the dead woman's passport and that will lend credibility to her statement. At the very least, it will raise doubts about our client's involvement in the killing. I'm hoping I can get the charges dismissed without having to go to trial."

Walking across the drawbridge, I felt awkward and uncomfortably exposed. Was Matt somewhere on the opposite shore, watching us through a pair of binoculars? Or had he just been bluffing? There were a few people fishing from the bridge, but no other pedestrians. I started to feel apprehensive about being followed by Sophie. If Matt was watching us from the opposite shore and saw Sophie walking across the bridge after us, he might realize that we were being followed. I would like to have looked back to see how closely Sophie was following us, but I was afraid that it would call attention to the fact that we were being followed.

Before long, we were approaching the bridge keeper's booth, which is located next to the draw span, about a third of the way across the bridge. As we walked past the bridge keeper's booth we briefly were hidden from view of anyone on the opposite shore, and I risked a quick glance back. Sophie was nowhere in sight. I wondered what could have happened. Had Sophie failed to pick us up when we left the office? Had she changed her mind about backing us up? All sorts of panicked thoughts began running through my mind. If anything happened to us now, no one would know where we had gone.

When Phoebe and I reached the mainland, we turned onto Bayshore Avenue and headed north until we reached the point where it intersected with Mays Landing Avenue, by the entrance to the parking lot for the Smuggler's Cove Bar and Grill. After a minute or so, Matt approached us from the direction of the bay front with a pair of binoculars on a strap around his neck. So he actually had been watching us cross the drawbridge.

"Do you have the money?" he asked.

"It's in here," I said, holding the briefcase up for him to see.

"Let me see it."

I opened the briefcase, extracted the accordion file, and handed it to him. He opened the file, looked at the money and then poked around in the file to make sure that there wasn't a cell phone or any kind of tracking device concealed in it. He performed a similar inspection of the briefcase. Apparently satisfied, he replaced the file in the briefcase and handed it back to me.

"Open the other case," he said, indicating the case that contained the portable printer. I opened that and he poked around in it as well. Then he patted us both down to make sure that we weren't carrying cell phones. Finally, he glanced around to see if we were being followed.

"Alright," he said, apparently satisfied with the situation. "Follow me."

We continued north along Bayshore Avenue, past the Land's End Marina, the Bounty of the Bay Seafood plant, and the Ranch House Motel. We then turned off on a side street and headed away from the bay front. We appeared to be headed toward a dilapidated shingled house that had a sign in front of it that read: "Emerson's Efficiency Apartments. By the Day, Week, or Month." A sagging stairway led to a large front porch with a couple of rickety-looking rocking chairs on it. The white paint on the porch's columns and railings was now a dingy shade of grey and peeling in several places. The front yard was mostly dirt with a few patches of dying grass. It didn't exactly look like the ideal vacation spot.

As we approached the apartment house, a man emerged from the front door, walked across the porch, and started down the stairs. He was a heavyset guy wearing reflector sunglasses and a black windbreaker, and had a knapsack slung over his shoulder.

"Hey, it's the security guy!" Matt exclaimed, pointing at the man. "He's got the woman's knapsack!"

The man on the stairs looked up at the sound of Matt's voice. When the man saw us, he froze in place. We froze as well. For what seemed like an eternity, none of us moved. The man on the stairs recovered his wits first. He reached inside of his jacket, pulled out a pistol, and fired a shot at us. A bullet hit the street at our feet and we scattered, diving for cover behind cars that were parked on the street.

The man's shot was answered by a rapid burst of fire from our left. A figure in a motorcycle helmet and sunglasses had appeared out of nowhere on the other side of the street and was crouched down behind a car with a pistol, returning the man's fire. It took a moment before I realized that it was Sophie. One of her shots hit the wooden railing of the stairway and sent a shower of splinters raining down on the man. The man vaulted over the railing, hit the ground, and started running toward a black car that was parked partway down the block with its engine idling. The man flung open the back door on the passenger side of the car, dove into the back seat, and the car tore away from the curb with a shriek of burning rubber, the door slammed shut by the acceleration of the car. I glanced across the street to where Sophie had been, but she had disappeared. A moment later, she careened around the corner from a side street on a scooter and took off after the black car.

I then remembered that Phoebe and I had been passed by a person on a scooter while we were walking across the drawbridge. Sophie must have rented a scooter in case the meeting wasn't located within walking distance from the office. When she saw that we were walking across the bridge, she must have decided that it was too risky to follow us on foot and instead used the scooter. She had arrived in West Oceanic Park before we did and picked us up after we had crossed the drawbridge.

"Oh, no, Irena!" Matt exclaimed. He got up off the ground and started running toward the apartment house. Phoebe and I followed him into the building, through a lobby furnished as a sitting room, up two flights of stairs, and into a bedroom.

A woman was sprawled on her back across the bed with her long blond hair spread out on the pillow, her arms outstretched, and her throat slit open, showing a horrid, gaping wound. The bedcover beneath her body was saturated with blood.

"Oh, no," Matt moaned. He went down on his knees alongside of the bed. "How could this have happened? I was only gone for a half an hour."

There was a phone on a night stand alongside the bed. I picked up the receiver and dialed 911.

"We need an ambulance immediately to Emerson's Efficiency Apartments in West Oceanic Park," I told the dispatcher as soon as she came on the line. "A woman is badly wounded. We also need the police."

"I'm afraid it's too late for an ambulance," Phoebe said. "No one could survive loss of that much blood."

"How did he find out where we were?" Matt moaned. "We were so careful." He was still on his knees next to the bed, sobbing. He had seemed like a rather slimy and cold-blooded sort of character, but now it was hard not to feel sorry for him.

I glanced around the room, which was a shambles. A lamp was smashed on the floor, a chair was overturned, a table was tipped onto its side. The woman on the bed must have known that she was fighting for her life and put up a terrific fight. But it hadn't been enough.

Shortly, we heard the wail of a sirens in the distance, coming closer.

"The police!" Matt exclaimed. "I've got to get out of here!"

"No, you have to stay and tell the police what she told you," I said.

"No, I can't talk to the police."

"But you have to."

"Look, I can't help you. I don't know anything. I've got to get out of here." With that, he bolted from the room.

As the sirens got closer, Phoebe went downstairs to the porch to direct the paramedics and police to the room upstairs while I remained in the room to make sure that no one disturbed the crime scene. The ambulance arrived first. The paramedics rushed up the stairs to the room, but there was nothing that they could do for the woman on the bed.

"It's a really deep cut," one of them said. "It nearly severed her head. She would have died almost instantly."

Sergeant Bartlett and another officer arrived in a police car shortly after the ambulance. Phoebe and I gave Sergeant Bartlett a quick summary of what had happened and a description of the security guy who had taken a shot at us and the car in which he had fled. Phoebe had had the presence of mind to get the car's license plate number. Sergeant Bartlett called in to the station and put out an alert for the vehicle. He also requested a forensic team to come and examine the crime scene.

After the forensic team arrived and Sergeant Bartlett had given them their instructions, he asked us to accompany him back to the police station to make formal statements.

At the station, Phoebe and I were split into different interview rooms to give our statements. My statement was taken by an officer named Derek Hewison, who I had met briefly the previous summer. After I finished my statement, he left me sitting in the interview room.

After awhile, Sergeant Bartlett and Chief Hadley entered the room.

"We've reviewed your law clerk's statement and allowed her to go," Hadley informed me, "but we have some further questions for you."

They sat down on the opposite side of the table from me.

"According to your statement, you were approached with an offer of information by a person named Matt, who said he worked as a concierge at the Oceanic Park Plaza. He said that he represented a witness to the murder who could provide a statement identifying the murderer."

"Yes, that's right."

"Why didn't you inform the police or the State's Attorney's office about this witness?"

"I told Matt that the woman should go to the police and make a statement, but he said that it wasn't possible for her to go to the police.

"Did he say why she couldn't go to the police?"

"No, he wouldn't say."

"So instead of informing the police or State's Attorney's office about the witness, you arranged to buy the information."

"Look, the information was really important and there didn't seem to be any other way of obtaining it. My client is facing a murder charge and the information would have cleared him."

"O.k., so you made arrangements to meet with the witness and take a statement from her. In accordance with these arrangements, you and your law clerk walked to West Oceanic Park, met this guy Matt, and started walking toward the Emerson Efficiency Apartments."

"Right."

"As you were approaching the apartment house, the security guy from the Plaza Hotel came out of the house and took a shot at you."

"That's right."

"And then a woman on the other side of the street returned his fire."

"Right."

"And you don't know who she was?"

"Uh...no."

"So, a passerby - a total stranger - reacts instantaneously and returns the security guy's fire?"

"Well...yeah."

"Doesn't that seem rather unusual to you?"

"Well, she probably saw that we were in trouble and thought we needed help."

"It's extraordinary that she happened to be in exactly the right place at the right time."

"It was rather lucky."

"And rather lucky that she just happened to be carrying a gun."

"Well, lots of people carry guns these days."

"So, you hadn't arranged for her to be there?"

"No, I told you, I don't know who she was."

"O.k. What did this woman look like?"

"I don't know. I didn't see her face. She was wearing a motorcycle helmet and sunglasses. Everything happened so fast, I didn't get a very good look at her."

"And after the security guy fled in a waiting car, she pursued them on a scooter."

"Well, she drove off on a scooter, I don't know whether she was pursuing the car."

"I wonder why this woman hasn't come forward."

"Perhaps she doesn't want to get asked a lot of pointless questions."

"Don't get cute with me!" Hadley slammed the palm of his hand down on the table, causing the table to jump. "I know that you're sitting there playing games with us. That woman was with you and I think I know who she is. When I prove it, you'll be charged with withholding evidence and interfering with a police investigation."

"I'm sorry, but you're mistaken," I said. "What you need to do is find the security guy who took a shot at us and fled in the car. Somebody paid him to kill the witness. You need to question him and find out who he's working for." I couldn't tell them about Dimitri Aleksashenko's ownership interest in the Oceanic Park Plaza or the possibility that the security guy was an FSB agent without revealing that I had gotten the information from Sophie.

"For your information, we have found him," Hadley said with a grim smirk on his face. "The car that fled the scene crashed on Piney Hollow Road, a couple of miles east of West Oceanic Park. It appears that the car went out of control on a sharp turn, skidded across the oncoming lane, careened off one tree, and then crashed into another. The gas tank was ruptured in the collision, and the car caught fire and exploded. Both the driver and the passenger were killed."

"Did you find the murdered woman's knapsack in the car?"

"The forensic people are still sifting through the wreckage, but, if the knapsack was in the car, the chances are that it was destroyed."

"What about Matt, the concierge from the Plaza Hotel?"

"We're still looking for him. So far, we haven't been able to find him. He hasn't been back to his apartment or to the Plaza Hotel. And now, unless you have anything further to tell us, I don't think that we have anything further to discuss."

It was early evening by the time I got back to the office. Phoebe had waited for me was working at her computer, as if nothing had happened, seemingly unfazed by the experience of getting shot at and then discovering a murdered body.

"Are you alright?" I asked.

"Yeah, I'm fine," she said, shrugging it off.

"I'm sorry for putting you in that situation. I didn't realize that we were going to get shot at and find the body of a woman with her throat slit."

"It was a change from working behind a desk. By the way, Sarah Cawthorne called a little while ago, to find out how things went. I told her what happened."

"O.k. I'll stop by the Sea Breeze this evening and talk to her. I have to return the money to her as well."

"Also Gary Rockwell from the *Oceanic Park Press* called. He has questions about what happened this afternoon. I told him that he'd have to talk to you."

"O.k."

"How do you think that security guy found out where that woman was hiding?"

"He probably followed Matt there. Matt must not have been as careful as he thought he was."

"What about that woman who shot at the security guy? Do you have any idea who she was?"

"Uh…no."

"The police seemed to think that you must have arranged for her to follow us and provide back up for us. They refused to believe that she just happened to be there."

"Yeah, they said the same sort of things to me."

"They asked me if I had seen Sophie after her boat blew up. For some reason, they seemed to think that it might have been her. Why would they think that?"

"Well, her body was never found. They're letting their imaginations run away with them."

"So, what do we do now?"

"Well, I think that it's apparent that the woman was killed to keep her from talking to us. That should be sufficient to raise serious doubts about Bradley Cawthorne's involvement in the killing. On Monday, I'll file a motion to dismiss the charges against him."

After leaving the office, I walked to the Sea Breeze Bed and Breakfast. Sarah Cawthorne and I sat in the living room. The south-facing room was dim in the early evening as the sun shifted to the west. Sarah Cawthorne appeared even more nervous and on edge than usual.

"Your law clerk told me what happened, that the witness was killed before you could speak to her," she said.

"Yes, that's right," I said. "We didn't need the money as it turned out." I handed her the accordion file with the money in it.

"Where does that leave things?"

"It's apparent that the witness was killed to prevent her from speaking to us. I think that undermines that prosecution's theory of the case. On Monday, I'll file a motion to dismiss and I think that it has a good chance of succeeding."

"I really hope so. This has been a terrible ordeal."

After leaving the Sea Breeze Bed and Breakfast, I headed for the Monte Carlo Motel. I took my usual precautions of taking a roundabout route and doubling back to make sure that I wasn't followed. Precautions were more important than ever, now that the police were looking for the mysterious woman who had returned fire outside of the Emerson Efficiency Apartments.

I climbed the stairs and walked along the second-floor balcony to Sophie's room. The door was propped open by a maid's trolley that was loaded with towels, soap, and other supplies.

I looked through the door and saw a maid stripping the sheets from the bed.

"Can I help you?" she asked.

"I'm looking for the woman who was staying here."

"She's checked out."

"Do you know how long ago she checked out?"

"No, I don't know. I was just told that the room had been vacated and that I should clean it."

"O.k., thanks."

So, that was that. I brooded over things as I walked back to my cottage. I wondered whether Sophie had played some role in the crash of the car fleeing the shootout at the Emerson Efficiency Apartments.

Had she caught up with the car, taken a shot at it, and caused it to crash? Where had she gone? And would I ever hear from her again?

I got a carryout dinner from the Bayview Restaurant, sat at the kitchen table, and ate it. As I was cleaning up afterwards, someone started banging on the front door. It was Gary Rockwell, standing at the screen door, with a computer case slung over his shoulder.

"Hey!" he exclaimed. "I've been looking all over for you. Didn't your law clerk tell you that I needed to talk to you?"

"Yes, but, after I got out of the police station, I had some other things that I needed to do."

"Well, I've caught up with you now. I need to know what happened in West Oceanic Park this morning."

We sat on the porch and I gave him a summary of what had happened, leaving out Sophie's involvement, while he took notes on his laptop. Like the police, he was interested in the mysterious woman who exchanged fire with the security guy and was skeptical when I said that I didn't know anything about her.

When Rockwell was satisfied that he had gotten all of the information that he could out of me, he went off to write up the story. I headed off on my evening walk. I had a lot to think about.

Chapter 19. Saturday, August 6, 2005

The next morning, I read Gary Rockwell's article about the killing of the woman in West Oceanic Park while I was eating breakfast at Java Joe's:

WOMAN KILLED IN WEST OCEANIC PARK. A woman was found dead in the Emerson Efficiency Apartments in West Oceanic Park yesterday afternoon. The deceased has been identified as Irena Erovinkin, an illegal immigrant from Ukraine. According to federal immigration authorities, Erovinkin entered the United States last summer on a tourist visa and remained in the country illegally after the expiration of the visa. Oceanic Park Police Department spokesperson Shirley Logan said that the cause of Erovinkin's death was murder resulting from a savage knife attack.

Erovinkin's death was reported to a 911 operator by local attorney Ned Johnston, who had gone to the apartment building, along with some associates, to interview Erovinkin as a potential witness in a case. As Johnston and his associates approached the apartment building, a man emerged from the building, fired a shot at them, and then fled in a waiting car driven by another person. An unidentified woman standing nearby returned fire and pursued the fleeing car on a scooter.

The car that fled the scene later was found on Piney Hollow Road, a two-lane country road outside of West Oceanic Park, where it had crashed into a tree, caught fire, and exploded. Both the driver and passenger were killed. Police are seeking information about the woman who pursued the car on a scooter.

Johnston is representing Bradley Cawthorne, who is accused of the murder of the migrant worker Silvia Viejo, whose body was found at the Angler's Haven Marina on Sunday, July 24. Johnston stated that he believed that Erovinkin had witnessed the killing of Silvia Viejo and was killed to prevent her from identifying the actual killer of Silvia Viejo. He said that he would be filing a motion to have the charges against his client dismissed.

The article left a lot unsaid. It omitted any mention of Matt and his connection to the Oceanic Park Plaza Hotel. The paper probably didn't want to alienate Eric Burns, who was a major advertiser. I wondered what role, if any, Burns played in all of this. If he was involved, was his involvement voluntary or was he being coerced into it in exchange for the financial bailout of the hotel? Since the Russian security guy had been killed in the car crash, we probably would never learn what sort of sting operations he had been carrying out at the Plaza Hotel.

"Hey!" Karen called to me from behind the counter. "There's a phone call for you."

"For me?" I was puzzled as to why anyone would be calling me at Java Joe's on a Saturday morning.

"Yes, we're even providing phone service for you now." She lay the receiver on the counter.

I walked to the counter, picked up the receiver, and said hello.

"Hello, this is Roy Parker, the warden of the Bay County Jail," a deep, rumbling voice said. I immediately felt apprehensive. "I'm sorry to disturb you on a Saturday morning, but it's a matter of some urgency. I managed to get hold of your law clerk and she said I might be able to find you at Java Joe's."

"It's no problem," I said.

"I'm afraid that I have some bad news. I have to inform you that your client, Bradley Cawthorne, hanged himself in his jail cell between 3:15 and 3:30 this morning."

I felt a sick, sinking sensation in my stomach.

"But…" I struggled to speak. "How is that possible?"

"He used his shirt. He tied one end around the bars of his cell and the other around his neck."

"What were the guards doing at the time?"

"The guards checked on him every 15 minutes in accordance with protocol. They checked on him at 3:15 and he was o.k. When they went back at 3:30 he had hanged himself. The guards immediately cut him down, performed CPR, and called for emergency personnel. The emergency team responded within five minutes. The paramedics put a tube down Cawthorne's throat and tried to revive him but were unsuccessful. Unfortunately, Cawthorne's larynx had been crushed. If it hadn't been for that, the paramedics might have been able to revive him."

"What about surveillance cameras?"

"Unfortunately, the surveillance cameras for that area of the cellblock are out of order."

I was so stunned I didn't know what else to say.

"I'm very sorry," the warden said after an uncomfortable silence.

"Have you informed his mother?" I asked.

"Yes, I spoke to her just before I called you."

"O.k.….well…thank you for letting me know." I hung up, and staggered back to my table in a daze. My mind was reeling as I struggled to make sense of this.

The timing of this was suspicious - it was just too convenient. The police and prosecutors knew that their case against Bradley Cawthorne was falling apart. I was planning to file a motion to dismiss on Monday morning, and, in light of recent events, it had a good chance of succeeding. The investigation into the death of Silvia Viejo would have to be reopened and Robert Oakley would be at risk of being discovered as the actual killer. Someone, I suspected, didn't want that to happen.

But what could I do now? The evidence that I had against Robert Oakley consisted of hearsay from Matt and circumstantial evidence based on the fact that Oakley was stationed at the U.S. embassy in Honduras at the same time that Silvia Viejo had been imprisoned there. Without anything more solid, I couldn't make a public accusation against Oakley.

I still might be able to get security video from the Plaza Hotel showing that Silvia Viejo had gone there the night that she was killed. But, unless the video showed her together with Robert Oakley, there would be nothing to implicate him. It seemed hopeless.

In the early afternoon I walked to the Sea Breeze Bed & Breakfast. When Sarah Cawthorne came to the door, she appeared distraught - her eyes were red-rimmed from crying and she had a handkerchief clutched tightly in her hands.

"You've heard the news?" she asked, as she led me into the living room.

"Yes, I'm terribly sorry," I told her, knowing that my words were inadequate.

We sat in the living room.

"There is no way that Brad committed suicide," she said. As she spoke, she alternately dabbed at her eyes with the handkerchief and twisted it into a ball with tense fingers. "I spoke to him on the phone last night. I explained what had happened yesterday. I told him that you were going to be filing a motion to dismiss the charges on Monday morning, and thought it had a good chance of succeeding. He was in good spirits. He had no reason to kill himself."

"I don't believe that he committed suicide either," I said. "But I'm afraid it may be impossible to prove that he didn't under the circumstances."

"The warden said that there would be an investigation by the Department of Corrections."

"I wouldn't put any faith in that. Those sort of investigations usually turn out to be whitewashes."

"I just don't know what to do. I've put so much work into this place, but I don't know whether I can stay here anymore."

Chapter 20. Sunday, August 7, 2005

The next morning, there was an article by Gary Rockwell about Bradley Cawthorne's death in the *Oceanic Park Press*. I read it while eating breakfast a Java Joe's.

> MURDER SUSPECT HANGS SELF IN JAIL CELL. Bradley Cawthorne, who had been charged with the murder of the migrant worker, Silvia Viejo, hanged himself in his jail cell early yesterday morning, according to jail officials. His body was found by guards checking on him at 3:45 a.m. Paramedics were called, but attempts to revive Cawthorne were unsuccessful.
>
> Cawthorne was believed to be a member of the Oceanic Park Vigilantes who had been conducting an anti-immigrant flyer campaign. He had been denied bail, and was in jail awaiting trial on the murder charge.
>
> The State Department of Corrections has announced that it will conduct an investigation into the circumstances surrounding Bradley Cawthorne's death.
>
> Oceanic Park Police announced that, with Bradley Cawthorne's death, they are bringing their investigation into the death of Silvia Viejo to an end. "We consider the investigation into the death of Silvia Viejo to be closed," Chief Hadley stated. "We are

satisfied that she was killed by Bradley Cawthorne. It appears that he was overcome by remorse and killed himself."

"There is no way he would have killed himself," Cawthorne's mother, Sarah Cawthorne, said. "I had spoken to him earlier in the evening about recent developments in his case. His attorney had uncovered new evidence and was going to file a motion to dismiss on Monday. Brad was in good spirits and very optimistic about his chances."

So, that was it. All of the loose ends had been tied up. The police and the State's Attorney's office were treating the matter as closed. There was little public outcry or concern over Cawthorne's death. Most people seemed to think that he had gotten what he deserved and saved the state the cost of a trial in the process.

Later in the week, Reverend Haycroft held a funeral service for Bradley Cawthorne at the Oceanic Park United Methodist Church. A few people from the Old Town community showed up to show their support for Sarah Cawthorne, but it couldn't help but be a sad and desolate affair.

Toward the end of the summer, there was a bit of good news. After holding a hearing on the request for a permanent injunction against the ordinance regulating artists and performers on the boardwalk, Judge Willis issued a written opinion in which he permanently struck down the ordinance as an unconstitutional restriction on free speech. So, the boardwalk remained unchanged. Boardwalk Elvis and the other artists and performers continued to ply their trade on the boardwalk and it retained its colorful character, much to the chagrin of the Merchants Association and the City Council.

In the early fall, the State's Attorney's office offered Walter Braddock a sweetheart plea deal on the assault charge for spraying Sean Taylor with pepper spray at the community meeting at the Oceanic Park Methodist Church. In exchange for a "no contest" plea, Braddock was given six months probation. Apparently, Sandra Rappaport's tough-on-crime policy didn't apply to Braddock.

Braddock seized on the fact that Irena Erovinkin was an illegal immigrant and cited her murder as proof that illegal immigrants were bringing gang violence to Oceanic Park. He portrayed Erovinkin's death as the result of gang warfare among illegal immigrants and used it to continue to push his anti-immigrant agenda. The actual reason for Erovinkin's death became lost amidst all of the inflammatory anti-immigrant rhetoric.

Also during the early fall, Robert Oakley announced that he would give up his House seat in order to run for the Senate in 2006. The announcement was greeted enthusiastically by business interests and conservative media pundits and Oakley immediately received the endorsement of several prominent figures in the Republican party. The Senate run was seen as the next logical step on Oakley's eventual path to the presidency. The FSB or whoever was blackmailing Oakley probably were having a good laugh at how well things were working out for them.

Later in the fall, the *New York Examiner* published a series of articles about Dr. Q, based on thousands of pages of documents that had been provided to the paper by a "confidential source." The articles detailed Dr. Q's role in helping wealthy clients, including several prominent Russian oligarchs, hide their money and evade taxes. The article also raised questions about criminal activity and money laundering. After publication of the articles, authorities in several countries indicated that they wanted to question Dr. Q, but he seemed to have disappeared. A couple of weeks later his body was found dumped in a back alley in Nicosia with a bullet in the back of his head. Apparently, Russian oligarchs didn't want to run the risk of Dr. Q revealing any of their secrets.

I had little doubt that Sophie had been the source of the documents that had been the basis of the series of articles. Now that Dr. Q was dead, perhaps it would be safe for her to come out of hiding.

I sometimes thought about Silvia Viejo. Outside of a handful of people, no one would ever know why she actually had been killed. The trauma that she suffered in Honduras back in the '80s had shattered her life and sent her off on a long, lonely journey. It appeared that she finally had built a life of sorts for herself as a crab picker, but she still was haunted by the past. She still carried all of the anger, hurt, and rage with her, because the cruel and evil things that people do to each other never really fade away. Then, in Oceanic Park, thousands of miles from home, she came face to face with her past. The desire for revenge must have been overwhelming, even after all of the time that had passed. It drove her to a desperate act and brought her lonely journey to an end. Perhaps she was at peace now, but I wondered.

Made in United States
Orlando, FL
08 July 2024

48746299R00152